DEM

MCCOY

BOYS

DEM
MCCOY
BOYS

SHELIA E. BELL

www.hispenpublishing.com

Douglasville, Georgia

ISBN: 978-1-944643-04-1

Library of Congress Control Number: 2017916575

Cover designed by Rebecca Pau
The Final Wrap
Thefinalwrap.com

His Pen Publishing, LLC
Douglasville, Georgia

Dedication

To all those called by God to minister.

"Courage is contagious. When a brave man takes a stand, the spines of others are often stiffened." Billy Graham

Acknowledgments

I take this time to acknowledge all of those who have supported me throughout my literary career. I can never emphasize enough just how important you are to me. You continue to motivate, inspire, push, and prompt me to keep doing what I know that God has called me to do, which is to write. Of course, I give thanks always and forever to God for taking me and molding me into the person He would have me to be.

What You Have to Say

"Oh my goodness! I was totally drawn into this book from beginning to end! My how we reap what we sow!!!! I can't say enough about this series!" Rachel Baldwin. (McCoys of Holy Rock)

"Twists and turns that I did not see coming! What a way to continue the series with the sons taking over the ministry!" N2Bookz (McCoys of Holy Rock)

"Oh my God. This book was totally awesome" GBond (My Wife My Baby…And Him)

"Wow another page turner from Shelia!" LuvAGoodBook (McCoys of Holy Rock)

"This series just gets better and better." Barbara Morgan (My Wife My Baby…And Him)

Chapter 1

"The best revenge is just moving on and getting over it."
Unknown

Khalil sat in Hezekiah's office gleaning over the way he had handled the situation with George. He was not anybody's pushover. He learned a lot when he was a youngster on the streets of Chicago shooting up dope, robbing people, and hanging out with gangs. He took the same hustle mentality he learned from the streets, and no doubt from his father, and put them to work at Holy Rock.

When he told Hezekiah about his decision to take over Holy Rock, Hezekiah mouthed some unintelligible garble. Khalil didn't try to decipher what the man was saying. At this stage, he didn't really care what his father thought. Hezekiah had done enough damage as it was and now Khalil was determined to be there for his mother and help her through the troubling times Hezekiah had put her through.

He did as he threatened and reported George to the police. When the police paid George a surprise visit coupled with a search warrant, they confiscated items from his home, but they also gave George a ride to the police station for further questioning.

Khalil had turned over the micro card, after making a copy of it, to the police so they had some more evidence. From what he found out from a friend who had a friend that worked at the police station, George was far more involved with young boys and pornography than Khalil could have ever imagined. From the items they confiscated, Khalil's friend said that George had literally hundreds of illicit pictures of young teenage boys filed away on his computer.

Khalil and Xavier held back the books and computer files they found on Hezekiah's computer. He wasn't letting Hezekiah off the hook, not by a long shot, but for now, he was going to take his time and play his hand well. Hezekiah had messed with the wrong boys, even if those boys were his sons.

"I need you to arrange a meeting with the trustees and deacons," Khalil told Sista Mavis, Hezekiah's administrative assistant. I want it scheduled as soon as you can get the majority of them together, preferably Tuesday morning after the regular weekly staff meeting."

"Yes, I'll get right on it. May I ask you a question, Khalil?" Mavis said cautiously.

"What is it, Sista Mavis?"

"How is Pastor McCoy? I've been praying for him and well, since the family still won't allow visitors, I...I'm well, I'm concerned about him."

"The family? You mean *me*, don't you, Sista Mavis?"

Sista Mavis Beechwood turned a shade darker than her already deep dark melanin skin. She tried her best to refrain from rolling her eyes and coming back with a smart mouthed rebuttal. How dare he talk to her like she was beneath him. Who did he think he was anyway? The pastor?

"No, I didn't necessarily mean you. I meant the whole family. I'm sure First Lady McCoy has her reasons for not allowing visitors, but it would be good to see Pastor McCoy even if it was for a few minutes. Will you tell him that I asked about him and that I'm staying on bended knees before the Lord on his behalf? And y'all should remember too, that God is a healer. And before you know it, Pastor McCoy will be back up in the pulpit sharing his testimony about how God brought him through."

"When you get that meeting arranged, give me a call or shoot me an email, Sista Mavis," Khalil said without so much as acknowledging what Mavis had said.

Khalil strolled off, leaving her looking like she could have been bought for a dime.

Mavis picked up the office phone as soon as Khalil completely disappeared down the hall and entered his office.

"Girl, something is brewing around Holy Rock. I don't know what it is, but I have a feeling that things around here are about to explode," she told the person on the other end of the phone line as she stretched her neck as far as she could around the corner to see if anyone was around who might hear what she was saying.

Khalil stood inside his office with folded arms. He wore his charcoal grey straight leg trousers, with a red pinpoint Untuckit shirt with the sleeves neatly rolled to his elbows, making him look like a male runway model. He made sure he dressed the part of a successful young man. With his matching expensive shoes, no one could tell him that he wasn't sharp. On top of his debonair attire, Khalil smelled good. It was enough to make any and every woman, young or old, swoon in his presence.

He walked over to his desk and stood behind it, looking down on it for a second or two before picking up the phone and calling Sista Mavis.

"Yes, Khalil," she said as soon as she put her call on hold and answered the interoffice call.

"Sista Mavis, will you call Omar and have him come to my office. I need him to move some things around."

"Yes, I'll get right on it."

"Thank you," Khalil said, and ended the call.

Omar was the junior building engineer. He and Khalil were a couple of years apart, with Omar being the oldest. Before Khalil assumed his self-appointed role as Senior Pastor of Holy Rock, he and Omar hung out from time to time, and had actually become friends. Khalil didn't allow too many people close to him, at least, not too many dudes that is. He was cautious about who he allowed in his inner circle. So far, Omar had turned out to be a cool guy. He and Khalil shared some of the same interests like sports and women. Omar was overall one of the good guys. He'd been raised up in the church and since becoming the junior building engineer two years ago at Holy Rock, he had transferred his membership to the church. He was dedicated and committed and possessed good work ethics. Omar loved people and he loved God.

While waiting on Omar, Khalil sat at his desk and called his mother.

"Hi, sweetheart," Fancy McCoy said when she answered her cell phone.

"Hi, Mom. Are you on your way to the church yet?"

"No, I'm still at home. I'm waiting on the nurse to come and relieve me. I've had a time with Hezekiah this afternoon," she complained.

"What do you mean?" Khalil asked.

"You know how he's been having these outbursts for the past few weeks. Now that he's regaining some of his speech and able to get around in that electric wheelchair, it's hell to tell the captain. You would think the man would be humble as a lamb but he's as wild as a boar. Mean as the devil. I thought he was going to hit me earlier when I tried to feed him."

"What? Hit you? Ma, are you okay?"

"Yes, I'm good; I dodged him. I think it's the meds they have him on. Some of that pain medicine from what I've heard makes some people irritable and plus he doesn't think rational all the time. That's from the stroke. You were there with me when we took him to the doctor last month."

"Yeah, but look, Ma, I don't want you putting yourself in harm's way. I think you should do like I suggested last month."

"Khalil, honey. I know your father has done some horrible

things. I mean, sleeping with that slut, Detria Graham, paying George under the table, and going behind my back embezzling money from Holy Rock, but I can't help it—I still love him. If he can just get better, I believe he would try his best to make up for all he's put me through. Actually, all he's put this family through."

"He needs to go to a nursing home, Ma. He needs around the clock care. All he's doing to you is stressing you out."

"Let's not talk about that now." A loud ring interrupted her train of thought. "Oh, dear, that's the doorbell. It must be the nurse. Look, I've gotta go. I'll see you shortly," Fancy said and ended the call without waiting on Khalil to say goodbye.

It had been several months since Hezekiah's massive stroke. He was showing marked signs of improvement. With the speech therapists working with him twice a week and both occupational and rehabilitation therapists coming in, Hezekiah was slowly regaining his strength.

He sat in his electric wheelchair out of Fancy's view and listened to her talking to that traitor son of his. When he got out of this chair and fully recovered, he was going to make all of them pay. He couldn't believe that his family had betrayed him the way that they had. How dare Fancy give her approval for Khalil to take over the ministry of Holy Rock. The boy didn't know jack about the Bible or how to run a mega church like Holy Rock. Was Fancy out of her mind? He had to find a way to communicate his feelings to her but it was still almost impossible for him to string a complete sentence together. He knew in his mind what he wanted to say, but he could never get the words out. But their day was coming.

And what was she talking about? Telling Khalil he had tried to hit her. That was a bold-faced lie. Yes, he did reach out and tried to grab hold of her hand to pull her back toward him. But that was only because she had told him that she was on her way to Holy Rock to help Khalil arrange a meeting with the trustees and deacons to make it official for Khalil to take over his pastorship.

Hezekiah prayed and prayed. Only God could help him. And only God would be able to help Fancy and his sons the day he would be able to get up out of this chair and walk back into Holy Rock. Yeah, God help all of their worthless, miserable, deceitful souls. They were going to pay the piper and they were going to pay him well. *Just you wait and see, Fancy, Khalil, and you too Xavier.*

Chapter 2

"You can fool some of the people all of the time, and all of the people some of the time, but you cannot fool all of the people all of the time." Phineas Barnum

Xavier looked in the mirror and surveyed the cap and gown that still hung in his closet. He was done with high school and ready to live the life he wanted to live. He had plans to attend Xavier University in Louisiana, the college that bore his name, and pursue his degree in law with a minor in African American studies, but that had been put on hold. With George putting his secret homosexual lifestyle on blast to his family, he caved in when Khalil pressured him into helping out in the ministry of Holy Rock. He felt he had brought shame to his mother and brother so the least he could do was adhere to their requests, for now.

He didn't want to forsake his college career for a life spent hanging around Holy Rock. He was tired of living life behind closed doors, fooling people, and hiding who he really was. Xavier wanted distance from his family and from the nosy, prying eyes of folks at Holy Rock.

He looked at his graduation attire one more time before removing the cap and gown from the rack, folding it, and taking it out of the closet and to the chest of drawers in his bedroom. He opened the bottom drawer and put the cap and gown underneath some other clothes he hardly ever wore.

"wanna go grab something to eat?" he texted Raymone.

A few seconds later his text notifier chimed. "Yeah, was just thinking about hitting you up. Pizza good?"

"Yeah, pizza is good. be there to scoop u up in 15," Xavier texted back.

"Cool."

"Xavier," he heard his mother call him on the bedroom intercom. "Xavier," she called again from the downstairs intercom.

He answered by grabbing his keys, leaving out of his room, and rushing down the stairs to see his mother standing on the outside of the foyer leading into the kitchen and garage.

"What's up, Ma?" he asked.

"I'm headed to Holy Rock. Do you want to come along? I think you'll benefit from sitting in on this meeting with your brother and me. We're going to discuss the official announcement about him taking over your father's pastoral duties. Plus, I want you to look over the rest of those files on Hezekiah's computer. We need to make sure nothing is on there that will show that your father was embezzling money from the church. You know now that the feds are all over George, he's probably going to sing like a bird on your father."

"And what if he does?" Xavier said, sounding fed up with talk about his father and Holy Rock.

"We have to have all of our ducks in a row just in case the tables are turned. You're the only one me and your brother can trust to clean that computer system. You're a genius when it comes to things like that," Fancy said. "And we have to stick together."

"Look, Ma, I told you. The only thing I know to do is replace the hard drive. If the feds want to find something out, they have their ways of doing it no matter how much I clean up the computer. And I don't know why you're so concerned about Dad anyway. He did what he did and he is who he is. He's a cheater in more ways than one."

Xavier became angry inside every time he thought of how his father had betrayed his mother. He was also worried that once his father regained his speech that he would tear into Xavier for being gay! He didn't want to hear anything Hezekiah might have to say. It was bad enough that his mother and brother refused to acknowledge that he was a gay man, even after George told them and showed them evidence.

Every time Xavier approached the subject, Fancy found a way to avoid it, and so did Khalil. It was always the wrong time according to the both of them. They even treated Raymone like he had AIDS or something. When Raymone came to the house, Fancy barely opened her mouth to speak or she would make sure she was gone or in her room out of sight. The one good thing about the whole situation was it seemed that his mother was giving him more freedom. She no longer kept him from driving his own car and she rarely said anything when he came in past his appointed curfew.

"It won't take that long, Xavier. Anyway, what could you have to do that's more important than helping your family and working in God's ministry?"

Xavier almost choked at his mother's statement. "Working in God's ministry? Are you kidding me, Ma? I'm far from being the one to work in God's ministry. Do you know how much Christians hate gays?"

"Xavier, now, baby, that is not true, and you know it. Sure, some people whether they're Christians or not, do hate gays and lesbians. But you shouldn't make all Christians wear that jacket. And anyway, I don't want to talk about homosexuals."

"No, Ma. You don't want to talk about *me* being gay. That's what this is all about. Every time I try to sit down and have a talk with you about the person I am, you find a way to skirt around the issue. You're always too busy or you have to run some errand, or whatever. I'm about to leave for college in a few months, Ma. And when I do, it'll be too late for talking." Xavier's voice began to rise. His frustration was obvious.

"First of all, don't you raise your voice at me."

"See, here we go. Now you're going to try to make it seem like all of this is on me. That I'm being disrespectful or something when you know it's not like that. Geesh!" Xavier said, biting down on his bottom lip.

Fancy looked at her youngest son and pointed her finger at him. Her long, polished, manicured nail could have pierced his eye if she got any closer to it.

"I thought we discussed you waiting to attend college next year? Your father is still recuperating, we have the work at Holy Rock, and so much more to contend with. Now is not the time for you to leave home and run off to college. I'm not saying attending college isn't important, but what I am saying is that you need to learn that blood is thicker than water and that sticking by your mother, the only mother you will ever have, is the right thing to do."

Xavier could have exploded; he was just that angry. "That's where you're wrong, Ma."

"What do you mean?" Fancy said, folding her arms and giving her son a cold, hard stare.

"The right thing for me to do is to be me. The right thing for me is to get out of this house and go as far away from here as possible. I have a full ride at Xavier, and I'm taking it. I'm not going to sit out and miss out on that. No way."

"You would walk out on me at a time like this? After all I've done for you and your brother? I've sacrificed my own dreams for this family and you can't sacrifice a few months?"

Instead of turning this into a full-fledged fight, Xavier didn't say another word. He turned and walked past his mother, and out of the house.

"Xavier! Xavier! Come back here," Fancy shouted. "Xavier,

where are you going?"

Again Xavier said nothing. He left the house, jumped in his car, and sped out of the circular driveway to go pick up Raymone.

Fancy waltzed into Holy Rock, still somewhat shaken about the confrontation she and Xavier had. She couldn't believe that he had walked out on her. That was so unlike her baby boy. She would have expected something like that from Khalil. Khalil could be hotheaded and subject to go off without a moment's notice like Hezekiah while Xavier kept his temper under wraps like she did. When she did reach the boiling point, she could be hard to contain. That's exactly how Xavier had reacted today. He had never once raised his voice to her or defiled her in any way. But he had done both today. He refused to come to the church to help her and Khalil, he was going to leave home in a few months even though she told him she wanted him to wait to start college, and he stormed out of the house without telling her where he was going.

That last part wasn't too hard to figure out. More than likely he was going to Raymone's house. She didn't care what George told her, what pictures he showed her, and she didn't care that Xavier admitted to being gay; Fancy refused to accept it. Xavier was just confused, mixed up, and needed to get himself a girlfriend. She hated to think it, but he needed a loose woman right about now. One who could turn his little behind out. Once she got things settled with Khalil taking over Holy Rock, she would have to work on just that—finding the imperfect woman for her baby boy.

Chapter 3

"Trials in life are not meant to make us fail; but to see how far we can fly." Ilifequotes

Stiles prayed that his life would get back to normal but it seemed that as time passed things got worse instead of better. He thought of the latest trial that God had allowed into his life. The mass shooting at Holy Rock seven months ago, discovering that Audrey, the woman he loved and knew as his mother, was not his mother, the tragic murder of his sister and brother-in-law at the hands of a deranged woman, Margaret who was his real mother, and to seal the deal, Hezekiah McCoy was his brother.

"God, I don't know what you have for me in all of this, and I definitely don't see how any of what's happened in my life these past couple of years and these last few months could work out for my good. No way. I know your ways are not my ways," Stiles said as he sat in his recliner in his man cave pausing from watching First Take to converse with God. "I know you called me to be a messenger of your Word, but I don't know how much longer I can hold up. I'm in a state of peril, Father. I need a word from you, a rhema word, Father God."

His cell phone rang in the middle of him pouring out before God. Stiles momentarily paused then ignored the ringing phone and continued his talk with his Father. For the next twenty minutes or more, he cried, he prayed, he pleaded, and beseeched God to deliver him from evil and restore what had been taken away from him.

In front of his congregation Sunday after Sunday, since returning to Houston and to his church family, he put on a face of contentment when inside he was hurting and heartbroken. His messages to the people of God remained strong and uplifting but Stiles didn't know how much longer he could put on a 'happy' face.

His phone started ringing again, moments after he finished his spiritual talk and returned to watching the last few minutes of his favorite sports talks show. He picked up the phone, recognizing it was Pastor's ring.

"Hello, Pastor."

"Hi, son. I was calling to check on you. We haven't talked in at least a month, maybe longer."

"Has it been that long?"

As Stiles thought about it, Pastor was right. He hadn't talked to him in almost a month. That told him that he had been consumed with too many other things in his life and that wasn't like Stiles. He always tried to make time to talk to Pastor. Tomorrow was not promised, and that had been made absolutely clearer than ever after everything that went down at Holy Rock during that awful Jubilee weekend.

"You must be pretty busy there in Houston, huh?"

"I should never be too busy to check in on you and Josie. How are you, Pastor? How is Josie?"

"Still blessed, son. Blessed and highly favored."

Stiles smiled at hearing Pastor still give praises to God after everything he had gone through. Margaret had practically shamed him, told all of his dirty secrets, and belittled him before the congregation of Holy Rock. She had slaughtered innocent people like Francesca, her husband Tim, and Pastor's closest friends, Rena's parents.

"That's good to hear, Pastor. I'm doing the best I can. Still been battling some spiritual issues in my life, but that's between the good Lord and me. I do remember the last time we talked you said you had returned to Holy Rock."

"Yes, I told you before you left Memphis that I was not going to allow Hezekiah to put me out of the church. He removed me from being one of the ministers and I can deal with that, but to tell me that I wasn't welcome at Holy Rock? No way. Me and Josie go there at least a couple of Sundays out of the month. She still feels a tad bit uncomfortable going since she knows how Hezekiah feels so I pacify her by visiting churches of some of my other preacher friends. I must say, I enjoy it but then again there's no place like home, you know."

Stiles could hear the hurt in Pastor's voice. It was sad that Hezekiah acted the way that he did toward Pastor. Sure, finding out that Pastor was his father and Stiles his brother was hard on Hezekiah. Stiles believed that was partially the cause of Hezekiah's stroke. From what he had learned, Hezekiah had suffered with hypertension for many years even though he was a relatively young man. The stress and shock from Margaret's revelation probably sent his pressure through the roof and it wasn't long after the mass shooting that Hezekiah had the stroke.

Stiles had reached out to his brother before he departed Memphis, but of course Hezekiah was still bitter about everything. Stiles couldn't blame him. After all, they're both human and the flesh can be weak and vulnerable when hit with the onslaught of what happened to them. But even with that, Stiles longed to have a relationship with his brother. He wanted to get to know the man Hezekiah and his nephews Khalil and Xavier. It was the only family he had now.

"Are you still there?" Pastor asked.

"Oh, yes, I'm here," Stiles said, having momentarily mentally checked out as a stream of thoughts raced through his mind.

"Anyway, like I was saying, me and Josie are hanging on. God is still good. I'm praying for Hezekiah's healing every day."

"Have you talked to Fancy?" Stiles asked.

"No, not since I told you me and Josie saw her in the hallway at church, but that was a while ago. She spoke to us. You know she's never been one to be mean-spirited. I asked about Hezekiah and she said he was slowly improving. Said he was able to say very short sentences and that with help he could stand up long enough to sit in one of those electric wheelchairs they got for him. You know it took some time for me to fully recover from both of the strokes I had, but I know if God healed me, He will do the same for my son. I just know He will."

"Yes, you're right, Pastor. Well, look, it's been good hearing your voice. I'll do better about calling. I'm really sorry that I've acted like I'm preoccupied."

"No need to apologize. I want you to spend time with the Lord. Ask him to deliver you from this burden you're carrying around. God is the one who wants to bear our burdens, son. He doesn't want us carrying around the weight of things we cannot change. He wants us to lean and depend totally on him."

"Yes, Pastor. Thanks for the word of encouragement. I love you. We'll talk in a couple days," Stiles said.

"Before you hang up, I want you to do something for me," Pastor said.

"Sure, what is it?"

"I want you to reach out to your brother, even if it has to be through his sons or Fancy. And next, I want you to open your heart to receive and give love again. This life is too short to hold on to hurt and unforgiveness. I know you've endured a whole lot. I mean a whole lot; more than some folks endure in a lifetime. You've lost your baby girl, your sister, and well, I don't want to go into it all. I just want you to know that God is still in control, Stiles. No matter how hard it is, He's still got you covered."

"I hear ya," Stiles said with a sound of sadness resounding in his voice.

"Gnite, son."

"Gnite, Pastor." Stiles pushed the END button on his cell phone, sat back on the sofa, and stared at the television as a dog food commercial played on the screen.

The sound of his cell phone ringing awakened Stiles. He looked around in a state of confusion. Another sports show was on and he was stretched out on the sofa, one leg on the sofa and the other one hanging off of it. He looked around, hearing his cell phone ringing but unable to find it. He looked on the floor and then reached underneath his backside and felt the phone.

It stopped ringing by the time he pulled it from underneath him. He looked at his call log and saw that he had missed two calls plus a text message from Kareena and his friend, Leo, from Memphis. He read both text messages.

"Guess you're either sleep or out partying, lol." The text message from Kareena read. "Call me later. Didn't want anything."

The text message from Leo read, "hit me up ltr. Just checking on ya, bruh."

Stiles hit the Call Back button and listened as Kareena's phone began ringing. It rung several times before going to her voicemail.

He looked at his phone. It was going on ten o'clock. Dang, he had been asleep for three hours! Slowly, he got up off the sofa and went to his bedroom. He looked at his phone again to see what time Kareena last called and texted him. It had been two hours ago.

He texted her back with the same message she had texted him about partying, smiling as he hit the SEND button.

Next, he undressed, and then went into his en suite bathroom and took a long hot shower. After he got done with that, he went into the kitchen, grabbed a bottle of water and an apple before returning to his man cave. He didn't feel like sleeping in his bed alone tonight. He would much rather camp out on the sofa and flick the remote back and forth until he fell back to sleep.

Kareena tossed and turned. She wanted so badly to answer her phone when Stiles returned her call, but she didn't. Her feelings were all over the place. She didn't want him to think that she was sitting around waiting on him to call her back. After all, she had friends; she had a life outside of Stiles and outside of the church.

Lately, she had been going out more with friends. She'd even met a nice guy who attended Full of Grace Ministries, too. River Garrett was his name. She hadn't mentioned anything to Stiles about him.

Stiles had made it clear on several occasions that the two of them could never be in a serious relationship; that they were only friends. So why not live her life and move forward? She was a young woman who wanted to have fun, go out on dates, take walks in the park, and ride on Ferris wheels. She wanted to share that with a man, someone who would fall in love with her. She was ready to open her heart and receive all that a man had to give to her. Yes, she had hoped that the man would be Stiles Graham, but Stiles wasn't ready. Kareena doubted that he would ever be ready, so it was time she accepted things for what they were.

She had called to talk to him, to hear his voice and when he didn't answer, Kareena took it as a sign that she should let him be. Later that same evening, when River called and invited her out to dinner she readily accepted. She had to admit that she had a good time. River was extremely easy on the eyes, a real hunk. He had relocated to Houston a few months ago and joined Full of Grace shortly thereafter. He had no children, had never been married, and before his job relocated to Houston he had been in a long term relationship that ended on a sour note when she told him that she was not willing to make the move with him even though he was ready to put a ring on it. They decided that they should go their separate ways and that was that, according to River.

After she returned home from dinner with River, Kareena went over some paperwork she needed to complete for tomorrow evening's church business meeting. Her text notifier chimed; it was a message from Stiles. When she read it, she smiled, laid her phone down, and went back to doing what she was doing.

Chapter 4

"There is no killing the suspicion that deceit has once begotten."
George Eliot

The deacons and trustees listened as Khalil and Fancy discussed Hezekiah's slow recovery and his wishes for his eldest son, Khalil McCoy, to reside over the congregation of Holy Rock while he continued to recover.

The duo presented a signed note from Hezekiah, which of course had been fraudulently signed by the best of the best, Fancy McCoy. Fancy had been forging Hezekiah's signature since back in the day when they were running their schemes. Hezekiah would often tease her, saying that she could sign his name so good that even he had a hard time determining whether he signed it or not. They would both laugh at that, but today was no laughing matter. Things were about to get real.

The deacons and trustees felt compassion and empathy as they listened and watched Fancy McCoy deliver a performance like an academy award-winning actress. She boo-hooed on cue and then told the most touching, loving stories of how Hezekiah was seeking God even in the midst of his stricken body. She gave them the story, along with the signed note, of course that Hezekiah had been led by God to have the ministry run by Khalil. He asked the deacons and trustees to give Khalil a chance and vote for him to become the interim senior pastor of Holy Rock until he was able to return. If God saw fit that he was not to return to the pulpit, Hezekiah stated in the typed letter that his wishes were for his son to be appointed as his permanent replacement.

By the time Fancy finished her award-winning performance, Khalil stood up and in a booming, confident voice that reminded the attendees of Hezekiah McCoy, he too delivered a powerful message about how God had spoken to him in a dream.

"The Lord is faithful. He takes care of His own. I know this is a big move we're asking of you to support. I know that you probably are asking yourself and one another how a young man can like me lead a flock like Holy Rock. Well, I've been prepared for such a time as this. My earthly father has been preparing me since I was a young boy," Khalil said, sounding like a mighty servant of God. "The Lord has brought us through a raging storm. He's seen us through some real turbulent times, but we're still standing!"

"Speak boy," one of the trustees said.

"Amen," said another one.

"God is a God that cannot fail. He's a God that makes no mistakes. Who would have thought that out of tragedy God would bring me to this very place at this very time? I know it's asking a lot of you, but I am asking you to not think of how young I am. Do not think of how inexperienced I am. Do not think of those things. Instead, think of what the good Lord says. Learning how to be led by the Holy Spirit is one of the most important things you can do. It doesn't matter a person's age or the stage they are in life. I had to get quiet and begin to listen to what the Holy Spirit was saying to my spirit. So, I stand here confidently before you. Isaiah forty-one verse ten says, do not fear, for I am with you. Do not anxiously look about you, for I am your God. I will strengthen you. Surely I will help you, surely I will uphold you with my righteous right hand."

By the time Khalil finished his mini sermon, the trustees and deacons were on fire praising God and welcoming Khalil McCoy as the new Senior Pastor of Holy Rock!

Fancy smiled and embraced her son after the meeting ended.

"We did it!" she said with joy. "Baby, you had the room on fire. You had those men ready to sign over everything they have if you had asked them to." Fancy paraded around the room like she was full of the Holy Ghost, dancing and shouting and waving her hands all up in the air while Khalil reared his head back and released a long loud laugh!

"Let's go celebrate, Ma. Let's go out to eat. And dinner's on me."

"I heard that. Let's do it." Fancy gathered her purse from behind the desk and walked toward the door.

"Hey, what happened to Xavier? He was supposed to be here."

"You're going to have to talk to that boy. He ran out on me."

"What do you mean by he ran out on you?"

"Called himself getting mad 'cause I was telling him that he needed to be here to help us clean your father's computer files and he needed to be at this meeting."

"He got upset because he says he doesn't want to sit out from college for a few months. Talking about what he wants to do is more important than his family."

Khalil walked in front of Fancy and opened the office door for her, allowing her to step out in front of him, before he turned around and locked it. "

"Ma, I've been thinking about that. Let him go on off to college. I mean he's already dealing with enough. My brother is a gay male; that's hard for me to accept and I know it's hard for you to accept. And even though Dad is a no good, lying creep, I hate to see and hear his reaction when he finds out that his baby boy is gay. So I'm saying that maybe Xavier does need to leave. We don't need any more unnecessary drama at Holy Rock...or at home. You feel me?"

"I guess, but he still could have come today. He hasn't left for college yet. I know he ran to that boy, Raymone. I tell you, Khalil, I'm hurt. I'm hurt and disappointed in Xavier. That's my baby. My baby boy."

Mother and son walked down the hallway and out of the church, onto the parking lot, talking along the way.

"You've got to do something about him," Fancy told Khalil.

"Do something like what, Ma? That's between him and God. He has to live his own life. Anyway, I get enough play for me and him from the ladies, young and old," Khalil teased.

"I'm serious, Khalil. You have to help me. I have to find a girl for your brother."

Khalil stopped in his tracks. "Ma, what are you talking about? Have you not heard anything that Xavier has said or that George showed us? Your son, my brother, is gay. G-A-Y, gay, Ma. No woman is going to change that."

"How do you know until you try? So promise me you'll help me find a girl for your brother."

Khalil looked at his mother, shook his head from side to side, and said, "Come on, Ma. We're taking my ride. We'll talk about Xavier over dinner."

"That's my boy," Fancy said and practically skipped the couple of steps to Khalil's sparkling candy apple red Lexus LC 500 coupe.

"Are you still angry with me?" The text message said.

Khalil read it while walking to their table. This woman had some nerve. Detria had been randomly texting him for God knows how long. He hadn't responded to any of them. He started to block her out, but he believed blocking people out of his phone was a female move and he was definitely no female. He left that up to his li'l bro.

He laughed to himself at the thought of his mother thinking that setting Xavier up with a girl would cure his gayness. He'd heard of some wild things, but this far outweighed them all. Yet, he knew that once his mother made up her mind about something, there was no way she was going to give up or give in until she got what she wanted. He decided that if she continued to press the issue that he would talk to one of the females in the youth program or better yet, maybe find one of those streetwalkers who he could throw a few bucks to. But now that he was the Senior Pastor he had to watch his back and his steps. He would have to remind his mother of that. They had to keep their hands as clean as possible.

"Ma, have you thought anymore about putting Daddy in a nursing home. You got too much pressure on you. Him being there twenty-four seven in the condition that he's in, is not good on you. You deserve to live your life in some peace and tranquility."

Khalil's text chimed again. "I just want a few minutes of ur time. We need to talk. Please. I won't bother you again if you promise to see me one more time."

Dang, this female constantly on my... he thought.

"I have to admit, it is difficult seeing Hezekiah in the state he's in and then remembering how he cheated on me. Then for him to act all mean towards me. I don't know; maybe you're right. Maybe we can find him a good rehab facility. You know somewhere that will give him all the therapy he needs, make sure he gets his meds and well...I don't know, Khalil." Fancy sighed deeply then used her fork to play around in her spinach and kale salad.

"I'll get right on it. I think I know of a couple of places that can accommodate him. You're going to be busier than ever helping me at the church, too. It's no way you can do both. He's lucky that you even want to be around him after what he's done. And what can he say? He knows he needs more specialized care than we can give him. I don't care if we *do* have nurses coming to the house. He'll get better use from his insurance if he's in a rehab facility and nursing home. You can go see him whenever you like."

"That sounds good, but at the end of the day I'm his wife.

Hezekiah and I have been through some tough times. You have to understand too, that I've been with your father since I was a young teen. He's all I know."

"All I'm saying is think about it. Pray on it. This is not about leaving the man. It's about getting him the help he needs; help you can't possibly give him. Look at you, you've lost weight; you're thin as a rail, you're always looking tired, you've lost your spark, Ma."

"Wow, thanks a lot, son." Fancy raised an eyebrow and looked a little hurt although she knew that every word Khalil said was true.

"I don't mean it like that. I'm just stating facts. Anyway, enough of the Dad talk. Let's enjoy this food and have a good time. Your son is the senior pastor of Holy Rock, Ma! Can you believe that?"

Fancy laughed, something she hadn't done in a while. It felt good. *Laughter really is good for the soul,* she thought, *and so is payback.*

Mother and son continued to enjoy their time together. When they were done, Khalil took his mother back to the church to pick up her car. He went back inside Holy Rock and asked Sista Mavis if she'd seen Omar.

"Yes, he was just here. I think he went over to the upper school. There were some bulbs that needed changing, and a few other things he needed to do over there," Mavis reported. "Do you need me to call him?"

"No…well, yes. Give him a call and ask him to come to my office."

"Will do," said Mavis and immediately got on the phone and called Omar.

Khalil turned to walk toward his office, paused, looked back over his shoulder, and then walked back the few feet to Sista Mavis' desk.

"Sista Mavis, I have some news to share about what the good

Lord has done in my life and the life of Holy Rock," Khalil said, smiling broadly.

"Tell me," she said anxiously. "She loved to hear a good praise report, and she felt special, extra special when the clergy confided in her. She was a gossiper, but she knew when and what to gossip about.

"Of course, you know First Lady Fancy and I met with the trustees and deacons."

"Yes, yes, and how did that go?"

"It went extremely well. Sista Mavis, you're looking at the new Senior Pastor of Holy Rock."

"What you say?" Mavis' eyes bulged and she almost wasted the cup of piping hot coffee that she'd just lifted up to her mouth to sip.

Khalil tilted his head back slightly and to the side. Laughter spilled from between his lips as he repeated himself. The look on Sista Mavis' face was priceless.

"Yes, God has called me to a higher calling. You know I thought working with the young people, with my peers, was what I was supposed to spend my ministry doing, but you know, Sista Mavis, God had other plans. I've been dealing with this in my spirit since Pastor McCoy's stroke, but I fought against what I knew God was directing me to do. But today sealed it. Today, during that meeting, the Lord spoke plainly and clearly."

"Well….uh…I…." Mavis sat her cup of coffee down on her desk. Words were difficult to get out. She was still reeling over the news Khalil had just shared. *This youngster is taking Pastor McCoy's place? Oh my, Lord. Umph, umph, umph.*

"I'm telling you, but I expect this to remain confidential for now. I'll be preaching Sunday and the official announcement will be shared with the congregation at all three services."

"Okay, Khalil. Oops, I guess I'd better get using to calling you, Pastor McCoy," Mavis slightly stuttered and grinned. "Congratulations. You must do what God calls you to do," she said. "If you're anything like your father, you're going to be one helluva....oh, forgive me Father," Mavis looked up toward the ceiling, lifting her hands.

"Well, I'm headed to my office. Will you send Omar down there as soon as you see him?"

"Sure thing, Kha...I mean Pastor McCoy." Mavis giggled. She watched until Khalil disappeared before she picked up her cell phone off of her desk and hit the keypads. "Girl, you won't believe what I just heard straight from the horse's mouth."

Chapter 5

"I felt like an animal, and animals don't know sin, do they?"
Jess C. Scott

Khalil sat back in his office chair. He went through several files and afterwards began preparing his sermon notes for this Sunday's service. He laughed to himself. *Him? Preparing sermon notes?* Never in a million years. He couldn't believe that he'd come this far in his young life. From the streets of Chicago, addicted to heroin and cocaine, robbing and stealing, to a juvenile detention center, to leading a congregation of over 15,000 members on the church roll. Who would've thought this would be his life?

He said a prayer thanking God for what He was about to do in his life as senior pastor of Holy Rock. Sure, part of his mission wasn't all directed toward God; he had a score to settle with his father, but Khalil felt that even in the midst of his disdain toward his daddy, God was still using him and he planned to do his best to serve the congregation and God. But he sure as heck wasn't going to cheat the people or steal from the church.

The knock on the door pulled Khalil from his thoughts. "Come in."

"Hey, what's up, man?" Omar said, entering into his friend's office.

"Hey, dude. How's it going?" Khalil asked.

"Everything's good. I came by here the other day, but you

were already gone so I didn't know what you needed. You called to hang out?"

"Yeah, sorry about that. And no, I wasn't calling to hang out. I need you to move me into my father's former office." Khalil spoke without reservation or hesitation. He sounded confident and determined.

"Whoa, that's a big move, my man," Omar said, standing in front of Khalil's desk.

"Yeah, it is. I'm sure Sista Mavis told you."

"Told me what?"

"Man, I know that woman can't hold water. I mean, she's good at what she does, but keeping her mouth shut is not one of her strong suits."

Omar laughed. "I ain't heard a thing," he said, showing both palms.

"Sure you haven't. Well, let me be the first to tell you."

"Tell me what?" Omar feigned surprise because Khalil had been right; Sista Mavis had told him about Khalil's promotion to senior pastor as soon as he stepped up to her desk. And in Sista Mavis fashion, she made Omar promise not to breathe a word.

"I'm stepping into my father's role as senior pastor of Holy Rock."

"*Whaat?* Get outta here!"

"Yeah, it's a done deal. The deacons and trustees cosigned on the change earlier today."

"Bruh, that's cool. I'm happy for ya. I think you're gonna do good, 'specially if you're as good as your pops."

"Thanks, Omar. So that's the reason I called you. Like I said, I want to move some things from my office over to his.

"No problem. You know I gotcha covered."

"My furniture can stay in this office, but I need the IT department to set up my electronic files. I do want some of the other things in my office moved over like some of these pictures and things on the wall, stuff like that. I also want to redo some things in my father's office. You know, make it my own."

"I hear ya. I'm on it."

"I knew I could count on you."

"You know it. We need to go out and celebrate. You know, get a couple of the ladies, and hit the M-town for some fun. Pretty soon, you're going to be too busy to even stop and blow your nose." Omar chuckled.

"You got that right. Set something up and let's do it," Khalil said.

"Consider it done," Omar replied. "I'll get things set up for the move. Let's say we start Thursday morning. In the meantime, let me know the changes you want to make in Pastor McCoy's office and what you want moved out of this office. How is he, by the way?"

"Things are progressing rather slowly, but he's hanging in there. It's just a lot on my mom, you know. I've been trying to convince her to send dad to a rehabilitation facility, but so far she hasn't budged. I mean he gets primarily around the clock care, but it's still not giving her any real, lasting relief from taking care of him."

"I hear you. Well, I hope he makes a full recovery. But thank God you're a real soldier, bruh. It takes heart, real heart to step up to a role like senior pastor."

"Thanks, man."

Omar turned, walked toward the office door, and opened it to leave.

"Oh, wait up. There's something else I almost forgot to talk to you about."

"What is it?" Omar asked.

"I want you to be one of my deacons. Don't get me wrong, my father has some great deacons and trustees, but I want to be surrounded by my dawgs, you feel me?" Khalil stated.

"Yo, man, are you sure you want me?"

"Yeah, I'm sure. Hey, man, on a serious tip. You're a cool

dude and from what I've seen you're committed to Holy Rock and you're committed to God."

Omar looked at Khalil. He was speechless at this point.

"What? You don't want it?" Khalil asked.

"Are you kiddin' me? Of course I want it. Thanks, man." Omar walked up and gave Khalil dap. "What do you think the other deacons are gonna say?"

"I'll break it to 'em gently." Khalil laughed and so did Omar "But seriously, I'll explain to them that I need my own fellas around me. And I'm not getting rid of all of them; I have a couple more guys I'm asking, too."

"You know I'm with you," Omar said. "Thanks again, bruh." Omar exited the office with a huge smile on his face. As he walked past Sista Mavis' desk, she stopped him. She wanted to find out what Khalil was up to, but Omar waved up his hand and said, "I can't talk right now, Sista Mavis. I'm in a hurry. Gotta go take care of something." Omar hurriedly walked past her desk, laughing to himself as he pictured the look on Sista Mavis' face.

Khalil returned to his desk and sat down in the office chair. He returned to working on his sermon when his text notifier chimed. "

"So you're just going to totally ignore me? That's not fair."

Again, Khalil did just that....ignored Dee's text. He didn't have time for her antics. The nerve of her. Sleeping with his daddy and him? *Dang, some of these females are scandalous to the bone.*

He returned to working on his sermon and for the next forty-five minutes, he worked harder than ever. He wanted his first official sermon as Senior Pastor of Holy Rock to be da bomb. He decided his message would be about hope. He had chosen several passages of scripture to preach from, but the main scripture he was going to use was Jeremiah twenty-nine and eleven: *For I know the plans I have you for you, declares the*

Lord, plans to prosper you, not to harm you, plans to give you hope and a future.

When he finished the rough draft, Khalil exhaled, sat back in his chair, and smiled. It felt good. No, he hadn't had any theological training, but he was not beyond studying the Word of God so he could grow into being a true man of God. He wanted to show his daddy that he could do this and he could do it better than Hezekiah ever could.

His interoffice phone rang. It was Sista Mavis.

"Pastor McCoy, there's someone here to see you. I told her that she would need an appointment but she insists on seeing you," Sista Mavis said, sounding perturbed.

"Who is it?" Khalil asked.

Sista Mavis lowered her voice. "You may not know her but I do. And I can't imagine why she's here."

"Who is it?" Khalil pressured Sista Mavis.

She lowered her voice even more. "It's the former first lady of Holy Rock. Her name is Detria Graham. What should I tell her? I don't think I can get her to leave unless I call Security."

"No, that's not necessary. Bring her to my office. No, on second thought, I'll come out and get her. Thank you, Sista Mavis. And Sista Mavis…"

"Yes, Pastor McCoy?"

"Hold all of my calls until I'm done with her. You understand? I'll be out there in a few minutes."

"Yes of course, Khalil…I mean, Pastor McCoy."

Mavis stared at Detria with her nose up in the air. Khalil wouldn't know Detria because he wasn't in Memphis when Detria and Stiles were the first couple of Holy Rock. So why was she here asking to see him? Initially, Mavis thought she was talking about Pastor Hezekiah, but Detria made it clear it was Khalil McCoy she wanted to see. How did she even know he was at this church? That woman was full of games and schemes and Mavis was determined that she was going to find out the motive of Detria's visit. The last she'd seen of Detria was before the accident that killed hers and Pastor Stiles' little girl, Audrey. *That woman ought to burn in hell for what she did. It's her fault that precious little baby is dead. If she hadn't been running around with that gigolo, Skip, when she knew she had a good man in Pastor Stiles, then her baby would still be alive.* Mavis had nothing good to say about Detria Graham. Not one ittty bitty thing.

Detria stood in front of Mavis' desk. She was dressed for the mounting cold weather outside. The forecast called for rain later that day. It was late fall, and the air was quite breezy. So far the skies were clear and the temperature hovered around fifty degrees. Detria made sure she looked good and smelled good. She wore a tangerine fitted trench coat made of Italian-woven cashmere. It tapered at her petite waist and she had on the matching belt, assuring a close fit. The matching rouched hat she wore and her stilettos didn't say 'church lady' at all.

Khalil stood up from behind his desk and walked around to the front of the rectangular walnut desk. Rubbing his head of short cut, thick black hair back and forth with his hand, he wondered what Detria was doing here. Why would she pop up at Holy Rock? This broad was too much. He walked out of his office, up the hall, and soon Detria's frame came into full view.

"Dang, she fine," Khalil said underneath his breath. He hadn't messed around with any females since he kicked Detria to the curb. That had been months ago, so of course his male testosterone was pumping. As he got closer, he felt his physical desire coming to a peak. He used his hand to smooth down his nonexistent mustache and proceeded to walk toward her.

"Sister, uh, Graham?" he said, extending his hand towards her. "I'm Khalil McCoy. If you're here to see my father, I'm sorry to inform you that he's on medical leave. My father suffered a stroke a few months ago."

"She massaged his hand lightly when he shook hers.

Her scent was enticing, and she was just as beautiful as ever in Khalil's eyesight.

"No, I'm aware of your father's stroke. I heard about it on the news. But it's definitely you I wanted to see. I need to talk to you about a highly confidential matter, if you don't mind. And uh," Detria pointed a finger at Mavis, "she told me that I would need an appointment, but please, young man, just give me a few minutes of your time. I promise you won't regret it," she said coyly.

Mavis rolled her eyes and shook her head from side to side, displaying her discontent with the floozy standing in front of her. And who exactly did Detria Graham think she was. Talking about 'she told me." *She knows darn well she knows who I am. If I wasn't in the church house, I'd call her a thing or two, but the good Lord wouldn't be pleased*, Mavis thought.

"In that case, come on back. I have a few minutes," Khalil said, turning to head back to his office. He looked over his shoulder. "Remember, hold my calls, and please no more visitors."

"Yes, Pastor McCoy," Mavis replied, watching as he and the floozy walked down the hall. Once again when she was assured that they were out of earshot, Mavis retrieved her cell phone and called her friend to tell her the latest.

"What do you want, Dee?" Khalil asked as they walked into his office and he closed the door behind them.

"First, what's up with that gossiping, nosy old hag up front calling you Pastor?"

"Not that it's any of your business, but that's who I am," Khalil answered in a condescending tone.

"You? A pastor? Since when? I thought you worked with the youth. What are you now? A youth pastor or something?" Dee asked, sounding confused.

"Like I said, not that it's any of your business, but I'm the Senior Pastor of this great church."

"You've got to be kidding me. You? The senior pastor of Holy Rock? Come on. What kind of shenanigans is Hezekiah up to now? Wait a minute—is Hezekiah? Is Hezekiah dead?"

Khalil chuckled. "Dead? No, he's still down but he's far from being dead. But since he is out of commission for God knows how long, he appointed me to take his place."

"Oh, my God." Dee began to laugh loudly. "That man knows he can come up with some real doozies! I can't believe it. Oh well, maybe I can audition for your first lady."

"Hardly," Khalil answered and walked toward his desk.

"Okay, Pastor McCoy," she said with emphasis and dripping sarcasm. "Tell me, why you won't answer any of my texts?"

"The last time I talked to you I told you to get out of my apartment and that I never wanted to see you again. I meant that, so what's unclear about that?"

"Khalil, we had a good thing going, and you know it."

"A good thing going? Are you serious? You were sleeping with my father, Dee, while you were sleeping with me. I don't see how you can let the words we had a good thing going part your lips. Something has to be wrong with you."

"Nothing is wrong with me. Yes, I was sleeping with Hezekiah, but would it have been any different had you found out I was sleeping with another man and not him? I don't think it would have been a problem. After all, what about you? You're a young, hot, fine, man. I know you were giving all that good loving to some little young girl other than me. Maybe even that little female that was all up on you that night we were at your parents' house. Remember?"

"Yes, I remember, and you're right. If it had been some other dude, I would still be a little salty about it but I probably would still mess with you. We weren't exclusive, never talked about it like that. But the thing is it wasn't some random dude; it was my father. That's too close to home for me."

"Look, I made a mistake, okay? I didn't even know you were

Hezekiah's son when we first met, and when I did find out, I was already feeling you. I didn't want to call things off. I planned on telling you and I also planned on calling things off with Hezekiah but things hit the fan before I could. Please, Khalil. Can't we just start over?" she said seductively, walking up on him.

Khalil gently pushed her away.

"Khalil, you know you miss me. I miss you," she cooed.

Dee took her good hand and began to expertly undo the belt on her trench coat.

"What are you taking your coat off for? You're about to leave, Dee. I'm done. Now please, just go. I have things to do."

Dee disregarded Khalil's demands and instead began to undo the buttons on the coat after she had undone the belt.

"I'll leave but not before I give you something."

"I don't want your gifts. I want you to leave me alone," Khalil said in a more demanding tone, frowning at her.

Dee undid the last button on her coat and then pulled the one side of the coat open, revealing her birthday suit.

Khalil gasped. "What the— Lord, have mercy."

"I've got your mercy," she cooed as she pulled the coat down over her shoulder allowing it to drop to the floor.

Khalil was frozen. He took in the beauty of her curvaceous body, inhaled her womanly scent, and when she closed the gap between them and pressed her body against his, he couldn't resist the fire that raged within his loins. He was good as gone and Dee knew it.

She wove her magic sexuality as she reached up, pulled his head down to meet her lips and gave him an overpowering, passionate kiss. Her tongue explored the crevices of his mouth and Khalil didn't fight back.

He took over; his mouth moved over hers with provocative intensity. His hands moved slowly over the familiar curves of her body. Lifting her up with one hand, he turned her around so that her bottom was on the edge of his desk. His hands continued to roam as he released his belt buckle.

Wrapping her legs tightly around him, she gave him what she knew he wanted. Dee smiled within as she said to herself, *Good things come to those who know how to deliver the goodies.*

Chapter 6

"If you are going through hell, keep going." Winston Churchill

Hezekiah had to find a way to communicate his feelings of discontent about everything that he had been hearing and seeing lately in his house. Fancy must have lost her mind, talking about putting him away in a nursing home. No way was he going to fall for that. And then there was Khalil.

Khalil had come to see him a few days ago talking about assuming the role of Senior Pastor of Holy Rock. Hezekiah couldn't believe his ears. He and Fancy must have been sipping on the same crazy juice or something because if they thought he would give up his ministry and let his thieving dope fiend son takeover, then they had another thing coming.

Hezekiah was determined to work even harder to regain his speech and mobility. He wanted to be able to communicate more than he wanted to walk again. If he couldn't talk, there was no way he would be able to stop the takeover of his ministry by his own flesh and blood.

Before she left for the day, the last nurse used the power lift to help Hezekiah transfer from the bed and into his electric wheelchair. He sat in his electric wheelchair in front of the television watching one of the popular religious TV channels. He usually remained in his electric wheelchair until Xavier came home to help transfer him back into the bed. Fancy didn't do as well when it came to things of that nature, but she did try.

Fancy entered his room and he gave her a look that hopefully sent her the message that he was not one to be played with;

stroke or no stroke.

"Good evening, Hezekiah," Fancy said as she walked further into the room she had set up downstairs for him after he had the stroke. He slept in the room alone, and unless one of his nurses was there he was all alone most of the time. Fancy came in from time to time, but that was only if she was relieving one of the three nurses that came throughout the day and evening. The last nurse left at nine o'clock at night. After that time, Hezekiah was left alone to think of how his life had ended up like this.

Fancy kept a baby monitor in his room so she could hear and see what was going on. There had been a few times when she came rushing downstairs to check on him after he had what was diagnosed as panic attacks.

"Khalil will be preaching his first sermon Sunday. I know you're going to be proud of him."

"No," he managed to say. He could say a few short sentences but no long words and if he got upset, he couldn't even say short sentences.

"Don't want him...Holy Rock," he said with more force. In frustration, he banged his good hand on his electric wheelchair sending a shooting pain throughout his fingers

His words surprised Fancy. "Sounds like your speech is getting better. That's good. Seems like the first words that would have come out of your mouth would have been I'm sorry. But like always, you only think of yourself, and frankly I'm sick of it."

"Don't you...," Hezekiah said and pushed the Forward button on his electric wheelchair and rolled up closer to Fancy.

"Watch it. Don't run over me, fool!" Fancy screamed.

Hezekiah stopped the chair and managed to grab hold of Fancy's wrist with the one good hand he had. It was his left hand and arm that he had regained a measure of strength and mobility. Not completely, but enough to be able to maneuver himself in his wheelchair by the push of the button throughout the downstairs of their lavish home. Latching on to her wrist, he refused to let it go.

"Lemme go. Turn me loose, Hezekiah. You're hurting me," she said as she pulled away from him, trying to get out of his grasp. The more she tried it seemed the tighter Hezekiah's grip became. She didn't know his strength had returned like this.

One thing about Hezekiah, he could be mean as a Pitbull, but he had never laid a hand on her. He used his words to attack her but things were obviously different now. Since he couldn't say what he wanted to say, he used every ounce of his strength to let her know that he wasn't going to give up his power at Holy Rock or in his house.

"Don't want him...Holy Rock."

Fancy jerked again and again but he still wouldn't let go of her. Without much thinking, she hauled off and slapped him as hard as she could.

Hezekiah broke his hold on her and then placed his hand on the wheelchair level. He headed toward her again and this time, since she was right up on him, he pushed the Forward button on his chair with full force, running up against Fancy's ankles and causing her to fall backwards and down on the hardwood floor, trapping her legs.

Hezekiah's' eyes grew large, but the scowl on his face remained. He backed up so she could get up off the floor.

"Nooooo!" His voice sounded like a grizzly bear.

Fancy scurried up off the floor and ran toward the door, hobbling and crying. She turned and looked back at him with fury and rage. "That's it. You've done it now. I'm getting you out of this house. You watch and see. And Khalil is the new pastor whether you like it or not. You're going to pay for what you just did. You're going to pay dearly!"

Fancy took off out of the room as Hezekiah headed toward her again.

Fancy managed to close the door on him before he ran her

down again. Still crying, she raced upstairs to her bedroom.

"Ma, what's wrong? Why are you crying?" Xavier asked, walking down the hall from out of his bedroom.

"Your father has gone mad," she said, pointing to her ankles. One of them was bleeding and the other had begun to swell.

"He almost broke my ankles with that electric chair."

"Did he lose control of it or what?" Xavier asked.

"Lose control? No, he did it on purpose. He's crazy. I've had enough, Xavier. He's going to a nursing home."

"Calm down, Ma," Xavier said as he reached out for his mother and helped her to her room. He led her to the sofa in her bedroom, sat her down, and then went into her en suite bathroom. Moments later, he returned with a cold towel and some triple antibiotic gel. He got ready to sit down next to her to tend to her ankles but Fancy jumped up. She almost fell back on the sofa, but she steadied herself by leaning on the back of the sofa. Tears were flowing heavier than ever. The more she cried the angrier she became. She took off out of her bedroom and toward the stairs.

"Ma, wait. Where are you going?" Xavier asked.

She dashed to the foot of the stairs and began screaming and yelling.

Hezekiah came out of the room behind Fancy and positioned the wheelchair at the bottom of the stairs. But there was no way he could run her down or grab hold of her again. She made certain of that by remaining on the stairs.

"I've been nothing but good to you, Hezekiah McCoy. I've stuck by you, accepted your mess, upheld you when you were dead wrong, even went to prison for you. All the time you've done nothing but use me and now you want to abuse me? You've cheated on me with that that witch, Detria. Only God knows how many other women there've been. Well, I'm sick of it. And I'm sick of you. First thing tomorrow morning, you're leaving here."

Xavier stood at the top of the stairs watching and listening. He wanted to make sure his mother didn't go all the way down the stairs and within his father's reach because if Hezekiah did anything else to her, Xavier knew that he would hurt his own father. He hated seeing his mother in tears. And for his father to run her down with of all things, his electric wheelchair, was sickening.

There was a time he respected his father; looked up to him, considered him his mentor and role model, but ever since he found out about his father sleeping with the same woman his brother was sleeping with, Xavier had lost all respect for the man. And his actions tonight proved that his father was mentally messed up. Xavier reasoned that his mood and behavior had to be a result of the stroke, but if he had now turned to violence against his mother, Xavier wanted his father out of the house, too.

"Ma, come on. Come back to your room. I need to check on your ankles," he said, looking at his father with red, blazing eyes. Xavier was so angry that his temples throbbed and his jawbones too. He went down the stairs to meet his mother.

Fancy turned around and headed back upstairs, meeting Xavier halfway. She allowed him to help her up the remaining winding staircase as her ankles throbbed. She limped all the way up the stairs while Hezekiah managed to say a few choice cuss words as loudly and as meanly as he could.

The following morning, Khalil arrived at the house. Xavier had called him the night before and so did his mother. He was ready to come to the house and yank his father out of that chair. It didn't matter that he'd had a stroke or not, but Fancy finally talked him down and convinced him to stay at home and just come to the house to make some calls about getting Hezekiah admitted to a long term facility.

The first shift nurse arrived, and after Fancy told her what had happened, she immediately made a few phone calls to check on room availability at a few of the rehab facilities. There were several hospitals in Memphis, but Fancy told herself that she wanted the best for Hezekiah. Deep down inside, she knew that she really wanted the best for *her* and the best for her was for Hezekiah McCoy to be as far away from her as possible.

The nurse contacted East Nursing Home and Rehabilitation Center in Nashville. It was an affiliate of South Nursing Home and Rehab Facility in Memphis so the nurse was able to provide much assistance in maneuvering through any red tape.

Within hours, after it was determined that they would accept Hezekiah, a local representative from the hospital arrived. She performed a pre-admission screening to coordinate the transfer. She talked to Fancy, Xavier, and Khalil. Last, she talked to Hezekiah; he was furious. His pressure had skyrocketed, his eyes were bloodshot, and the few words he could say were cuss words. At the end of his screening, she determined that first Hezekiah needed to be transferred immediately to downtown Methodist University Hospital to get his blood pressure stabilized and to get him calmed down. Within the next 24 hours, she explained to Fancy and her sons that they could then transfer Hezekiah to East Nursing Home.

Within a couple of hours, after she completed her screening, a transport ambulance arrived. Hezekiah was sleeping because the nurse had given him a sedative to calm him down.

Fancy had tears in her eyes as she watched them put him inside the ambulance. They told her that she could ride along but Fancy refused. She wanted this done as quickly as possible. She had had enough for now and plus her ankles were still swollen and hurting.

Khalil told her he wanted her to see a doctor and get some x-rays taken to make sure nothing was broken. After Hezekiah left, he told Xavier to take their mother to the doctor right away.

Things were about to change drastically in the McCoy household now that dem McCoy boys were in charge.

Chapter 7

"Health is not valued until sickness comes." Thomas Fuller

Hezekiah woke up, looked around, and felt confused about where he was. The last thing he remembered was being at home in his electric chair and talking to a nurse about his high blood pressure. Now he had awakened here in this sterilized, cold room. He looked around the room and realized that he was in the hospital. What had Fancy done? Had she made good on her threats to have him put away like he was some stray animal? If she had, she would pay. He would make sure of it.

He saw that he was attached to tubes and had an IV in his left arm. He saw the button to call for the nurse but he couldn't use his right arm so he couldn't call for assistance. He had questions that he wanted answers to.

As if someone read his mind, a nurse entered his room. "I'm glad to see that you're awake," the polite sounding young, overweight, blonde-haired, white girl said. "I'm Marcia, your evening shift nurse." She erased the previous name off the white board that was on the wall in front of Hezekiah's bed and wrote her name on it.

"Where?"

"You want to know where you are?"

Hezekiah nodded slowly.

"You're at Methodist University Hospital. Your blood pressure was at stroke level so we had to bring you here to get it stabilized. You've already had one stroke. I know you don't want to have another one. You're going to have to learn how to remain calm and not stress yourself out. Next time, you might not be so lucky, Mr. McCoy. Okay?" she said as she studied the machine he was connected to, checked his IV, and then told him to open his mouth wide so she could take his temperature.

Hezekiah did as he was told.

"Your temp is normal, but your pressure is still up a bit. But continue to get some rest. They should be bringing in your dinner shortly. If you need something, just push the button on the side of your bed."

"Can't," Hezekiah mumbled.

"Excuse me?"

"Can't." Hezekiah shifted his eyes from the nurse to his hand.

The nurse followed his gesture with her eyes. "Are you able to push the button?"

Hezekiah shook his head from side to side. "No."

"Okay, here then." The nurse removed a corded buzzer from above Hezekiah's bed and placed it next to his right hand. "Will this do?"

"Other," he said and looked at his left side.

The nurse moved the corded buzzer to his left side. "Better?" she asked and smiled.

He nodded.

"I'll be back in to check on you a little later. Oh, before I leave, do you need anything? You have a catheter inserted so you don't have to worry about going to the bathroom unless of course you have to, well if you need to have a bowel movement."

Feeling embarrassed, Hezekiah again shook his head for no.

The nurse noticed his pressure going up. "It's nothing to be embarrassed about Mr. McCoy. It's a natural occurrence you know. Please, keep calm. Remember, we want to get your pressure stabilized so you don't have to be stuck up in this hospital for any longer than needed." She smiled that bright smile. "Okay?"

The nurse exited the room, closed the door behind her, and seconds later, the door opened again. A short, dumpy man with locs walked in with a tray of food. He spoke while he positioned the side table over Hezekiah's bed so Hezekiah could reach his food.

"Do you want me to let the head up on your bed a bit?" the older man asked.

Hezekiah nodded

The man raised Hezekiah's bed up and then removed the top off the tray of food to reveal the usual hospital food of two vegetables, two pieces of baked chicken, a dessert, a glass of water and some tea.

"Here you go. Enjoy," the man said and left out of the room.

Hezekiah stared at the tray of food and tears began to form in his eyes. He didn't want to cry and he was going to do everything he could to keep his tears at bay, but he couldn't help but feel distressed over his present situation and the choices he'd made that helped land him there.

The thought that Fancy and his sons wanted to get rid of him was more than he could possibly conceive. All that he had gone through with that woman and she wanted to push him out of her life the way that she did was too much. And learning about his true identity, his dead birth mother, Margaret and his new brother, Stiles was enough to send him into cardiac arrest, or rather a stroke.

He looked at the phone and tried to reach it as it started ringing, but he couldn't. He felt helpless and hopeless. The phone rung several more times before it stopped. He turned his head away from it and then looked at his tray of food before using his one good hand and arm to sweep the plate off the tray and onto the floor.

Hezekiah remained in the hospital for three days before he

was told that he would be transferred to East Nursing Home and Rehabilitation Center.

I'm not going to anybody's rehab, and definitely not one out of this city, Hezekiah complained to himself when the nurse and doctor told him that today was his transfer date.

He put together as many words as he could muster to relay his discontent with being transferred.

"From what we understand, you have no one to adequately care for you at your home, Mr. McCoy. Of course, we can't force you to go to East, but I do strongly urge you to do what's best for your long-term care. It's not like you would be there on a permanent basis, only until you're able to be more ambulatory and do things on your own."

Hezekiah shook his head as forcefully as he could. "No. No."

"I understand your frustration, but I'm telling you that being upset like you are is not good for your health or your blood pressure. If you want to regain the use of your limbs and improve your speech, the best place is at a rehab facility or nursing home. If you insist on not going to Nashville then I can see if there are beds available at one of the facilities here in the city. Would you like me to do that?" the doctor asked.

"Yes," Hezekiah said.

"I'll look into it right away." The doctor turned and walked out of the room and so did the nurse.

Later that day, Fancy and her two sons came to say their goodbyes to Hezekiah, only to be told that he had been discharged and transferred to a facility out east off Primacy Parkway. Fancy was enraged.

"Why didn't anyone call me?" she said to the nurse situated at the front nurses' station outside of Hezekiah's former hospital room.

"Ma'am, I'm sorry. I just came in. The transfer was done during the last shift. But in checking the doctor's notes, your husband refused to go to Nashville. Dr. Kuykendall was able to get him a bed at the nursing home and rehab facility on Primacy Parkway."

"That is not where he was supposed to go!"

Khalil walked up and put an arm around his mother's shoulder. "It's okay, Ma. At least they sent him to a place where he can get some help and the proper care and attention. It'll be a load off of you, regardless."

"Yeah, Ma, and you can go see him any time you want to since he's still in Memphis," offered Xavier.

Fancy turned and looked at Xavier, rolled her eyes, pursed her lips, and then looked back at the nurse. "You all haven't heard the last of this. This was totally inappropriate. My husband is not mentally stable enough to make decisions," she snapped.

The nurse looked frightened. "I'm sorry, Mrs. McCoy. I really am. All I can do is call your husband's doctor. Maybe he can tell you what to do next," she offered.

Fancy inhaled and then slowly released a deep breath. "Thank you, but that won't be necessary. I know how to contact Dr. Kuykendall. Thank you. Let's go," she turned and looked at Khalil then at Xavier.

The three of them headed out of the hospital with Fancy walking in front like she was the leader of the pack.

Arriving at the rehab and nursing home twenty minutes later, Fancy, Khalil, and Xavier entered the doors of the facility and Fancy asked where she could find Hezekiah.

"Ma'am, I'm sorry, but that information is confidential," the front desk clerk stated.

"He is my husband," Fancy told her.

"I understand, ma'am, but your husband has stated and signed on his paperwork that he wants no visitors. He specifically stated that he didn't want to see anyone from his family or his church unless they were listed on his visitation form."

Fancy looked at Khalil and then turned to the other side and looked at Xavier. "What's going on? she asked.

"Look, are you sure, uh, uh, Ursula," Khalil asked after reading the woman's name tag. He flashed a smile at her. "There has to be some kind of mistake. My father has been under a lot of stress lately due to a stroke. My mother should have been informed that my father was being admitted to your facility. Is there any one we can talk to that can help us get this problem resolved?"

The young woman looked like she had been transformed to another space and time as she looked dreamily into Khalil's eyes.

"I'll see what I can do," she said as she tapped the keys on a laptop. "I'll see if the director's assistant can help you. Let me call him and see if he's in his office."

"Thank you so much, Ursula." Khalil flashed another smile and reached over the counter and extended his hand toward the woman.

She met his hand and he caressed hers more than shook it. She picked up the phone and within a minute or two she ended the call.

"The medical director's assistant is James Burlington. He's on the third floor, room 326. The elevators are to the right. When you get off, go to your left, and follow the green footprints to the next hallway on the right. His office will be down that hall. If you get lost, there's another receptionist on that floor."

"You've been so kind," Khalil said.

Fancy mouthed a quick "thank you" and walked off with Xavier trailing behind her.

Khalil hung back for a few minutes and talked to Ursula. By the end of his conversation, Khalil had found out that she was a single mother of two girls, had been living in Memphis for less than a year, and had been working at the facility for a little less than two months. He invited her to attend Holy Rock and she had promised him between blushes that she would love to come hear him preach.

Khalil strolled off and caught up with his mother and brother just as they were stepping on to the elevator.

"You're just like your father," Fancy said when Khalil approached. "A charmer…a real charmer." She smiled and Xavier pushed the button to the third floor.

The director's assistant gave Fancy information about Hezekiah which included the location of his room. Fancy had explained that her husband was mentally unstable as well as physically unstable because of the stroke and was therefore not in a position to make sound decisions regarding his health care. As far as financial responsibilities, she told Mr. Burlington that she was the one who handled his affairs in that instance as well. Hezekiah's insurance would pay much of his health care bills, but there was also out of pocket expenses that would have to be paid. She assured the man that if he wanted to make sure that they received the monies due them for Hezekiah's length of time spent at the facility, then he needed to keep her abreast of everything that would be going on with him during his stay.

At the end of the twenty-minute meeting, the four of them walked out of Mr. Burlington's office and he escorted the McCoy family to Hezekiah's floor and room.

When Fancy walked into his room, Hezekiah's eyes bulged.

She walked over to him and gave him a peck on the cheek, smiling like she was glad to see him.

Fancy looked back. "Thank you, Mr. Burlington. Thank you for everything," she said.

"You're quite welcome. Mr. McCoy, you're in good hands at our facility, sir. I'm glad we cleared up the misunderstanding about your wife and family."

"Thanks, man," Khalil said, and extended his hand out to shake the man's hand.

James Burlington was tall, dark, and handsome and Fancy almost drooled when she saw him. He was definitely pleasing to look at and he had an enticing scent that wafted up her nostrils and aroused her femininity. That was definitely something she missed since Hezekiah's stroke; their lovemaking. She walked back over to him as he prepared to leave them with Hezekiah. "I can't thank you enough," she whispered as they stood at the door. "Please, let me do something to show my appreciation. I was worried sick about my husband. I mean he's been unable to do much of anything since his stroke a few months ago." She batted her eyes at him and tugged gently on his hand.

"You don't owe me a thing, ma'am. It's my job," James said, trying to maintain his own composure. This woman was just like he liked his women. Beautiful, petite, smart, and in control. If he wasn't a married man, he would definitely give her a few things she could do to repay him.

"That's nice of you, but if you think of anything, please by all means, call me. My number is on file now that we've updated my husband's paperwork," she said flirtatiously.

"Yes…uh, I'll keep that in mind. Now, if you'll excuse me, I need to get back to my office. But let me also remind you that you can reach out to me anytime if you have other concerns or questions."

"Definitely," she whispered. "Definitely." She turned slowly and with an extra switch in her step, she walked back inside Hezekiah's room, feeling James Burlington's eyes glued to her backside.

Walking back inside Hezekiah's spacious room, Fancy didn't waste a moment blasting him out. "You honestly think that after you tried to break my ankles that I would let you get away with trying to pull something like this? Well, that's exactly why I call the shots now, Hezekiah. Remember, you're not mentally stable enough to make decisions of your own."

She shot Hezekiah a devious look. "You proved that you didn't give a care about me when you did what you did, but now it's my turn, and I told you that payback was coming. I'll let you stay here in this dump, because that's exactly what it is – a dump. I tried to send you away to somewhere nice but noooo, you wanted to outsmart me. I should have let you lay up in here and rot, but because I still care about you, I couldn't, in good conscious, do that. I can't believe you tried to go incognito on your family. You never cease to amaze me."

Khalil stepped up. "Look, Dad, what Ma is saying is that as long as you abide by the rules here and do what these folks tell you to do, then you'll probably be allright. But if you want to do this on your own, then go for it. Without us, though, I don't think things will be looking good for you anyways. You know what I mean?" Khalil smirked.

"You did this to yourself, Dad," Xavier spoke up. "What goes around comes around. Isn't that what you've always said?"

Hezekiah looked sick. His complexion grew darker and his face filled with concern and uneasiness. Was this the family that once loved him, respected him, and looked up to him? Had he done things so badly that they were ready to leave him for the wolves to devour? Sure, he was wrong for running Fancy down with his wheelchair. He was wrong for sleeping with Detria Graham. He was wrong for stealing from the church. He was wrong for trying to keep them out of his life by telling the staff that he didn't want any visitors. Yes, he was wrong about so many things and now he felt the pain, the anguish of regret, and the cost of his bad decisions. He loved Fancy, he truly did, but maybe he had gone too far. He saw how she flirted with that dude right in front of him. But what could he do? He knew Fancy had needs and he couldn't fulfill them, not a single one of them. He had done so much wrong to her and running her down was the lowest of low. He never wanted to hurt her but his rage had overtaken him when she told him she was going to send him away and that Khalil had taken over his ministry. Everything was just too much. Was this God's way of paying him back?

The past year was like living someone else's life. His mother wasn't his mother; his brother was Stiles Graham; his sons hated him; and only God knew what else had gone wrong since he had the stroke.

He looked at Fancy. "Fancy, love you. Sorry," he managed to say with spit flying out of his mouth as he spoke.

Fancy stared back at him, and the love she had in her heart for the man who had been in her life since she was a teen girl resurfaced. She looked at him with pity, love, and resentment in her eyes.

"I...I know you do," she said, but she did not say the words he thought she would say. She did not tell him that she loved him. "Look, like Khalil said, you need to get accustomed to being here for as long as it takes for you to get better. If they don't treat you right, you just let me know and I'll get you out of here and somewhere else. I just can't bring you back home, Hezekiah. I can't take care of you the way you need to be taken care of. As for the church, you need to trust Khalil. He's going to make you proud. I know he will." Fancy smiled.

"G...George?"

"George is paying the piper," Khalil spoke up. "We know you were paying him under the table to keep his mouth shut about a lot of things that I don't care to go into right now. Just know that we know all about it, and we learned a lot about George, too. I don't know how much you knew about your head of Security, but what we found out about him can send him to prison for some years. He's already been questioned by the police. He's bad news, something you should've known, but it is what it is. I'm handling it."

Hezekiah couldn't imagine what Khalil could have been talking about. What had George done that could send him to prison? The guy was a scumbag, that much Hezekiah knew but what exactly had Khalil unearthed about him? So much was going on right under his nose and he couldn't do or say anything about it. If this was the way his life was destined to be, he would rather be dead. He wouldn't be able to live like this for the rest of his life. Either God was going to have to hurriedly heal him or take him out.

"What...do?" Hezekiah asked.

"I don't want to get into it here," Khalil said while Xavier looked like he could poop in his pants, afraid that his brother would divulge his secret.

Xavier didn't know how much his brother would willingly tell his father. If Hezekiah learned that he was gay, Xavier felt that he would be disowned by Hezekiah. Then again, the more Xavier thought about it, the less he cared. After all, his father had betrayed and deceived his family so what could he have to say about Xavier's life?

Xavier was ready to get out of Memphis anyway. He wanted to go away and live his life, a life void of ridicule and shame because of his sexuality. He wanted to be free to explore life without being made to feel like he was on a straight path to hell with no return ticket. He was sick and tired of Christians condemning other folks, and Hezekiah was no different. He could practically hear the venom his father would spew at him when he found out that his youngest son was gay. For now, Xavier hated to admit it, but he was relieved that Hezekiah could barely talk and that he was out of the house.

Khalil and his mother pressed him about remaining in Memphis and helping them with the ministry, but Xavier was determined that he was getting out of Memphis while the getting was good. He could do him and no one would interfere with his life ever again. He loved his family but not as much as he loved Raymone. Enough was enough.

Chapter 8

"Find your tribe; love them hard." Danielle LaPorte

Stiles had reached out more than once over the past few months to Hezekiah but each time he did, he hit an impenetrable wall. Today when he called him on his cell phone, the recording on the other end said that Hezekiah's phone was no longer in service. Stiles hoped and prayed that Hezekiah was doing better since having a major stroke because he desperately wanted to see about making amends with his biological brother. He had no one in his life now, except Pastor and Josie. His mother, both his biological mother Margaret, and Audrey, the woman who raised him were dead. Francesca was dead. Tim was dead. Rena's parents. Dead. And his poor little baby girl, Audrey. Dead. He had lost so much and now though his brother, his only brother, was alive it felt like he'd lost Hezekiah too because Hezekiah had made it clear that he wanted nothing to do with him.

Pastor had suggested time and time again that he should give Hezekiah some time to digest the fact that he had a brother. How much time did Hezekiah need? It was coming up on a year since everything went down at Holy Rock. Members called that day the Jubilee Tragedy; and indeed it was.

Stiles heard Pastor's voice in his head but he felt that he needed time to digest a lot of things, too. He had lost far more than Hezekiah could ever imagine. Both of them were men of God but where was Hezekiah's forgiving heart? Why did he blame Stiles for the sins of their parents? He had lost just as much and he longed to have his brother as a part of his life.

He called Holy Rock again and asked for Hezekiah. In the past, he was told that Hezekiah was not available and that was that. His call was sent to Hezekiah's voicemail and of course the guy never called him back. This time when he called, he actually talked to someone who he knew from when he was senior pastor of Holy Rock. He didn't know when she became the receptionist or administrative assistant, or whatever her role was, but he was glad.

"I'm sorry, Pastor McCoy is on an extended leave. Can someone else assist you?" the woman on the other end of the phone asked Stiles.

"Sista Mavis? Is that you?"

"Yes, this is Sista Mavis? How can I help you?"

"Sista Mavis, it's Pastor Graham. Stiles Graham. How are you?"

"Pastor Stiles, oh my Lord, it's good to hear your voice. I knew you sounded familiar, but so many people call this church in a day's time until everyone sounds alike." She laughed into the phone. "How are you? I haven't seen you or heard from you, well since the terrible tragedy. I'm so sorry."

"I'm okay. God is good."

"Yes, all the time. Well, you know Pastor McCoy had a stroke shortly after that crazy woman, oops, I'm sorry. He hasn't returned to the church. From what I've heard he still can't talk much and he's confined to a bed and an electric wheelchair."

"I'm sorry to hear that. That's why I was calling; I wanted to speak to him, see how he was getting along."

"I'm sure you do. After all, he *is* your brother," Mavis blurted again. "I'm sorry. This mouth of mine is going to get me in trouble."

"No worries, Sista Mavis. It's not like it's a secret or anything. Margaret made sure before she died that everyone knew that. And knowing that Pastor McCoy is my brother, I want the chance to get to know him. I want him to be in my life."

Stiles continued talking to Sista Mavis for several minutes. Though she could be a gossip, Sista Mavis was a good listener. Stiles laughed to himself. Maybe she was a good listener because she wanted to know everything there was to know about everybody at Holy Rock.

"Now that Khalil has taken over the ministry, I think things will be different. I'm not sure if that's going to be good or not."

"What did you say?" Stiles was stunned. Surely he hadn't heard Sista Mavis correctly. "Did you say that Khalil has taken over the ministry?"

"You haven't heard? I thought sure old man, uhhh, Pastor Graham would have told you."

"Told me what?"

"Well, if anyone asks then you didn't hear it from me, but Khalil is the new Senior Pastor. From what I've heard, Pastor McCoy's recovery isn't going too well. Did you know they had to put that poor man in a nursing home, but you didn't hear that from me. I heard he tried to run down First Lady Fancy with one of those heavy-duty electric chairs. Said it almost amputated her legs at the ankles. That's probably why I haven't seen her around here in a few days. He still can't say a word and he can't even walk. That man might not ever walk or talk again. You know how strokes can be. They can leave you crippled for life."

"Yes, yes, that's true, but nothing is too hard for God," Stiles told her, still trying to decipher if what Sista Mavis told him about Khalil taking over as senior pastor was really true.

"Where did you hear that Khalil was going to be the senior pastor, Sista Mavis?"

"From one of the associate ministers; I won't say which one."

When Sista Mavis finished explaining that Khalil would be preaching his first sermon this Sunday, Stiles remained in a state of shock. He didn't know that Khalil had been called to the ministry but he could understand why Hezekiah would want his son to take hold of the reins and keep the church moving forward. He didn't know why Pastor had said nothing about it; it had to be because he didn't know about it. From what Mavis said, it hadn't been officially announced to the congregation as a whole, so maybe Pastor hadn't heard about it for that reason. He was no longer on staff and he and Josie often visited other churches ever since Hezekiah excommunicated him from Holy Rock.

"Is Khalil there?"

"No, he hasn't come in yet. He's usually here around nine o'clock but today he won't be here until eleven. He said he had some errands to run this morning."

"Look, do me a favor, Sista Mavis."

"What is it, Pastor Stiles? I sure wish you would come back to Holy Rock," Mavis continued babbling.

Stiles disregarded her last comment. "Will you send me to Pastor Khalil's voice mail?"

"Sure thing. You hold on, and please pray about coming back. Your brother needs you."

"God bless you, Sista Mavis. Take care."

Stiles left a voicemail for Khalil telling him that it was urgent that he speak to him. He needed to find out exactly what was going on and where his brother was. If what Mavis said was true and Hezekiah was in a nursing home, he needed to make a trip to Memphis to see about him. He didn't care if Hezekiah wanted him there or not, he was going to do whatever he could to help his brother. He couldn't lose another family member or loved one because this time he didn't know if he would be able to bounce back.

Khalil finished getting dressed. He looked at his wrist and saw that it was already ten-thirty five. He had told Sista Mavis that he would be at the church by eleven. At the rate he was going it was unlikely that he would meet that timeline. Maybe closer to noon, but so be it. He was the senior pastor and he didn't answer to anyone but God himself.

His text notifier chimed. It was his mother. "Are you at the church yet?"

"No. should be there by noon. Everything ok?"

"Yes. I'm still in the bed. Enjoying a late sleep in. it feels good not to hav to get up and check on Hezekiah."

"That's good, Ma. I'm getting dressed. Hit me up if you need me."

"Hav u talked to ur brother?"

"Nope."

"He didn't come home last night. And he's not answering his phone."

Khalil didn't have the time nor did he have the desire to check up on his brother. He suspected that he was laying up somewhere with Raymone and that's where he wanted to be. He definitely hated his brother's choice but hey, that was on Xavier, not him.

"I'm sure he's good. No need to exchange one worry for another. Chill out n relax. U deserve it. TTYL."

"I don't want you to leave."

"You know I got things to do. I'm already going to be later than what I anticipated." Khalil continued to get dressed, tying his tie and straightening it around his neck. His white starched shirt, slim leg Levis, and jacket fit his personal taste perfectly. He surveyed himself in the mirror as the woman walked up behind him and grabbed him below his belt while standing on her toes to nibble at his neck.

"Stop it, Dee. I need to get outta here. I have a lot going on today at the church."

Dee stood on her flat feet and then walked in front of Khalil as he stepped away from the mirror.

"I'm so glad you're giving us another chance. You won't be sorry. I promise."

"I don't know about that. I'll make that decision later, after I see if you're a woman of your word."

"I told you that I was going to help you, didn't I? And that's what I meant. All you have to do is tell me what you want done, when you want it done, and I've got your back."

Dee walked off, went over to the other side of her massive master bedroom suite, retrieved her designer purse, pulled something out, and walked back over toward Khalil as he headed to the bathroom.

"Here. This is a little surprise for you." She pressed a MasterCard Gold Card into the palm of his hand and folded his fingers over it. The 24k gold-plated card would open doors for him that twenty something year old men like himself could only dream of. Sure, he was going to make a boatload of money by being the senior pastor of Holy Rock, but it would never give him the kind of riches and luxuries being with Detria could give him.

"What's this?"

"Let's just say it's reserved for the special man in my life. And if you have to ask the limit on it, then you're not ready for it," she purred. "Use it wisely, but don't think about screwing me over by spending all your goodies on some young stupid li'l girl." She reached up and pulled his face down to meet hers. Kissing him with fervor and passion she began undressing Khalil.

"Dee, I told you. I have to get to Holy Rock." He said, slightly resisting her, but his manhood betrayed him every single time.

"I know, but let me tend to this rock right here first and then you can be on your way."

Khalil was not one to resist the seduction of a woman, especially the likes of Detria Graham. Dang, the woman had just given him a credit card worth God knows how much. She had his back. All he had to do was play his cards right and he would be on top of the world.

While he finished undressing, he thought about his next step. Now that he was Senior Pastor of Holy Rock, the congregation would most likely be expecting him to get a first lady. *Not such a bad idea*, he thought to himself as he swooped Detria up in his arms and had his way with her against the bedroom wall. *Detria McCoy. Ummm, nice ring to it. Money and power. What more could a man ask for?* He smiled wickedly as he satisfied Dee's needs and that of his own as well.

Xavier pulled out of the downtown hotel parking lot and headed to drop Raymone off at his new job. He had secured a position working at International Paper in their IT department. Unlike Xavier, he didn't care whether he attended college or not, but he didn't want Xavier to leave him either. The position with International Paper started him off at $35,000 a year, a good start for a nineteen year old with no degree. It wouldn't have been possible without the clout of his father who was a high-level executive at the company. Raymone had been working every summer at the company since he turned fifteen years old so just about everyone who mattered knew him and that made it even easier for him to be offered a position.

"Why don't you let me put in a word for you. I can get you on at IP, too," Raymone offered as Xavier drove down Madison Avenue heading toward the interstate. Raymone worked at the Hacks Cross location of International Paper or IP as most called it.

"Naw, I don't think so. Anyway, how many times do I have to tell you that I'm outta here come September? I have a full ride to Xavier and I'm taking it. I know you don't want to go to college just yet, but I still want you to come with me. I know your dad will help you cop a job in Louisiana just like he did here."

"I don't know. I mean, I love you, Zay, but I don't want to

disappoint my dad either. He's supported me and stuck by me all of my life. And when I told him that I was gay, he didn't bat an eye. He accepted me for who I am. I can't turn my back on him." Raymone looked away from Xavier and out of the passenger side window of Xavier's white on white Acura TLX, a graduation gift from his parents.

Xavier felt his anger mounting. "You don't love me. You can't possibly love me if you're putting your father over me. I'm glad your dad is the way he is. I mean, he's helped me too. He's accepted me and not judged me, but I want to be free to live my life on my own."

"I don't want to argue with you about this. I hoped you would understand."

"No, I hoped *you* would understand," Xavier bit back as he accelerated the car and got over in the far right lane. "You know the situation I'm facing at home with my family. They won't even mention the word gay. After George did what he did and took those pictures of you and me, they haven't said a word. And when or if my father finds out, then I'm going to have a whole new set of worries. I can't live my life like that. I *won't* live my life like that." Xavier yelled and pressed his foot harder on the accelerator.

"Slow down. You're going to get a ticket," Raymone warned.

"I can't do it. I'll come visit you every chance I get, but I can't go with you, Zay. I'm sorry." Raymone looked at his best friend and his lover. He wanted to have a life with Xavier but he loved his new career. It was a once in a lifetime opportunity and he didn't want to give it up. He could see himself growing in the company and with his father being as important as he was, Raymone could see himself living out his dreams as a young executive on the rise.

Xavier grew angrier and angrier the more he thought about everything. He was tired of being put off and pushed to the side. It seemed that everyone in his life was ready and willing to dismiss his feelings.

"If that's the way you want it, then we may as well be done. I'm not going to deal with you or anyone else for that matter that won't support my dreams."

"*Your* dreams? What do you mean *your* dreams? Don't you think I have dreams too? Why can't we both live our dreams? Why does it have to be all about you and what you want!"

"It's not all about what I want! This was supposed to be about us. I want to go to Xavier, get my law degree, and build a future, a real future for us. You can get a job at any IT department. It's not like International Paper is the only corporation in the world."

Xavier turned and looked at Raymone with red eyes that revealed his rage while Raymone had tears flooding from his.

"It's me or nothing. Make your choi—"

"Zayyyy!" Raymone screamed, but it was too late.

The car catapulted in the air flipping several times over after slamming into the vehicle and then a guardrail before landing in the middle of the interstate.

Chapter 9

"Double, double toil and trouble." William Shakespeare

Kareena knocked on the door of Stiles' office at Full of Grace Ministries. Outside of handling the daily affairs of the church they hadn't seen each other beyond office hours. Kareena willed herself to keep moving forward with living her life. It was hurtful because out of nowhere it seemed that she and Stiles' friendship had suffered tremendously and she had no idea why. He had become withdrawn, sullen, and irritable.

"Come in," he said from the inside of his office.

Kareena turned the knob and slowly opened the door and walked inside.

"Good afternoon, Kareena. How can I help you?" he said coldly.

"You asked for the print out of the monthly membership and tithes." She walked over to his desk and laid the report down on his desk.

"Thanks, Kareena. How does it look?"

"Excuse me?"

"The report? How are the membership stats and the tithes and offering? Any increase? Decrease?"

"Actually, we're on the rise. Membership has increased by five percent since last month and tithes and offerings are at a steady pace, which is good considering that during the summer months we had a decrease in giving."

"Yeah, people seem to forget all about the church during the summer. They go on their vacations and outings and I guess they think the church does the same. But fall is approaching and hopefully we'll see an increase again. There are still some things I want to do around here to improve the church."

"Yes, I know, and you'll get there. God has been good to Full of Grace under your leadership. We're growing. It may not be at the pace you'd like, but it's still a blessing. And the new children's and youth ministry we started this summer was a great suggestion on your part."

"Thanks. I think the kids and youth are having a good time. I want to expand what we're able to do for them and be more visible in the neighborhood. So much is going on and it shows. After Hurricane Harvey rushed through here, it's been tough to get back on track."

"Yeah, people are still hurting and there is much work that needs to be done. So many are homeless and have nowhere to go."

"It's during times like these that I wish we had the financial resources and connections to help more than we have. I'm thankful that our building suffered only minor flooding, but so many others lost everything," Stiles lamented. Not once had he looked up at Kareena. His face remained glued to the report she'd laid in front of him.

"Stiles, talk to me," she finally said.

This time Stiles did look up. Kareena was beautiful in his eyes. She always had been, and he found it hard to restrain himself at times. Looking at her his mind reminded him of the two times they'd made love. His heart skipped a beat at the thought but he refused to let her see the effect she had on him.

"Talk to you about what?"

"Look, I know you. I know you've been troubled about a lot lately. The flood, your family back in Memphis. I'm so sorry for all the heartache you've experienced. But I do know that God will see you through it all."

"How many people do we still have living at the church since the flood?" he asked, totally ignoring what she'd just said. Inside, his wounds ran deep. Hearing her say what she said made him know just how much Kareena knew him. She could easily tell when he was upset or bothered by a situation and that made him feel vulnerable. He didn't want to appear vulnerable to anyone. He wanted to be tough and strong and in control of his thoughts and feelings. That was difficult to do at times. It seemed that every time he felt like he could rise above the problems, God knocked him down with another one. This time it came in the form of his nephew, Xavier. He may not have personally known the youngster but he was still his blood, his family, and he wanted to be there for him in any way that he could.

When he didn't get a call back from Khalil after a few days, he called the church office again. That's when Sista Mavis told him that Xavier had been involved a bad car accident.

"That child, Lord, have mercy. It was a bad accident on I-240. It was all on TV. And poor boy, it was his fault. He fractured a couple of bones, but basically walked away, but his best friend wasn't so fortunate. He sustained life-threatening injuries and they say he's paralyzed from the neck down."

"Oh, my God, Sista Mavis. Thank you for telling me. I know this may be a bit much to ask but can you give me First Lady McCoy's cell phone number…and Khalil's, too."

"I guess I can. I just don't want to get into trouble."

"I promise you. I won't say a word. I just want to check on my family, Sista Mavis."

"Did you hear me?" Kareena asked, watching Stiles look past her in a daze like he had something that was blocking his thoughts.

"I…I'm sorry. What did you say? How many are there?"

"We have a family with five children, a husband and wife in their fifties, and two men in their late sixties."

"We need to work on finding them suitable housing, but until then make sure they are well provided for and taken care of with food and clothing."

"That is already being done. It may be some time, at least a few more weeks, maybe even months before we're able to find them housing, especially the family with children, but I'm doing all I can."

"I know you are, Kareena" Stiles stood up, walked from behind his desk, and stood in front of Kareena. He embraced her. "Thank you." He pulled back and stared into her eyes. "I don't know how I would do any of this without you. I know we haven't been seeing each other outside of church lately. I hope you're okay."

Kareena stared aimlessly at him. The beats of her heart were rushing nonstop as she savored the feel of his embrace. "I'm good. I've been busy anyway so I guess you can say that neither of us have had the time to hang out like we used to do. As a matter of fact, I'm actually…" she paused. "dating, if that's what you call it." She forced a fake smile.

"Oh, I see. Well, good for you. Anyone I know?" asked Stiles.

"You should remember him. He joined Full of Grace a few months ago. His name is River…River Garrett. He relocated to Houston when his job transferred here."

"Oh, yes, I remember him. He's been a faithful member since he joined. He's one of the volunteers isn't he?"

"Yes, he's been one of our dedicated and committed volunteers, helping around the clock with the makeshift shelter we set up in our small fellowship hall."

"I've talked to him briefly. He seems like a good guy. I'm happy for you."

Pressing the palm of her hand against his chest, Kareena said, "Hold up. Don't make it into something more than it is. It's not like we're walking down the aisle. He's simply a friend. We've enjoyed a couple of meals together and a movie. That's it."

"He's lucky to have you as a friend. And if he has any sense, he'll recognize that."

"And you?"

"And me what?"

"Do you recognize it?"

Stiles looked but said nothing. Instead he paused, looked away, and walked back behind his desk like he was seeking sanctuary. "I may have to go to Memphis."

Realizing that she'd obviously approached a bridge that he didn't want to cross she fell in place with his change of conversation. "Why? What's going on? Is your brother all right?"

"Hezekiah is in a nursing home."

"A nursing home? Are you serious?"

"Yes, very. On top of that I just learned that his youngest son, my nephew, was in a serious car crash."

"Is he all right?" asked Kareena with concern clearly resonating in her tone.

She walked over behind his desk and stood in front of him again.

"Physically he's going to be okay from what I've been told. Mentally, I don't know. His best friend was in the car with him and seems like the accident was Xavier's fault. His friend is paralyzed from the neck down. He may never walk again."

Kareena threw her hand over her mouth. "Oh, God. That's terrible. Have you talked to First Lady McCoy or your nephew, Khalil?"

"No. I had been calling Holy Rock to try to reach Khalil but every time I called he wasn't in the office and he hasn't called me back. I just got First Lady Fancy's cell phone number and Khalil's too. I plan on calling them when our meeting is done."

"Go ahead. I don't have anything else to share…unless you have something else you need me to do. Is there anything I can help you with?" she offered.

"No. You've been more help than you can possibly know,

Kareena."

Stiles embraced her again, and like before he pulled back but this time he held her firm by her shoulders and looked into her eyes before he kissed her on her forehead.

Kareena cleared her throat. "Okay, I guess I'll go check on our guests. I'll continue to work on housing for them."

"Thanks," Stiles said, watching her as she turned and walked to the office door and opened it.

"Oh, I think when all of this is done, I mean with the guests we're housing that we should do something special for the volunteers. There's no way we could do what we do without them. Many of them have suffered loss themselves."

"Yes, I know and agree with you. I'm grateful that neither of us sustained serious damage in the area where we live."

"God is faithful. And if you need to go to Memphis, then go. Everything will be fine here, Stiles. See you later," Kareena said and walked out the office, closing the door behind her. Once on the other side of the closed door, she leaned against it, closed her eyes, inhaled then exhaled as she tried to still the beat of heart.

Stiles walked up to the door, laid his palm against it and softly whispered, "*Kareena, Kareena.*"

Chapter 10

"There are no accidents; there is only some purpose that we have yet to understand." Deepak Chopra

"Holy Rock, let's give God some praise this morning." Khalil waded across the purple-carpeted floor where the podium once stood like he'd been preaching for years. He had the podium removed and opted for a more casual delivery that complimented his style of dress. He'd seen numerous preachers, especially the younger ones, delivering their sermons in jeans, button down shirts or polos and loafers, so he felt more than comfortable doing the same rather than wearing a stuffy suit. Initially, he had chosen to wear the traditional suit and tie, but at the last minute, and after one of his before church service rendezvous with Detria, he changed his mind.

His message was just as smooth and together as he was. His voice was strong but inviting and his swagger was on point. His melanin skin and glistening white teeth matched his perfect manly physique. With every word, every movement, he seemed to hypnotize the congregation gathered to hear his second sermon. The message he delivered the previous Sunday was a hit because he received numerous phone calls and emails afterwards. The church phone lines were on fire just like Khalil.

It's been a rough week as I'm sure most of you have heard. My little brother was in a serious car accident. He has a fractured left arm and some internal and external bruising, but God is good; he's going to be okay. His best friend and passenger, however, has a long road ahead of him. He's paralyzed from the neck down, but again God is good and there's nothing too hard for Him."

The crowd began to clap and the voices of the people rang out with praise. Some of them stood on their feet like they were at a rap concert.

"I'm asking you to keep Raymone Sanders in your prayers. Lift him up before God on a daily basis. Let's unite and believe that God will heal him and perform a miracle in his life. I also ask that you pray for my brother. He's having a hard time dealing with what's happened. He's blaming himself for his friend's condition. Any of you who know Xavier and Raymone, you know they are inseparable.

Khalil listened to the words he was saying. *If they only knew just how inseparable.* "Xavier's mental state right now is fragile, to say the least, and so is Raymone's. But God's word says that we are to rejoice in hope, be patient in affliction, be constant in prayer. He's promised that when we call on Him, He will answer; He will be with us in trouble. We've gone through the flood, but even in that God promises that when we're in over our head, He will be with us. When we're in rough waters, we will not go down. When we're between a rock and a hard place, it won't be a dead end. Can I get an Amen and a hallelujah?"

The packed church was in an uproar shouting praises.

Khalil continued his message for the next twenty minutes. He preached the Word of God even more elegantly than Hezekiah. He left Holy Rock on fire.

Detria sat mid-way the large sanctuary with a huge smile plastered across her made up face. She hadn't been inside Holy Rock since she lost her role as First Lady. Well, not in church service. She spent as much time as possible in Khalil's office, much to the chagrin of that nosy witch, Sista Mavis. But Detria could care less. She was getting exactly what she wanted when it came to her relationship with Khalil.

He may not have said the words I love you, but she believed

that it wasn't too far off before she had him so far gone for her that he would be begging her to become his first lady. Initially, it had been difficult to show back up at Holy Rock but there were so many people who she didn't know and who didn't know her that she felt at ease. Of course, there were still many of the old members who remained at Holy Rock, including her parents. There were some who frowned at her and gave her unpleasant looks, but they didn't pay her bills and whatever they had to say about her, she shook it off.

Watching and hearing Khalil preach reminded her of ex-lover, Hezekiah. She had never heard Hezekiah preach in person, but she had watched a number of his church services on live stream. He could deliver the Word, that much was for sure, but still no one was better than Stiles when it came to holding an audience captive. Yet, Khalil was pushing close to beating Stiles out.

She hadn't seen or heard from Hezekiah since his stroke. She was the one who called 9-1-1 that night. They had just finished making love. It was one of the scariest nights of her life other than when she had the fatal accident involving her baby girl. She hoped that Hezekiah was doing better, but she doubted that he was because knowing him the way that she did, there was no doubt that he would have returned to Holy Rock by now if he was in any way able to do so. She didn't ask Khalil about him because she didn't want to stir up mess. Talking about his father was a sensitive subject for him.

The last she'd heard and that was from nosy, gossiping Sista Mavis, Hezekiah was in a nursing home. Sista Mavis hadn't told her that, but on one of her pop up visits to see Khalil, she heard Sista Mavis talking about it to someone on the phone. How could Fancy McCoy do such a thing? She should have had plenty of money to take care of him and Detria was certain that Holy Rock was going to take care of him; they practically worshipped the ground the man walked on. Some wife Fancy was. Had that been her man, her husband, or whatever, there was no way Detria would ship him off somewhere, especially to a nursing home and rehab facility. Those places could be horrific and most of the staff didn't give a rat's behind about the patients. Some kind of wife Fancy was and she had the nerve to turn her nose up at Detria.

Detria departed Holy Rock after standing in the long line to shake hands and greet the pastor at the end of the second church service. When it was her turn to shake Khalil's hand, he extended it out towards her but to keep from using her one good arm and hand she leaned in and hugged him with her good arm instead.

Khalil inhaled her sweet fragrance. Whatever the fragrance Dee wore, it drove him wild. It was like a magic love potion; it was just that exotic and captivating. He returned her hug but made it sweet and short so as not to get anyone suspicious.

Sista Mavis stood a few feet away watching the whole ungodly scene. She was no dummy; she knew there was something going on between that slut, Detria Graham and the young, naïve Khalil McCoy.

"Look at her," Sista Mavis leaned in and whispered in the ear of her good friend, Sista Regina. She and Sista Regina had been attending Holy Rock for at least fifteen years so they'd seen a lot of changes at the church. "How she mess around with a child? Doesn't that woman have morals at all?"

"You know she don't. She was messing with the building engineer, got knocked up with his child, so what makes you think she would have scruples now?" Sista Regina whispered back.

They stood in the cut and watched the scene playing out before their eyes and then followed Detria with their cutting eyes until she moved away from Pastor Khalil and exited the church.

"Humph, hope she has no intent of coming back to Holy Rock on a permanent basis. We've had enough drama around here to last a lifetime."

"You sho right, girl," said Sista Regina to Sista Mavis. "You sho right."

The two women moved up in the line until each one of them had their turn shaking the young pastor's hand and complimenting him on delivering a powerful message.

Chapter 11

"Guilt is to the spirit what pain is to the body." Elder David Bednar

Xavier wanted to go see Raymone before he left the hospital. He had been discharged an hour or so earlier but he wasn't allowed to walk inside the hospital due to safety precautions.

"Baby, I don't know if it's a good idea to go see Raymone. You need to do some more healing and his room is way on the other side of this hospital. It's not a short walk, you know," Fancy told him.

"Look, Ma, just say that you don't want to wheel me over there to see him. I can do it myself. You can go on home. I will call an Uber to bring me home, but I'm not leaving this hospital until I see Raymone," Xavier insisted.

Fancy shook her head. She was at her wit's end. It was bad enough that Xavier could have killed himself and Raymone, but thank God the good Lord saw fit to let both boys live to see another day. She hated that Raymone was a quadriplegic, but she was grateful that her son was going to be just fine. He had some emotional wounds that far outweighed the physical wounds, and that was the real reason she didn't want him to go see Raymone. She believed that Xavier would completely break seeing the young man in the state that he was in. Then again, she knew that she was not about to leave Xavier by himself so she gave in to his demands and agreed to take him to see him.

Xavier was still somewhat weak from the effects of the accident, combined with the pain meds so it was good that he was traveling around the massive hospital in a wheelchair pushed by his mother.

When he arrived to the Neurology/Neurosurgery floor, he stopped at the nurses' station and asked the room number for Raymone Sanders. He'd tried calling Raymone several times, but his parents, rather his mother, refused to let him talk to him. He hated that his mother was so angry with him, but he understood because he was angry with himself.

As Fancy pushed him up to the door to Raymone's room, he knocked lightly.

"Come in," he heard Raymone's mother say.

He pushed the door open with his good arm. His other arm was still in a cast that he would have to wear for the next six weeks. That meant he would be going away to school with his arm still in a cast, but at this point in time, Xavier didn't know if he would be able to go to college. He was riddled with guilt and couldn't see his life continuing when Raymone's was ruined.

"What are you doing here?" Mrs. Sanders asked when she saw Fancy pushing Xavier inside the room. The room was dark and Xavier was immediately brought to tears seeing the love of his life lying in the hospital bed with tubes running in and out of his body.

Raymone managed to turn his head less than an inch. He followed more with his eyes at the sound of his mother's voice.

He rolled up close to Raymone's bedside and took hold of his hand. Caressing it and massaging it slightly he told Raymone, "I'm sorry, Raymone. I'm so sorry," he cried. "I'm here for you. I won't leave you; I promise," he confessed. At that moment, he knew there was no way he could leave Raymone and go to Xavier University. Not after seeing him like this.

"You should be sorry. This is all your fault," Raymone's mother cried out. "Do you see what you've done?"

The blood pressure monitoring machine suddenly began to wail. Mrs. Sanders looked at it and immediately pushed the button for the nurse.

"Look what you've done. You've got him all upset. You need to leave, Xavier," she ordered and walked over to the door, opened it, and waited for Fancy to turn Xavier around and push him out of the room.

Xavier was heartbroken and distraught.

Mrs. Sanders followed them out of the room and into the hallway. "How dare you bring him up here. What were you thinking?" she chastised Fancy.

"You know that Raymone and Xavier are best friends. How could I not bring him to see him? And you don't have to be so mean. Xavier is suffering, too. This was an accident, a horrible, horrible accident, and I can understand you being upset, but to take it out on Xavier like this just isn't right. He already feels terrible. This hurts him more than you can imagine."

"Who are you to come up here and tell me what isn't right? Until you walk in my shoes or better yet until you can sit day in and day out with your child and know that because of someone else's negligence his life is ruined, then don't you come up here and dare try to tell me how to act or behave." Mrs. Sanders turned her attention toward Xavier. "Raymone cared deeply for you, Xavier."

Xavier dropped his head as tears flowed from his eyes and down his cheeks.

Focusing once again on Fancy, Mrs. Sanders said, "And for your information, Miss holier than thou First Lady Fancy McCoy, Raymone and Xavier were more than best friends. As much as you hate to say it, they're gay; they were lovers and you know it, but now my baby, my poor child's life is over. All because of your son's carelessness. Xavier gets to leave here and go home. In a few weeks, he'll be good as new, but my poor Raymone," she said looking at Xavier again with red tear-filled eyes that penetrated through him like steel, "will never ever walk again. He's paralyzed in his legs, hands, and triceps. He only has use of his biceps, wrists, and right index finger.

Because of this he will not be able to even get in and out of the bed or a chair independently. He has to wear a catheter because he can't control his piss or his bowels! He won't be able to dress himself. He'll forever be dependent on someone else to care for him. So don't you dare preach to me about what's right!"

Fancy proceeded to push Xavier away from the woman as she fought back tears of her own. It was heart wrenching to hear the words that spewed out of the woman's mouth. It hurt like hell, and Fancy could only imagine how hurt Xavier was seeing Raymone laid up like he was and hearing his mother blame him for everything. She pushed the wheelchair up the hospital corridor toward the elevators as fast as she could.

Xavier began to wail like a wounded animal as they got on the elevator. He couldn't control the agony in his heart. What was life without Raymone, his first true and only love? His life was over; it was done. He wanted to die.

On the drive home there was nothing she knew to say except that he should pray for Raymone. Xavier wasn't hearing it. He didn't want to hear anything about prayer or God; he wanted everything back the way it was. So rather than disrespect his mom, he remained silent all the way home.

At home, Xavier went straight to his room, shut the door, locked it, and turned on his laptop to research ways that he could kill himself without leaving a mess for his mother to clean up.

Fancy called Khalil on the phone to express her concern about Xavier.

"What's going on?" Khalil asked when he arrived at his mother's home.

Fancy was in the kitchen preparing something to eat. "You want a sandwich?" she asked.

"Yeah, sure. Is that turkey?"

"Yes, you want your cheese melted?"

"Yes, you know how to do it up, Ma."

"Xavier is in a bad way. I took him by Raymone's room to

see him before we left the hospital. His mother was there and she went clean off on Xavier and me too. And seeing the boy lying in the hospital bed totally helpless didn't help the situation either."

"Well, Ma, you and Xavier have to put yourself in his mother's shoes. I mean, this is something serious. Her son is paralyzed all over his body. I mean that's a tough pill for anyone to swallow, you know?" Khalil walked over to the oversized kitchen island, pulled out a stool, and sat down.

"Yes, but that doesn't help Xavier any. My child is depressed and sad."

"He needs to man up. Suck it up. I don't mean to sound insensitive, but it is what it is. There's nothing he can do about what happened. All things happen for a reason; sometimes we have a hard time accepting that, but it still rings true."

Fancy continued making the sandwiches with all the trimmings but paused just a second to give Khalil a strange stare.

"What?"

"I had to look at you for a minute; you sounded just like Hezekiah."

"Speaking of dad, how is the old man?"

"He hates that place. I can't say I blame him. It's second class and the times I've gone to see him, it smells like a pile of crap."

"He's only been there for a couple of weeks, Ma. Give it some time. Maybe the smell will give him the will to work hard to improve his speech and his ability to get around."

"He can get around in that chair, but the thing is he still needs help to get in the chair from the bed. And that catheter easily sets up infection. He has another urinary tract infection."

"TMI, Ma. Now back to Xavier. Only the good Lord can change the situation with Raymone. Until He does then Xavier needs to grow up, and stop acting like a little punk."

Xavier appeared in the doorway of the kitchen just in time to hear his brother's remarks.

"You don't care about anyone but yourself. What do you know about friendship and love anyway?" he scolded Khalil.

"Man, you need to stop acting like a little broad. Okay, so your partner is out for the count. What are you gonna do? You gonna go down too?"

"Maybe."

"Well, you're even weaker than I thought. No wonder you're gay," Khalil shot back.

"Stop it," Fancy screamed at the two of them. "I will not have this name calling and fighting in my house."

Khalil stood from the stool and walked toward his brother. Pointing a finger at his chest, he let Xavier know exactly what he felt. "Okay, so you wanna take yourself out cause of something that was an accident. Go ahead then. Take the easy way out, sucka."

"Stop it, Khalil," Fancy ordered again.

"No, Ma, this fool needs to hear the truth. You think you're the only one that's messed up? Yeah, that's your partner or whatever y'all call one another, but it's nothing you can do to change what happened. Try to be a better man for it. Do what you can to help dude but don't crawl up in a corner and die. That's a sucka move, a weak move, a little boy move. You're a grown man, or you're supposed to be. Where's your backbone, bruh?"

Xavier stared at Khalil. At first he was mad but then his brother's words began to sink in. Maybe the best thing to do was to stick by Raymone, to show him how much he cared about him and how sorry he was for what happened. If it took the rest of his life, he would never stop trying to help Raymone see that his life wasn't over and neither was their relationship. Right now, he understood that Raymone was in a deep state of depression and denial, and maybe it would take a while, a long while before he would be able to see him, especially since his mother was acting like a gatekeeper. But someway somehow he was going to make things right.

Xavier didn't say a word in response to Khalil's words. He turned, walked out of the kitchen, and back up the stairs.

Fancy and Khalil heard his bedroom door slam shut behind him.

"How could you be so cruel?" Fancy asked.

"Ma, he's not a little girl. He's a grown man. Either he's going to take heed to what I said or he's going to shut himself off up there in that room and give up. It's his choice. Either way, you need to stop catering to him. That's why he's a punk now."

"What did you say? Are you blaming his sexuality on me?"

Khalil walked over to the stainless steel double wide refrigerator, opened it, and retrieved a gallon jug of tea."

Fancy passed him a glass.

Khalil filled the glass with ice, opened the tea, and poured himself a glass before he returned to his stool.

"Naw, I'm not blaming you or anybody else for him being the way that he is. But I am saying that you've always babied him. It's time to let him be a man. He needs to get to work at the church or get outta here and go to college cause running off to his room and having a pity party ain't gonna work."

Fancy pushed the plate with his turkey sandwich, a side of potato salad, and potato chips in front of him. "Eat your food. I'm going upstairs. We'll talk tomorrow."

"That's how you gonna do?"

"I'm tired, Khalil. I'm so tired." Fancy broke down and started crying.

Khalil got up again from his stool, walked over to his mom, and held her in his arms. "Don't cry, Ma. Please don't cry," he said rubbing her head gently. "Everything is going to be all right. You'll see."

Chapter 12

"Sometimes people just need someone to listen." John Short

After Khalil left, Fancy took a long hot bubble bath, climbed in her bed and prepared to relax her mind. She called the nursing home, like she did most nights, to check in on Hezekiah. The nursing staff always assured her that he was doing fine. They gave him a mild sedative nightly to help him sleep through the night.

Fancy curled up in the king sized bed, pulled the covers up around her neck and turned on the television to watch one of her favorite reality shows when her cell phone started ringing. She picked it up from off the nightstand next to the bed and looked at the number.

"Ummm, who is this calling from a 346 area code? Probably a telemarketer." She shrugged her shoulders and decided to answer it anyway. "Hello."

"Fancy?"

"Yes, this is Fancy."

"Hi, it's Stiles."

"Stiles? Stiles Graham?"

"The one and only," Stiles quipped.

"How are you?"

"I'm good. The question is how are you and how is the family? You know word gets around pretty quickly in the church realm, which is the reason for my call."

Fancy positioned herself comfortably in her bed by propping three fluffy pillows behind her back. "I guess I was wondering when I would hear from you."

"Well, it's not from lack of trying. I've tried calling Hezekiah, but I think his phone service is off. I left a couple of messages with Khalil through his church voicemail and I called you a few days ago and left you a voicemail."

"I'm sorry that I haven't gotten back to you. It's just that so much has been going on. I feel like I'm being yanked and pulled in a million and one directions sometimes. Please forgive me."

"Believe me, I feel ya. So how is Xavier?"

"He's having a rough time dealing with the repercussions from the accident. His best friend was severely injured; probably will never walk again."

Stiles listened and heard the hurt and concern in Fancy's voice. "I'm sorry to hear that. And what about Hezekiah? How is he?"

Fancy spoke slowly like she was weighing her next words carefully and cautiously. "I...I had to put him in a rehab and nursing home facility. I had nurses coming to the house but he still wasn't getting the around-the-clock care he needed. Plus, he had become mean, moody and—"

"And what?"

"And violent," she said after pausing for several seconds.

"What do you mean violent? Towards you? The nurses? Who?"

"He was mean toward the nurses. Short tempered with them but with me it was that and more. He even ran me down with his electric wheelchair. Almost fractured my ankles," she cried.

"What?"

"That's when I knew I had to do some things differently. I just couldn't take it. I'm tired, Stiles." Fancy continued crying into the phone

Stiles listened to her as she released her tears. He knew his decision. He was going to Memphis. "Don't cry, Fancy. Everything will be all right."

"I don't know. It's just hard. And I don't know if you heard, but Khalil is the senior pastor of Holy Rock, at least until Hezekiah returns. I don't know when that will be or if he will ever grace the pulpit at Holy Rock again. But Khalil is doing a great job so far. It's like he was made for this." She reached over on her nightstand and pulled out a couple of tissues from the tissue box, wiped her tears, and a small smile formed on her face.

"That's good to hear. Although I must say that I am a little shocked that Khalil assumed such a giant role. Being a senior pastor is not easy, and overseeing a church the size of Holy Rock makes it even tougher."

"Yes, I know, but I know a lot of what goes on behind the scenes, and so does Khalil. He worked closely with me and Hezekiah before all of this happened. And you know he was youth director before this," she explained.

"Yeah, but being a youth director and a senior pastor is like trying to compare apples to oranges."

"God is gracious and he's showing favor on my son."

Stiles detected some irritability in Fancy's tone so he backed off from that subject. "Listen, I'm coming to Memphis in a couple of days."

"Oh? Do you have a speaking engagement or are you coming to see your father?"

"No, I don't have a speaking engagement and yes I'll see Pastor when I get there, but the main reason I'm coming is to see you, Hezekiah, and the boys."

"But why?" Fancy didn't understand the reasoning behind Stiles' decision to come to Memphis. Hezekiah hadn't spoken to him since Margaret went on her murdering rampage. So what was his real reason? Did he think he could come and get Holy Rock back? If that was what he had planned, he was in for a rude awakening because she was not going to let anything or anyone steal that crown from the McCoys of Holy Rock!

"Fancy, you're family. You need me there. And before you

think that I have some ulterior motive, let me assure you that my motive is to get closer to my family, especially my brother and my nephews. You need someone there for you, someone who understands what you're going through. And believe me, you know if anybody understands, it's me."

Fancy listened to Stiles. She began crying all over again. "Unfortunately, you do understand. You've been through so much. And I do need someone. I mean, Khalil is here for me, but between him being the pastor now and trying to live his own life, he shouldn't have to be worried about me. He's been such a blessing."

"Look, don't you worry about a thing. Give me a couple of days to get things straight here. You know we had a huge hurricane not too long ago and we still have some people staying at the church, but I'll work all of that out."

"I'm sorry. I didn't think to ask you if you were affected by the floods. I read that it was pretty bad down there."

"Yeah, it was. But it could have been worse. My place was spared and so was the church. We experienced very little flooding, just a lot of rain."

"Good. Thank God for that. Many people weren't as lucky as you."

"I know and that's why we immediately opened our church doors to accommodate as many people as we could, given the size of our church. We are a small congregation and a small church in building size, but God is multiplying that small space. We're housing people in our fellowship hall. At the height of the storm we had close to a hundred people."

"Oh my, Lord," Fancy said, still sniffling but wiping away the last few tears.

"We're down to about seven people who still require our assistance. We're working to find them housing."

"God bless you. In light of all that you have going on, please don't come here, Stiles. I can manage. You have your own congregation and your own life there in Houston."

"But I have my family in Memphis. I'll call or text you sometime tomorrow to let you know when I'll be leaving out. Now get you some rest. Oh, and I don't think you need to mention to Hezekiah that I'm coming. I don't want to get him upset."

"Don't worry. I had no plans to tell him anything. He'll see you when he sees you. And don't worry about a place to stay. You can stay here. We have plenty of room."

"I don't want to impose on you so I plan to stay with Pastor and Sista Josie, or I can easily get a hotel."

"I insist that you stay here. Like you said….we're family."

Stiles grinned. "See you in a couple of days." They ended the call.

Fancy nestled her head back against the pillows and smiled. A sense of relief mixed with anticipation flooded her heart and her spirit. She laid her cell phone down next to her on the bed, closed her eyes, and allowed sleep to overtake her.

Stiles held his cell phone in his hand as he got up off of the couch in his man cave and retreated to his bedroom. His phone rang. It was Kareena's ringtone.

"Hi there. To what do I owe the pleasure of this phone call?" He chuckled.

"Just thought I'd check in on you. At church today you were having a pretty rough day. Have you given any more thought about going to Memphis for a visit?"

"As a matter of fact. I have. I was going to talk to you about it tomorrow when I got to the church. I just spoke to Sista McCoy."

"How did that go?"

"Actually far better than I expected, but then again I've known her and Hezekiah since they first came to Holy Rock. She's always been a cool person. It's her husband who can be, well let's just say he can be difficult to get along with."

"Yeah, he was the associate pastor when you were there."

"That's right. Fancy is a good person. After talking to

her, I knew more than ever that she needs somebody. I mean, she's basically like me. She has no family other than her sons in Memphis. I'm not sure where her parents or other family members are. I assume they're still in Chicago."

Kareena listened as Stiles discussed several things he wanted her to handle while he was away. They talked for the next twenty-five minutes, taking moments to laugh and talk about things outside of Full of Grace before ending their call.

The following day, Stiles went to his church, talked with his associate minister and Kareena, and then visited and prayed with the remaining guests staying at the church. Afterwards, he called Pastor and told him about his plans. Pastor agreed that it would be a good thing for him to come see his family.

"I didn't know anything about that boy taking over," Pastor told Stiles. "He's just a child."

"I can't believe it myself," Stiles replied. "Fancy said Khalil officially announced it a couple of Sundays ago. Maybe that was the Sunday when you and Josie visited Community of Faith. I remember you saying that y'all had been invited to their pastor's anniversary service around that same time."

"Maybe so. Seems like somebody from Holy Rock would have called and told me or Josie; they tell us everything else." He sounded a little perturbed.

"Joe called and told you," Stiles heard Josie saying in the background.

"Joe ain't told me nothing," Pastor retorted.

"Hold up, Pastor it's no need to argue with Josie about it. It's okay. We all forget things sometimes."

"I didn't forget a darn thing. Joe hasn't called here, and nobody told us anything."

"Okay, Pastor. Anyway, I just wanted to let you know that I would be there later this week. Sister McCoy extended an invitation to me to stay at their house."

"You be careful about that, son. Hezekiah is still upset with me and you. I don't know why he's got it in for you when I'm the one that's his daddy. I understand him being upset with me, but I've tried to make things right. He won't have a thing to do with me, so all I can do is pray for the man. Give it to the good Lord. Did you know he hasn't preached in God knows when?" Pastor stated, sounding agitated.

Stiles crinkled his brow. What in the world was Pastor saying? He knew full well that Hezekiah hadn't been able to preach or attend church since his stroke. "Well, Pastor, hopefully when I get there I can make arrangements for him to attend one of the church services. I'll have to check with Sister Fancy and the rehab staff first, of course."

"What rehab staff? What you talking about, son?"

"I guess you didn't know this either. But Hezekiah's in a rehab facility because he needs around-the-clock care."

"Why would he be at a rehab facility? Did he have some kind of accident or something?"

Stiles was growing concerned now. Pastor acted like he didn't know that Hezekiah had a stroke. Was his memory failing him or what? "Pastor, remember. Hezekiah had a stroke some time ago."

Pastor was silent for a few moments. "Stroke? Oh, yeah. Of course I remember that he had a stroke. What do you think, that I'm crazy or something?"

"No, Pastor. Look, I'll call you when I get to Memphis. Okay?"

"Okay, son."

"I love you. Kiss Josie for me. See y'all soon."

"I love you too. Goodbye"

Ending the call with Pastor, Stiles pushed back his concern about Pastor's sudden memory lapse.

Chapter 13

"You never have to say 'sorry' to me because I go out of my way to make sure that you are." Unknown

Stiles called Fancy to tell her that he was leaving out later that morning. The phone rung until it went to her voicemail. He left her a message telling her of his plans. "She's probably gone to see Hezekiah," he mumbled as he gathered the last few things he needed out of his office and prepared to go give a final goodbye to Kareena. He texted Fancy as he walked to Kareena's office. "Left u a msg. leaving Houston in a couple of hours. Should arrive in Memphis around six."

Khalil had decided rather than return Stiles' phone call, he would wait to talk to the dude when he came to Memphis. His mother had told him about Stiles' call to her a couple of nights before. He had his suspicions about why Stiles wanted to suddenly reach out and touch them. Things had been going rather well these past couple of months in his new role and Khalil didn't want Stiles or anyone else interfering with his road to success.

He had plans to make several changes with the ministerial staff, deacons, and trustees. He had several younger men in mind, including Omar, the building engineer. He would share his plan at the weekly staff meeting the following week. Khalil wanted people surrounding him whom he felt like he could fully trust and who would work with him. Unlike his father, he didn't want to take the chance of getting someone like that snake, George Reeves, on his team.

As for George, Khalil had recently learned that George was waiting to be indicted on charges of possessing child pornography. The man was definitely a sick, filthy pedophile. One of Khalil's soon to be appointed young deacons worked for the prosecutor's office. He told Khalil that George had been questioned many years ago by Chicago Police Department for sexual misconduct, but no charges were ever officially filed against him.

Khalil was just glad that he'd gotten rid of George. The only thing left for him to do was to make sure no matter how much his father's health improved that Hezekiah McCoy never graced the pulpit of Holy Rock again. Whatever it would take, Khalil was ready to do to destroy his father's life and legacy just like Hezekiah had destroyed Fancy's trust. His mother deserved better. Khalil could only hope and pray that soon she would come to the same realization.

He went over his sermon notes, counselled a young couple who wanted to get married, had lunch in the church cafeteria, and then prepared to leave to go pay his father a visit. He hadn't seen him since the man entered rehab, and he wasn't looking forward to seeing him today either, but he had to do what needed to be done. As senior pastor, it was his responsibility to visit the sick and shut in as much as he possibly could. There were several other ministers who did the bulk of the visitations, but being that Hezekiah was his father, he owed it to the man to at least check in on him personally.

"Sista Mavis," I'm leaving. I'll return later this afternoon for Bible Study."

"Yes, Pastor Khalil. Be safe out there. You know this city isn't what it used to be."

"Yes, ma'am. Have a good evening. I hope to see you tonight at Bible Study."

"I won't be back tonight. It's my baby sister's birthday; me and my other two sisters are going to take her out to dinner."

"Okay, well enjoy yourselves. I'll see you tomorrow morning. Gnite."

Khalil exited the church, walked to his car, got in, and drove off the parking lot and onto the street. He had driven less than a mile when he saw the flashing lights of the "Boys in Blue" as many people referred to the Memphis Police Department. This sight unfortunately was not uncommon but what made him take a second look was the car they had pulled over. As he slowed down with the traffic he took a concentrated look at the vehicle. He saw a young man, spread-eagled and leaning against the car that looked identical, including make and model to one of his father's three cars. The doors and trunk of the car were opened, which immediately signaled to Khalil that the police were doing or had carried out a search.

"Man, I hate to see that kinda bullcrap. Been there done that," Khalil said with empathy in his voice as he drove slowly pass. He looked back one last time and his eyes met the face of the young man they had against the car. He almost caused a collision as he quickly maneuvered to the far right lane and turned into the parking lot of a strip mall. He pulled his car halfway into a parking space, turned it off, and jumped out. He could see the young man's face even clearer now. He ran the few yards that separated him from where the police had pulled Xavier over.

"What the…" Why would the cops be searching the car? Xavier was not one to do drugs. He didn't know him to drink or do anything like that. He raced over to where they were.

"Hold up!" one of the big, white, burly cops said. Another police car pulled up around the same time Khalil ran up.

"That's my brother," Khalil yelled.

"I don't give a…." the police said with an uncalled for expletive pouring from his thin red lips. "I said get back."

Khalil knew that if he was going to get anywhere with this cop, he had to settle down and not show how pissed off he was.

"Officer, I'm sorry. I mean seeing my brother as I passed by, shocked me. I'm the senior pastor of Holy Rock, that large church about a mile up the street. I was passing by and noticed this is my father's car. Can you tell me what happened?"

The police officer eyed Khalil up and down and then arrogantly said, "Drugs. Maybe you should have been preaching to him cause he's about to take a ride downtown."

"Drugs?" Khalil looked over at Xavier.

"I didn't have anything, bro. I don't know what they talking about."

"That's what they all say," another officer said as he walked over to where Khalil and the first police officer were standing.

"You say this is your brother?"

"Yes, sir. My baby brother. That's my father's car. He was on his way to the church."

"Guess he made a little detour 'cause we found his stash, pulled him over for running the light. We detected a suspicious odor when we pulled him over."

"I didn't run that light," Xavier said, turning his head and looking over his shoulder at the officer while still being pinned down against the car spread-eagled. "And I don't know what kinda suspicious odor they're talking about."

"Shut up," the officer holding him ordered loudly, followed by a couple of expletives.

"Hey, let the preacher boy see what his little brother is riding around with," the first officer yelled to a third officer who was sitting in his police cruiser with his door open and one leg out of the car.

The officer raised up a mini-sized clear plastic bag filled almost to the brim with a white substance that looked like sugar. Khalil knew better than to think that it was sugar or salt; it was cocaine. What was going on? Had his father been doing coke and left it in his car? No one had driven that car since Hezekiah had the stroke. Fancy told Xavier he could drive it until he got a new car, being that his was totaled when he had the accident.

Khalil rubbed the top of his head back and forth and paced

nervously as if trying to think how he was going to get his brother out of this bad situation.

"Hold tight, Xavier. Be cool. We're going to handle this," he tried reassuring him.

"Well, right now, we're going to handle it," the initial officer barked. "Get him in the car," he said and the officers jerked Xavier and proceeded to all but drag him to the police car.

Xavier stumbled and they ordered him to get up. His arm was still partially bandaged, but the officers didn't seem to care, they yanked and pulled on him without mercy. Xavier struggled to get up.

"Hey, there's no need for all of that. He was in a recent accident. That's why his arm is bandaged. Go easy."

"You wanna take a ride wit 'em?" one of the officers said, looking at Khalil with angry, black eyes that said he would do exactly what he wanted to. "Shut the....up!"

Khalil was furious but he maintained his composure. He knew far too well how police could go from zero to a hundred and things could turn real ugly.

"I said, get up," the officer yelled as Xavier continued to struggle. It was difficult for him to stand up with two officers crowding his space. He had barely stood up when he went down again. One of the officers pulled out his club and hit Xavier on the thigh.

Xavier yelled out in tears. This was not looking good at all.

"You don't have to beat him," Khalil yelled.

"I said, you'd better shut up," the officer yelled again and walked up on Khalil, poking a club in his chest. "Preacher boy or no preacher boy, you're going to take a ride with him. I swear. As a matter of fact, get in your car and get outta here," the officer ordered.

Khalil's eyes grew bloodshot red but he turned and walked away. He looked back at Xavier once more. They were pushing him inside the police car. His brother looked like a frightened little boy as tears flowed heavily down his face. He was not meant for this; he wasn't meant for it at all.

As Khalil approached his car, he opened the door and flopped down inside. Putting his head in his hands, he shook his head and then looked out toward the two police cars, one with his brother inside. He started his car and then drove a short distance to a parking space in front of one of the stores on the strip where he still had a view of the scene. His mind went into overdrive. Something wasn't right. How could this have happened? Khalil waited in his car for the next half hour until he finally saw the police cars pull off. He revisited the thought about the drugs they said they found in the car. Like a lightbulb turning on, Khalil suddenly thought about the last person who had driven his father's car. It was all beginning to make sense…George.

Khalil started the ignition and sped off the parking lot and headed straight in the direction of Dee's house.

Chapter 14

"You are only one decision away from a totally different life."
Unknown

Khalil pulled up into Dee's driveway and slammed the brakes, bringing his vehicle to a complete stop at the drop of a dime. He turned off the ignition, hopped out of the car, and ran up the walkway, up the steps, and pressed heavily on the doorbell, then alternated by pounding on the door with the massive knocker.

Priscilla opened the door, looking alarmed, obviously concerned with whoever was on the other side knocking on the door like a madman.

"Khalil, what's going on?" she asked in an alarming tone.

"Where's Dee?" he asked as he walked into the foyer without being formally invited to come inside.

Before Priscilla could reply, Dee appeared.

"What's wrong? You sound upset?" she asked as she walked up on him, grabbing him by his elbow.

"Those pigs!" he said. "I'm trying to stay on the straight and narrow, but they're pushing me, Dee. They're pushing me to my limit."

"Who? What are you talking about? Come on, let's go into the office."

She took him by his hand and they walked to the office. She opened the door and ushered him inside, closing it behind her. Priscilla was trustworthy so she wasn't worried or concerned about her overhearing their conversation, but she felt like whatever had Khalil upset like this warranted some private time.

"You look like you're about to explode, baby. Tell me what's going on."

"The police. They have Xavier."

"What do you mean they have Xavier? Have him where?"

Nervous, Khalil rubbed his head back and forth while pacing across the hardwood floors of the beautiful office that Dee hardly ever ventured into.

"Baby, please tell me what happened."

Khalil went through the whole spill about seeing the car that looked like his father's to seeing them abuse and arrest Xavier for what Khalil said had to be a jacked up charge.

"Are you sure Xavier doesn't do drugs? I mean, maybe he had someone with him who left drugs in the car," Dee told him, trying to make some sense out of what Khalil had told her. She heard what he said, and she understood that he didn't want to believe that his brother could be using or even selling drugs, but from what Khalil explained, the bag of cocaine they showed Khalil was pretty substantial. This could mean a stiff sentence for his little brother.

"I know he doesn't do drugs and he doesn't sell drugs, Dee! I'm telling you, this was a set up, and I think George, maybe even my father, had something to do with it."

Dee was shaken to hear him mention George. She knew firsthand how George could be an evil, vindictive, and sometimes violent person. She'd dealt with him many times during her illicit affair with Hezekiah. George monitored the downtown condo where she and Hezekiah met up. She never understood why Hezekiah trusted George so much. But the more time she spent with Khalil and kept her ears wide open, the more she learned about the retired cop. She thought again about the drugs inside the car. She and Hezekiah enjoyed their share of doing drugs; something Khalil never suspected. She kept that part of her life hidden. She would find the right time to let him know and from the type of past he once lived, she hoped he would be cool with her method of chosen relaxation.

"Why would you think that George Reeves had something to do with it? The drugs were found in Hezekiah's car and Xavier was behind the wheel. That's cut and dried, Khalil. I'm sorry, but all I know that you can do is call a lawyer. I can contact my lawyer and see if he can recommend a good criminal defense attorney," she offered, hoping that suggestion would get her in even closer to Khalil.

Khalil sat down on the edge of the office desk. He looked terribly sad and troubled. "Would you? I need some legal advice, but I also need someone to believe in me and what I'm saying."

"I do believe you, Khalil. I just want you to see things the way they are. Even if the police or someone else planted the drugs in the car or left drugs in the car, you can't prove it. I mean they have those police cams, but were they running? Did you notice?"

"I don't remember seeing police cams. If they were running it will show them punching and kicking my little brother for no good reason. I'm telling you Xavier is no fighter, no dope fiend, and he's definitely not violent. For God's sake, he's as gay and docile as they come."

"Gay? Xavier?" Dee's shock was evident in her voice. "I thought he had a little girly girl demeanor but I didn't actually think he was gay." She laughed out loud. She wondered if Hezekiah knew that. If he did, he never said anything to her about it, and they had some serious conversations from time to time. He'd told her mostly about Khalil's past troubles but he never mentioned his son's names and she'd never seen pictures of his kids. That's why she didn't put two and two together right away when she and Khalil initially met.

Khalil stopped talking immediately and looked up at Dee.

Dee quickly recovered from the shock, stopped laughing, and assured Khalil that it made no difference what his brother's sexual orientation, that she could care less. Other people might judge him but she'd done too much and seen too much to judge anyone.

"Everything will be fine. I'm here for you. Whatever I can do to help your brother I promise you that I will do it. Okay?"

"We'll see."

Dee walked up to him, laid her hand on his chest, and then moved her arm up to wrap around his neck. She slightly pulled his face toward hers and kissed him hard.

"Yes, we will. But for now I want to make you feel all better."

Later that evening, Khalil and Dee went to see a bail bondsman to find out if a bond had been set for Xavier, and it had. Detria paid the bond and the two of them waited well into the night for Xavier's release. When Khalil saw him come out of the jail, Xavier looked like a frightened little boy.

"Are you all right, Zay?"

"I just want to get outta here and go home," he said, looking at Dee strangely and walking past his brother.

As they walked outside the jail, Dee walked in front of them, allowing the brothers to talk as they headed to the parking lot across the street from the jail.

"Isn't that the broad that Daddy was messing with?" Xavier asked.

"Yes, but forget that right now. You owe her a debt of gratitude. This broad posted your bail."

"I didn't ask her to. Ma would have done it. I don't want to be obligated to your sluts."

Dee stopped in her tracks and looked back at Xavier and Khalil after overhearing what was said. "You can turn around, take your scared, punk behind right back inside there for all I care. I only did this on the strength of your brother."

"Hold up. You are out of line," Khalil said to Xavier. "Way out of line. Is this the way you treat someone that has gone out of her way to help you, to make sure you didn't sit in a cell overnight? And she got you one of the best lawyers in the city on top of that. We're supposed to meet him in his office first thing tomorrow, but like Dee said, if you want to do this on your own, then have it your way."

"I didn't do anything. I was set up," Xavier yelled as tears poured from his eyes. "I have no idea how those drugs got in that car."

"The fact of the matter is they have you charged with possession. You're lucky you even got out of jail tonight. And you're going to need a dang good lawyer to beat this case whether it's a set up or not."

Dee started walking again, this time with haste as she crossed the street before the traffic light changed. She wanted to tell Xavier exactly where he could go and it wasn't heaven either, but because she wanted Khalil all for herself, she was willing to do whatever it took to make him see that having her in his corner could pay off nicely. She wanted to become his wife and the First Lady of Holy Rock...again. Whatever she needed to do to accomplish that she was going to do.

She made it to the car, and rested against it, as she watched the brothers talking and walking slowly toward her. *That little arrogant punk*, she thought to herself.

"Did you tell Ma?"

"No. That's for you to do. But her, I want you to apologize to Dee," he whispered to assure that this time Dee didn't hear their conversation even though she was already at the car and they were still crossing the street.

"That's the same broad who was screwing our father while she was doing you. How can you take her money and how did she even find out what happened?"

"I know what I'm doing, and who I smash is none of your business. You have bigger things to worry about, like staying out of jail." Khalil seethed, standing up on his brother so close that it was hard to tell there were two people. "Now, if you want to handle this little problem you've gotten yourself into alone then tell me now and I'll tell Dee to keep her money and she can keep spending it on me. What's it going to be?"

Xavier looked at his brother with anger in his eyes, but then exhaled and walked toward the car. When he made it across the street to where Dee was still leaning against Khalil's ride, he walked over to her. "I apologize, Ms. Graham. Thank you for bailing me out and for getting me a lawyer. I…I don't know how I would have been able to spend the night in that cell."

Khalil unlocked the doors with his key FOB while Dee walked around the front of the car and to the passenger side. "No apology required, but apology accepted," she said.

Xavier rushed behind her, opened the door for her, and waited on her to get inside before he closed her door, climbed in the back seat, closed his door, and laid his head against the leather seat. He was tired, smelly, still frightened, and ready to get home.

The car remained quiet except for the music playing on the radio. Xavier thought about Raymone. After court tomorrow morning, he had made up in his mind that he was going to try again to see him.

Khalil focused on the highway but his mind was actually on his father. It was time he paid him a visit. After he saw what they were going to do at his brother's arraignment tomorrow morning, he was going to make it his business to try to see him again.

Dee's thoughts were on how she was going to go about with her plans to become Mrs. Khalil McCoy. Khalil was in her debt but she was not going to make him feel as such. She wanted to play her cards just right. He was young and ripe for the picking and all she needed to do was use her womanly wisdom to reel him in again. She had to make him see that she could help him get everything he wanted in life: money, status, power and of course…Holy Rock.

One thing she learned while being married to Stiles and being the first lady, she had the inside scoop of how things actually ran and connections that could take him farther than Hezekiah ever imagined. He was young, handsome, and charismatic, qualities that the people of Holy Rock loved. All he needed was a little more grooming for the position he temporarily held and before he knew it, he would be the permanent pastor. It wouldn't matter if Hezekiah came back with full strength or not, once Khalil won them over, Hezekiah would be a done deal.

If she got Khalil to marry her, she knew she would run into quite a bit of opposition from the long time members of the church, but again, with Khalil being young, young people were flocking to the church in droves and soon the old timers wouldn't have a say at all. She would have to play her hand just right, and that she was going to make sure she did, starting with this foolish, sweet as sugar, Xavier. If she could help him beat this trumped up charge, then everything else would fall into place.

They arrived at Dee's house. Xavier had fallen asleep in the back seat but woke up when he heard the door closing. He popped his head up in time to see Khalil walking Dee to her door. He watched as they exchanged words and shared an intimate kiss.

Xavier turned his head and looked down at his phone, which was dead, so he couldn't attempt to call Raymone though he wanted to hear his voice so badly. He laid his head back against the seat again when he saw his brother walking back toward the car.

"Hey, wake up. Get in the front seat. I'm not your chauffeur," Khalil ordered as he opened the door and got inside.

Xavier pretended he was just waking up. "Oh, okay," he said drowsily. "Where is uh, Dee?"

"Inside."

Xavier opened the back door, got out the car, opened the front passenger door, and climbed into the front seat. "I'm sorry. I wish you had woke me up. I wanted to tell her thanks again."

"You'll have time for that in the morning."

"She's coming with us to court?"

"Yeah, no doubt. What? You got a problem with that?"

"Naw. I was just thinking; she's already done so much. I

don't want to put her out of her way, you know. And I don't wanna owe her what I can't already pay back."

"You better be glad somebody is doing it, cause getting lawyered up don't come cheap, li'l bruh. It don't come cheap at all."

Chapter 15

"Only those who care about you can hear you when you're quiet." Unknown

Stiles and Fancy had been conversing on the phone back and forth for the past several days. He initially had plans to drive to Memphis and stay for a few weeks, but there was so much going on at Full of Grace Ministries, that he had to change his plans at the last minute. One being that a long time member of the church who had been ill, died. Stiles could not see himself leaving at this time for a lengthy period. He wanted to be there for the man's family, his widow who was up in age, and his children and grandchildren, all faithful, loyal members of Full of Grace. The guest evacuees would be there for a couple more weeks too, so the day he was to leave, he changed his mind about driving to Memphis and instead had his administrative assistant to book him a flight for the weekend, and he would return on Monday. He would be back in time to eulogize Mr. Johnson and make plans to return to Memphis a couple of weeks after that.

He didn't take Fancy up on her offer to stay at her and Hezekiah's house, but chose to stay with Pastor and Josie this first time around. Soon after his plane landed, he picked up his rental car and drove straight to Pastor and Josie's house. He spent a couple of hours with them before he called Fancy and told her he was in town.

"I'm glad you had a safe flight," she said.

"Thanks, Sista Fancy."

"Are you sure you want to visit Hezekiah this evening?"

"Yes, that's the main reason for my visit, and of course to see about you. I'm only here for the weekend as I told you due to the death of one of my members."

"Yes, I know. I'm sorry to hear that."

"We all have to make that journey one day. Anyway, send me that address again, and I'll save it in my phone and then I'll be on my way. You don't have to go with me, you know."

"I know, but I want to. I haven't gone to see him in almost two weeks. I usually try to go at least once a week but it's been so busy and there is a situation at home that, well that's weighing heavily on me. I didn't want to project that onto Hezekiah. He knows me too well; he'll know that something isn't right."

"Let's talk."

"Maybe we will, but as for now, you just concentrate on your brother. He needs someone to get through to him 'cause God knows I can't," Fancy said.

Stiles detected her frustration in her voice. He couldn't understand why Hezekiah was so angry with Fancy and even with him when it was none of their faults what occurred between Margaret and Pastor. He wanted to have a relationship with his brother and now that his sister and brother-in-law were dead, he really wanted to make things work with Hezekiah. He longed for family and to have a brother was something he always wanted.

Stiles finished getting dressed, said a quick goodbye to Pastor and Josie, and left to go see his brother and of course Fancy, too.

Stiles was pleasantly surprised to hear Hezekiah's speech was beginning to improve somewhat. He remained wheelchair bound and unable to walk. Most of his words still came out tangled, but if he took his time talking like the speech pathologist taught him, sometimes his words could be deciphered.

When he first saw Stiles enter into his room, Hezekiah showed total dissatisfaction. "What the....?" he managed to say.

Disregarding Hezekiah's less than accepting greeting, Stiles said, "Hello to you, too." He understood that Hezekiah still had a lot of anger inside of him, but as his brother, he was willing and ready to look past that and work on building a relationship with him. Perhaps they would never grow close as brothers, but Stiles hoped that they could learn to be civil toward one another and cordial. He wanted Hezekiah to know that regardless of how things happened in the past, that he wanted them to forget those things that were behind and look to their futures as blood brothers and men of God.

Fancy stood behind Stiles looking on. She had warned Stiles that Hezekiah was not easy to get along with. He still treated her like she was garbage. He couldn't get past the fact that she had 'put him away' as he described it. But it wasn't her fault that he had abused her. She wasn't going to have it, not ever. Even when he got well enough to come home, Fancy didn't know if she would remain in the house with him or not. Instead of absence making her heart grow fonder, absence was making her heart wonder.

She made up in her mind that on Stiles' next visit that she would tell him about Hezekiah and Detria's nasty affair. Hezekiah would say that she was betraying him, but again, her feelings for her husband were diminishing by the day. She had prayed about it more than once, but each time she thought of him, instead of the love she once felt for him she felt anger, distrust, and disgust. Those combinations were not good—not good at all.

"You're my brother. I had to come to see about you," Stiles continued.

"No need," Hezekiah struggled.

"Oh, but there is. Whether you like it or not, we were born of the same woman. We come from the same womb. We share the same blood. What my mother—what Audrey--did was wrong and it was deceitful and cruel. Our mother, Margaret, paid the ultimate price for it, but that is not our fault. There is no need for us to war against one another. We are not Cane and Abel, Hezekiah. I am your brother; I want to have a relationship with you. I want to be here for you."

"Why?"

"Why? Have you not heard anything I've said? We're brothers. Do I need any reason other than that?"

"Want nothing…..with….you…father."

"You mean your father, don't you? Pastor is your biological father, not mine. I could be angry about that, but I'm not. The man raised me."

"I'm going to give you two some time alone," Fancy finally interjected. "I'm going downstairs. Visiting hours are over in," she looked at her cell phone that she held in her hand, "forty minutes. Hezekiah, I won't be back up here. I'll check on you later this week."

"No," he said. "Go," he turned and said to Stiles.

"I think we have more to talk about, a lot more."

"Go…no brother," he said.

"Oh, Hezekiah, stop being so stubborn and evil. You sound so foolish! Don't you see that your brother is reaching out to you? He's extending an olive branch to you and you have the nerve to turn it away. None of what has happened is his fault! You should be grateful that he wants you in his life!" Fancy yelled. She was sick of Hezekiah and his mean ways. "Start acting like the man God called you to be."

"Out. Go…no….come back!" he yelled. His words were slow but they were exact and vengeful sounding just the same, perhaps even more so since each word was heavily pronounced.

Hezekiah turned his electric chair away from his two visitors, bolted out of his room, almost knocking poor Fancy over once again, and took off down the hall and out of sight.

Fancy ran out of the room and didn't stop until she approached the elevators. Stiles was right behind her. Fancy pushed the elevator button, and then held her head in her hands and cried. The elevator opened. No one was on it. Stiles held the door back and ushered her inside.

"Don't cry, Fancy. He's just going through a lot." He gathered her in his arms as the door to the elevator closed.

She looked up at Stiles. "I can't take it. It's too much. If I really thought he was behaving this way because of the stroke, then I think I would be able to tolerate his actions more, but I don't think it has anything to do with the stroke," she said, stepping back, looking into her purse, and pulling out a tissue to wipe her face.

"What else could it be? I mean I'm sure this stroke has taken a toll on him, Fancy. I remember when Pastor had his stroke, he became distant, on edge, and depressed. And if you consider everything that's happened with Pastor, Margaret, the shooting, the man is going through a lot. Even I'm still having a hard time digesting everything that's happened."

The doors to the elevator opened and they both stepped out. Stiles put an arm around her shoulder as she continued to sniffle and cry. They walked outside to the car and he opened the door for her.

"Why don't we grab something to eat," he suggested. "Maybe it'll take your mind off this and you can tell me what else is going on."

"I'm sorry. I didn't think to offer you anything to eat when you came to the house."

"I didn't stay, remember. I just came and scooped you up to come here. It's all right anyway. We're going now."

"What would you like to eat?"

"Let's go to Déjà Vu. Are they still open? Stiles asked.

"Yes, they should be. I'll check on my phone."

"Okay, then Déjà Vu it is."

"Do you remember how to get there?"

"Sure, I do."

At the popular Cajun and soul food restaurant, Fancy and Stiles dined on an array of food, all delicious and filling. They laughed and talked about the good times they enjoyed at Holy Rock when Stiles was senior pastor. For a while, Fancy felt the burdens and weights of her family problems being pushed aside. Laughter truly proved to be like a good medicine.

Deep into their dinnertime, the conversation turned serious when Stiles inquired about what had her so troubled, other than Hezekiah.

She initially thought that she shouldn't talk about what Xavier came home a few nights ago and told her. His ordeal with the police, his night in jail, and the drug charges he faced, but she needed someone she felt that she could trust. Her spirit told her that she could release her troubles on the trusted ears of Stiles, and so she did. She slowly began to open up to him and before long she freely talked. She told him everything that had been going on and then she told him about Hezekiah's affair with Detria and that the harlot had twisted the mind of Khalil as well.

After they were done eating some two hours later, they prepared to leave the restaurant. As they walked downtown toward Stiles' car, she began crying all over again when they arrived at the car.

Stiles, much like he did in the elevator, pulled her against his chest, smoothed back her hair, and whispered, "When you pass through the waters, I will be with you; and when you pass through the rivers, they will not sweep over you. When you walk through the fire, you will not be burned; the flames will not set you ablaze."

"That…that's one of my favorite passages of scripture." She moved away from him, not in haste, but slowly and looked into his handsome face and his dark brown eyes. "How did you know?"

"I didn't. The Holy Spirit has a way of knowing what we need when we need it." He looked at her, took her hand into his, and continued ministering to her. "You have to remain strong, Fancy. Remember, there is nothing too hard for God. You know that. I know it's difficult. Xavier in trouble; Detria playing these sick, sin-filled games, Hezekiah, an adulterer and troubled man,

Khalil's new position at Holy Rock. It's a lot. But I want you to know that I'm here for you, and I'll do whatever I can to help you."

He stroked her natural hair and she allowed her tears to flow while they stood at his car and people passed them by. Minutes later, he opened the door and she got inside the car. They drove in silence to Fancy's house.

"Do you want to come inside?" she asked him, as she wiped fresh tears from her face. "I'm so sorry that I've put all of this on you."

"I'll walk you to the door, and there's no need to be sorry. You need someone to talk to. Being a first lady makes it hard to know who you can trust and who you can turn to during times like these. Of course, we know you are to rely on God, but as humans, in this flesh, we yearn to hear the words of another person sometimes. We want to have someone to do just what we did earlier, have a shoulder to cry on. I'll be that shoulder for you, Fancy as long as you need me to. I promise to come to Memphis as often as possible until much of this is resolved."

They got out of the car and Stiles walked her to the door as promised.

"You sure you don't want to spend the night? I have plenty of room," she offered.

"No, maybe tomorrow night. I promised Pastor that I would spend tonight with him and Josie. I plan on going back to the rehab facility to talk to Hezekiah tomorrow."

"But you heard what he said; he doesn't want you back. He doesn't even want me to come back."

"We say and do a lot of things when we're hurt and angry. I'm going to try to talk to him again."

"I hope that you'll come to church Sunday."

"You know I can't pass up a chance to visit Holy Rock whenever I come to Memphis. It's part of me, so of course I'll be there. Tomorrow after I leave from seeing Hezekiah, I want to see if I can meet up with Khalil and Xavier, separately, if possible. Is Xavier home tonight?"

"He probably is. He parks in the garage. He's not one to venture out much, and it's even less since he caught that ridiculous charge," Fancy said, finding herself growing upset all over again.

"I didn't mean to make you upset again. If you will, text me his number. I'll give him a call and see if he'll meet with me sometime tomorrow. I'll do the same for Khalil."

"Thank you, Stiles." Fancy stood on her tiptoes and kissed him on the cheek. "God bless you."

"Hey, what's a brother-in-law for?" he chuckled and so did Fancy.

"Now go on inside. I'm going to Pastor's house and hit the sack. It's been a long eventful day and evening," he said and smiled again.

"Goodnight, Stiles."

"Goodnight, Fancy."

Fancy walked inside the house, closing the door behind her as she heard Stiles' drive away. She smiled as she walked in the kitchen, sat her purse on the kitchen island, removed her shoes, and went to the refrigerator. She removed a bottle of wine, poured herself a glass, and took it upstairs to her bedroom.

Xavier stepped out of his room. "Oh, hey, Ma."

"Hi, sweetheart."

"You been to see Dad?" he asked.

"Yes. I think you should go see him. You and Khalil have only been there twice since your father's been there."

"He doesn't want to see us," Xavier said dryly.

"I understand, but you should still try. Pastor Stiles, your father's brother, is in town this weekend. He went with me today to see him."

"I bet Dad wasn't too happy about that."

Fancy took a sip of her wine. "No, he wasn't to say the least."

"That bad, huh?"

Fancy nodded. "Yes, but enough about Hezekiah. How are you? Were you able to see Raymone today? I know you said you were going to try to see if he would finally agree to see you."

Xavier's head hung low. "No, he still doesn't want anything to do with me. I feel so bad, Ma."

"I know, baby. But give him time. He's going through a lot. He has to learn how to live his life in a whole new way."

"All because of me," Xavier cried.

"Xavier, don't do this to yourself. You have to forgive yourself, honey. Listen, I gave Stiles your phone number. He wants to talk to you while he's here. And please, before you tell him no or before you get upset with me about giving him your number, will you just listen to what he has to say? We all need someone to talk to, someone to give us Godly counsel. Someone who will not judge us or look down on us for the mistakes we've made. Please, Xavier. If he calls, don't brush him off."

Xavier wiped his tears. "I'm going to go pick up a pizza I ordered. I'll be back," he said and walked off.

"Xavier, wait."

"What is it, Ma?"

"Have you thought anymore about attending Xavier? You only have a few weeks before it's time to leave. I'll go do some college shopping for you next week. There's so much you're going to need for your dorm room."

"Do you even have to ask about whether or not I'm still going to college? Don't you see, Ma. Any hopes of going to Xavier University are gone....done...over," he said forcefully. "I screwed that up. First, with the accident, and now with this charge. So don't ask me about Xavier anymore."

"Honey, it's not over. You can still go to college. Xavier University is where you've had your sights on going since you were in middle school. You can't let what's going on here stop you. We'll work it out. I promise," she said as she walked up on her son and stroked his arm tenderly.

"I already contacted them and let them know my circumstances have changed and I wouldn't be attending. I turned down the scholarship, too so just leave it alone. Leave *me* alone already," he yelled, stormed down the stairs, went into the kitchen, and Fancy faintly heard the door leading to the garage open and shut.

She shook her head slowly and walked the rest of the way to her room. She took the glass of wine to her bathroom, set it on the bathroom vanity, and started running a warm bath for herself.

In her mind, she repeated the passage of scripture Stiles shared with her earlier as she undressed. *When you pass through the waters...*

Chapter 16

"Change nothing and nothing changes." Unknown

Stiles was pleasantly surprised that Khalil and Xavier both agreed to meet up with him. Khalil suggested that Stiles meet him and his baby brother for breakfast before Stiles got back on the highway to Houston.

"How does it feel to fill such a huge role at Holy Rock?"

"A little strange; a little scary but on the other hand I know that I'm doing exactly what God wants me to do at this point in my life. All things work together for good."

"To those who love the Lord and are called," Stiles immediately added.

"According to his purpose," said Xavier.

All three men laughed lightly and exchanged friendly banter back and forth. They discussed sports along with finances and the latest in literature, being that reading books by controversial and African American authors was Xavier's forte.

"I'm proud of you guys, and I'm sure that your father is as well."

"I don't know about that, but then again, I'm not living to please my father. Not my earthly father that is," Khalil stated and put a forkful of pancakes in his mouth.

"Xavier, have you made a decision about attending Xavier in the fall. You know that's right around the corner. It'll be time for you to leave this city."

"Yes, my calling is to remain here and help my brother and my mother in the ministry." He wiped his mouth nervously with his napkin and then picked up his glass of soda and took a couple of deep swallows.

"So you're not going to accept that full ride? You do have a full ride scholarship, don't you?"

"Yes, I do, but it is what it is."

"I see," said Stiles hearing an uneasiness in Xavier's voice and tone. "All I'm going to say on that is be sure you're doing what *you* want to do, Xavier and not what you think others expect of you."

"No one expects him to do anything other than what he feels is best for him," Khalil said forcefully.

"My brother is right; this is my decision and mine alone. I'd rather not talk about it anymore."

"Sure, no problem," Stiles said.

They continued eating their breakfast and making small talk.

"I want you two to know that I'm here for you. I'm just a phone call away. If you need me, I'll hit the road with no questions asked. You hear me?"

"Yes, sir," Khalil responded respectfully.

"Being the senior pastor of a huge church like Holy Rock won't be easy. You're going to have a lot of opposition but you have to stand your ground. If God is calling you to do something then do it. Preach the Word, study the Word, and keep your head on straight. And being a young, handsome, smart and *single* man, like yourself," Stiles emphasized 'single' "the women are going to be all over you, if they aren't already. Just be careful, nephew. Real careful," Stiles said, taking a sip of his coffee followed by a taste of his hashbrowns.

Khalil couldn't be sure if Stiles knew about him and Detria or not, but he didn't care one way or the other. Detria was a single woman, and yes, she had been married to Stiles, and had an affair with his father, but all of that was in the past. If he wanted to smash her, that was his business. Like Hezekiah, he had his purpose for what he did and who he did it with…and messing around with Detria was no different. He had his reasons and his purpose.

"Well, I better get ready to hit this highway," Stiles said after he took a final bite of his meal.

"It was good talking to you, Pastor Stiles," Xavier said.

"I'm your uncle. Call me Stiles or Uncle Stiles. I know your father doesn't like the fact that we're brothers, but I hope one day he will welcome me into the fold," Stiles said and chuckled as he pulled out a ten-dollar bill and laid it on the table for the tip. "Oh, and breakfast is on me."

"My father has his reasons for everything he does," Khalil said. "I'm sure this is no different, but on the other hand, I am my own man. I make decisions according to how things are played out before me, so I have nothing against you, *Uncle Stiles*," Khalil said.

"I'm with Khalil. I have nothing against you."

"Good, Stiles said, and wiped his mouth one final time with his napkin. He pushed back from the table and stood, followed by Xavier and Khalil. They shook hands and the three of them walked to the front of the restaurant. Stiles paid for the meal and the three men walked outside.

They shook hands again. "Have a safe trip," Xavier said.

"Yeah, be safe," Khalil said.

Stiles gave each one of them dap and walked away towards his car. He stopped and turned around for a brief second. "Hey," he called out. "I meant what I said. If you need me for anything, hit me up."

"Fa sho," Khalil said.

"Yeah, fa sho," Xavier said.

Khalil welcomed and introduced to others his new staff at Holy Rock's weekly staff meeting. Sista Mavis sat at the other end of the long conference room table with her mouth poked out like she had a mouthful of tobacco tucked inside her bottom lip. She was still holding a grudge against Khalil who had told her a week ago today that he was replacing her as his administrative assistant. She couldn't believe that he had reassigned her to act as one of the administrative assistants to the associate ministers. The same thing had happened to Sister Gloria Wooten when Stiles stepped down from Holy Rock. Pastor McCoy sent her packing in the exact same way when he became Senior Pastor. Now it was happening to her and she was more than upset, she was absolutely dumbfounded over his decision.

As the meeting continued and he introduced one person after another as newly appointed deacons and trustees, Sista Mavis watched as some of the older deacons displayed frowns that could have scared the worst of the worst away.

"We have a lot of changes going on at Holy Rock, but I want you to know that it is only to make things better for this church and for its members."

Xavier sat on the opposite side of his brother, looking handsome in a pair of jeans, bright mango-orange button down shirt and matching bow tie. A young man at the other end of the table eyed the handsome McCoy boy in wonderment and pleasure.

"I want to take this time to also introduce another role, or should I say two roles, I have filled at Holy Rock. One is my prior position of Youth Director. As you know, First Lady McCoy has been graciously filling that role since I took over the position of senior pastor. As some of you may recall, my mother was quite active with the children and the youth when my father was associate pastor. But seeing that not only is my father ill, she has other obligations that she fulfills and she has expressed that returning to such a consuming role is not what she desires to do at this time. Therefore, I want to announce that my brother, Xavier McCoy, is assuming the role."

Some of the members could be heard clearing their throats

and a couple of others gave sideway glances at each other, but no one said anything out loud.

Xavier was touched that his brother believed in him enough to place him in such a high profile position, but he tried to explain to Khalil that he had no desire to work in the church to such an extent. He didn't know where his life was headed now that he had the drug charge pending and his hopes to attend Xavier University had been dashed. By all means, he understood that he needed to do something productive with his life if he had to remain in Memphis, but he had not given much thought to playing such a pivotal role at Holy Rock. When Khalil approached him about what he wanted to do, Xavier bucked against it. What would people say about him being over the youth and young adults, especially those who were against homosexuality. The last thing he wanted to do was cause an uproar at Holy Rock. As it stood, the only thing going for him now was the fact that George was no longer a threat to him or to the future of Holy Rock, at least he hoped he wasn't. The last he'd heard about George had been from his brother. Khalil told him that his sources reported that George was facing at least five to fifteen years behind bars for his crime of possessing child pornography and it had been recently alleged that good old George had been crossing state lines to have sex with minor boys.

"I also want to inform you that Xavier is also our new financial administrator. Brother Pickens has submitted his resignation. Brother Pickens nodded. "Where we will hate to see him and Sister Pickens leave Holy Rock and Memphis, we will keep them in our prayers as they enter retirement and relocate to the west coast."

The room grew eerily quiet at the huge announcement. Sista Mavis swallowed so hard it looked like she had an Adam's apple. She couldn't wait to pass this news on to her sista friends. *Who does this boy think he is coming in here stirring up all this mess? He is definitely his father's son because Hezekiah McCoy did the same thing when he took over as senior pastor.* Mavis wondered how many people would leave after hearing this latest news.

"Would you like to say something, brother? Or should I say Brother Xavier?"

Xavier cleared his throat. If he was uncomfortable or unsure of his new roles, it wasn't revealed in his speech. "I just want to say that I am grateful to be part of Holy Rock and to serve as the Youth Director and Financial Administrator. I will work as if I am working for the Lord, and will do my best to make Holy Rock better in these areas. I am only as good as those around me so I will be calling on you. If any of you work well with youth and you want to be part of this growing ministry, please see me after this meeting."

Malik, one of Holy Rock's seven associate ministers, batted his eyes slowly and smiled again discreetly as he listened to Xavier. He was especially attentive, and seemed to cling to every word Xavier spoke.

"I hope that this is the beginning of a fresh start for Holy Rock," Xavier continued, purposely avoiding eye contact with the handsome deacon. "Thanks to my brother, our senior pastor, Holy Rock is drawing in younger people by the droves and I am grateful to God for that," Xavier said as he sat back down.

Khalil stood. "Thank you, Xavier. It's all God. He's working on our behalf."

A knock on the door interrupted the meeting and in walked his mother and a young lady that made Khalil's breath catch in his throat.

"Come in, Mother."

"I'm sorry to be late, but I was waiting on your new administrative assistant to arrive."

"Good morning, Pastor McCoy. Good morning, everyone," the young woman said as she followed Fancy all the way into the conference room.

"Hello, gentleman....Sista Mavis," Fancy spoke. She walked over to the empty seat two chairs down from Khalil's end of the table and the young lady walked next to her and prepared to sit in the chair next to Fancy's chair.

"This is Eliana Hodges," she introduced.

"Welcome to Holy Rock, Mrs. Hodges," Khalil immediately rose from his chair and walked over to shake her hand.

Khalil swallowed hard and simply stared. He had given his mother charge to find a suitable administrative assistant to replace Sista Mavis. From looks alone, his mother had definitely come through.

Sista Mavis was good at what she did when she did it, but Khalil admitted to his mother that he wanted someone younger, who had a more pleasant attitude, and who wasn't a church gossip. There were too many confidential matters, especially surrounding his family that he couldn't chance getting out. He didn't have full proof that it was Sista Mavis leaking personal matters, but he had been warned many times that it was her, and he had overheard her talking to her friends on the phone on several occasions.

Eliana was beautiful. Petite as she was, she strolled in with exuberant confidence and her hips swayed from side to side like a mild wind blowing on a spring day. She appeared to be in her early twenties. She had shiny black hair with skin that matched dark eyes deeply set under prominent eyebrows. She wore her thick black hair in Medusa-styled locs and her sensually soft fragrance was alluring but not overpowering. Her smile further transformed her face and made it even more captivating.

"Nice to meet you, Mrs. Hodges," Khalil greeted her again as he extended his hand. "Mother," he said once more and leaned forward and kissed his mother on her cheek. Fancy smelled just as sweet but not in the same way as Eliana.

"Please call me Eliana," the young lady said.

Everyone else nodded and spoke to Eliana and Fancy while Sista Mavis barely mumbled.

Khalil returned to his chair. "Everyone, Eliana will be joining us for the next several weeks to see if she is a good fit to fill the position of my personal assistant. Eliana, tell us a little about yourself."

"Here is my resume Will you pass that to him? she said to the gentleman on her left. The young man nodded, took the resume' and passed it to Khalil while smiling with lust in Eliana's direction.

"Impressive," Khalil said as he reviewed it.

"As you will see on my resume', she said looking directly at Khalil and then at the others gathered, "I have worked in the church for most of my life. I have a bachelor's degree in business administration and management with a minor in human resources management. I am working on my master's degree now. I love the Lord and I love working in the church ministry. My grandfather was a preacher in Alabama for many years. My parents raised me and my four siblings in the church and not just in the church, but they taught us about God and gave us the foundation on which to make our lives rich in faith and belief in Him."

Many of those sitting at the table nodded their approval, all except Sista Mavis who sat quietly with her arms folded. She refused to admit that she too was impressed with this young girl's words. She was not only pretty, she was articulate and smart.

"I know how important it is to maintain confidentiality," she went on to explain without Khalil having to inquire about it. "I must admit that I have not worked for a church this size, but I am sure it is no different than the small church of which I have been affiliated with most of my life. All of us have problems, trials, and situations that arise in our lives and many times we run to the church, or should I say the pastor of the church," she emphasized and flashed her eyes directly at Khalil. "It is imperative and necessary to uphold the privacy of that individual and or families when they come to the pastor for help."

"I must say that I am quite impressed, Mrs. Hodges."

"It's *Miss* Hodges, she said, but again, you may call me

Eliana if you so choose."

Khalil nodded, clasped his hands together, and rested them on his elbows on the table. "Of course, Eliana. Everyone, please take a moment to introduce yourselves."

The staff did as Khalil asked. When it got to Sista Mavis, she put on a forced smile and introduced herself.

"Sista Mavis will be doing most of your training over the next couple of weeks," explained Fancy.

The meeting ended shortly after Eliana and Fancy's entrance and Khalil instructed his mother and Eliana to join him in his office.

"I hope you enjoy being part of Holy Rock," Khalil stated as they walked up the hall. Along the way, he pointed out her office area where Sista Mavis sat gathering her personal things to make room for Eliana to take her place. She slightly rolled her eyes as the girl passed. Fancy saw her and returned Sista Mavis' stare with a penetrating gaze of her own that seemed to warn the woman not to cross her. Sista Mavis quickly shifted her eyes away and resumed gathering her things, stopping when the phone started ringing.

"Good morning, Holy Rock Ministries," she said in the most polite voice she could muster.

Fancy smiled and continued her stride to Khalil's office.

"I'm sure that I will love working here," Eliana said. "As I stated in the meeting, I am going to school for my master's, but it should not interfere with my duties and responsibilities."

They arrived at his office and Khalil opened the door and stepped aside to allow his mother and Eliana to enter.

"That is something I wanted to discuss," said Fancy. "You will be required to attend most services including Sunday services and weekly evening services which are held each Wednesday night. Hours can be long here and we serve a congregation of over 15,000 on the church roll."

"Will that be a problem?" Khalil asked as he offered Eliana

and his mother a seat before he walked around to his desk and sat down.

"No, I do my classes online, but I am required to actually attend classes one weekend every six weeks. I hope that won't be a problem."

"I think we can work around that," Khalil stated quickly.

"As long as we know in advance," Fancy immediately added.

"Oh, I can give you my schedule, and I have less than a year before I complete my studies."

"Good for you."

"Have you discussed salary and benefits with HR?"

"Yes, I have, and it is more than generous. Thank you," Eliana said.

"Good. Do you have any questions for me?" he asked, looking boldly into her eyes that seemed to hypnotize him as she returned his look with a softness that made his young tender heart go pitter patter.

"When do I start?" she giggled lightly.

"How about first thing Monday morning?" Fancy said.

"That will be fine."

"Do you have a church home?" Khalil asked.

"Yes, I do, but my church family understands the commitment that is required when working for a church."

Fancy watched as Khalil became almost lost in this young girl who she had taken the pangs to choose carefully. She was set on making sure she chose someone who would be able to turn her son's head and mind away from that treacherous Detria Graham. Eliana Hodges, Fancy believed, was the one she hoped would do it. So far, it looked like things were off to a good start.

"Well, if you'll excuse me, Pastor Khalil, I'm going to my office to handle a few things before I go see your father. Eliana, why don't you take some time to get to know the man you'll be spending a lot of time with." Fancy smiled, rose from her chair, and nodded as she walked to the door.

"Yes, I'd like that," Eliana replied.

"So would I. I'm anxious to learn all about you…Eliana." Khalil threw up his hand, displaying a gentle wave and smile. "We'll talk later, Mother."

Chapter 17

Brooke and Detria enjoyed shopping and hanging out for the better half of the day. They went from mall to mall in search of nothing in particular, just enjoying some much needed sister time. There once was a time that the two sisters were inseparable but their relationship had taken some hard hits all because of what happened between Detria and Skip.

Brooke was never on board with her sister having an affair with Skip. She loved and respected Stiles and believed that Detria was responsible for her severed family. She certainly was not fully blaming Detria for little Audrey's death, but still the fact remained that all that had happened was directly tied to her sordid relationship with Skip who was a no good, slick talking, shyster dude who only wanted to use Detria, and that he did. Brooke did blame Detria, however for practically giving her one surviving child and son over to Skip. Detria had never been the motherly type; it seemed like Detria and children were not a match made in heaven. Talking sense into Detria was like talking to a concrete wall; she had a hard head and a stubborn spirit.

The day she found out about the tragic accident that killed little Audrey was one of the most horrifying times of Brooke's life. Such a sweet little, precious and innocent child she was. Brooke expected that Detria would go all out and pour out love and affection for her baby boy, Elijah, but it had been just the opposite. It seemed that after she realized that Skip didn't want her and had gotten married on her, that she handed the child over to Skip and his wife to raise. Brooke and her family rarely saw him or heard from Elijah because Skip didn't bring him around and Detria didn't press him to.

The sisters sat across the table from each other at The Cheesecake Factory initially talking about the items they'd purchased and catching up on sister-to-sister chat.

"How is Elijah? You know mother and father would like to see him, and so would me and the boys."

"He's good. And if you want to see him so badly, you all know where to find him. He's with his father, so don't start with the shenanigans, Brooke. We've been having a good day and I wouldn't want to see it ruined because you want to play Miss Holier-than-thou."

"Not at all; I'm just saying that we want to see Elijah. Come on, Detria."

"Come on what?"

"How can a mother not miss her own child? It's probably been God knows when since you've seen him. I know it's been at least a year since any of us in the family have seen him. We probably wouldn't know him if he walked up on us, and you probably wouldn't either."

"I'm not going to sit here and entertain this foolishness, Brooke. Elijah lives with his father. If y'all missed him so bad then you know how to call Skip or go to his house or even find him at one of his many Subway Restaurants, but I don't see you, mom or dad doing any such thing. And I see my son when I see him, and that's that on that. End of that discussion. Tell me; how are my nephews?"

"You're concerned about Jayce and Jayden but you aren't thinking about Elijah?" Brooke wiped her mouth and did a feigned chuckle. She couldn't get over her sister and her disregard for her family and her child. It never ceased to amaze Brooke, yet she loved Detria. Always did and always would.

She prayed that one day Detria would see the error of her ways before it was too late.

"Yes, I'm concerned about Jayce and Jayden. They're my nephews, for goodness sakes. The good thing about that is I'm not responsible for their care so I don't have to worry about failing at being a good parent, you know," she said and looked deep into her sister's eyes.

Detria understood that she would never win a mother of the year award and she had made peace with that, particularly after baby Audrey's death. She would not take on the physical burden of being responsible for another person's life, namely her child. Skip was doing a far better job at raising him along with that hussy wife of his, and when Skip would bring the boy over, Elijah always whined and cried about going 'home' within an hour or so after arriving at her house. The last time Skip brought him to her house she decided right then and there that enough was enough and she would never force him to come see her again. He had any and everything a child could want at her house plus his own room with tons of toys, but he still wanted his father and Meaghan. There were a few times when she missed him, but for those times, she chose video chat over personal visitation. She paid a handsome penny for child support and she had made Skip's life quite cozy and comfortable with all the money she'd given him when she got her settlement. She was not going to allow anyone to make her feel bad about her decision and that included her parents and Brooke.

"Jayce and Jayden are doing pretty good. Here, let me show you some of these pics, girl." Brooke proceeded to remove her phone from her purse and flipped it around to show Detria tons of pictures of the boys.

Detria did the same after Brooke was done, only the number of pictures of Elijah that Skip had sent her were far outnumbered by the tons Brooke had of Jayce and Jayden.

"He is so handsome," Brooke said. "I miss him."

"Girl, please. Like I said, if y'all miss him so much then go knock on his daddy's door. Skip is not going to keep y'all from seeing him. He may be a low down cheating dog, but he's not going to deprive his son from seeing his grandparents, aunt, and cousins. But I must admit," Detria said, raising up a finger on her one good arm. "He is not going to volunteer either." Detria giggled lightly then used her fork to stab into her almond crusted salmon salad, then placed a forkful of it inside her mouth.

"You need prayer," Brooke said, shaking her head.

"So how's my brother-in-law?" Detria asked, totally ignoring Brooke's remark.

"John's good. Our tenth wedding anniversary is coming up next month. I'm thinking about having some type of party or dinner. You know, something special that we can share with our close friends and family."

"That sounds lovely," Detria said, trying not to sound sarcastic but failed at her attempt.

Brooke rolled her eyes at her sister.

"Ten years, huh?"

"Yep. If you had been the kind of wife you should have been, you and Stiles would be celebrating your lives together." Brooke picked up her glass of iced tea and took a swallow.

"What does the Bible say?" Detria said, taking another bite of her food before proceeding. She chewed a couple of times and then said, "Brethren, I count not myself to have apprehended it, but this one thing I do: forgetting those things which are behind, and reaching forth unto those things which are before."

"You know the Word; too bad you don't live the Word," Brooke chastised her, then she picked up her mushroom burger and took a bite of it.

"I love spending time with you," Detria laughed again while Brooke slowly chewed her food and rolled her eyes.

"Whose life are you ruining now? Do I know him, cause if I do, I'd like to warn him to steer clear of you," Brooke said sarcastically.

"Since Mom and Dad stopped going to Holy Rock after Stiles' departure, I'm sure you don't hear much about what's buzzing around there, but they have a new young tenderoni serving as the senior pastor."

Brooke eyed her sister cautiously. "Please don't tell me you're robbing the cradle, Detria. Surely, even you have some standards and morals."

"Of course I have standards and morals. Contrary to what some people say, I am not a loose woman, sister."

Brooke couldn't help but laugh. "I love you, Detria," she said. "With all of your flaws and imperfections, I love you."

"And I love you too, sis. Now, let me tell you all about that fine specimen of a man, Khalil McCoy, the newly appointed senior pastor of Holy Rock!"

Chapter 18

"Not everything that is faced can be changed. But nothing can be changed until it is faced." James Baldwin

Xavier made a promise to himself to visit his father at least twice a month. This would be the third time in the past two months that he'd kept that promise. At first, Hezekiah didn't have two words to say to him, but Xavier talked to him anyway. He told him everything about what had happened with Raymone, about him giving up the scholarship at Xavier and staying in Memphis to work at Holy Rock. He poured out everything to Hezekiah, even told him about the drug charge, but excluded information about him being gay. He already knew how his father would deal with that realization and Xavier wasn't up to battling with the man, at least not right now.

Hezekiah seemed to listen to his son. He had little to say, but Xavier did feel that Hezekiah gave him a look of understanding as the man nodded while Xavier told him what had been going on. He wished he could say the same for Raymone, but unfortunately that situation hadn't changed and Xavier had resigned himself to accept that what he and Raymone once shared had to be put in the past. Their relationship was over, done, finished, kaput. He had tried unsuccessfully numerous times to talk to Raymone and finally just a few days ago after visiting Hezekiah, Raymone had agreed to see him.

The visit was not pleasant at all and Xavier left Raymone's house feeling lower than low. Raymone made it clear and so did

Raymone's parents that their friendship was no more. He didn't want to see Xavier ever again. It crushed Xavier like a mountain of boulders had been placed on top of him. That night and the days that followed Xavier remained pinned up in his room. He barely ate, he refused to answer his phone and texts, and each time his mother knocked on his door he adamantly refused to see her. Khalil had called and came over too, but Xavier refused to open up to him as well. He needed time to come to terms with what he'd done. No matter what people said to try to make him feel better, it didn't work; Raymone was a cripple because of him and he would never ever forgive himself. On top of that, he was facing the drug charge.

Khalil's candy lady, Detria Graham, had paid good money for a lawyer to represent him. The attorney tried to alleviate any worries or fears by explaining to Xavier that in Tennessee, first-time drug possession charges were classified as a misdemeanor. "Whether you're charged with possession of marijuana, cocaine, heroin, or meth, you will be charged with a Class A misdemeanor. In your case, it was cocaine. If convicted, you could face up to a year in jail and fines but I am confident that we can get the case thrown out."

The preliminary hearing had gone off without a hitch, and even when Xavier's lawyer told him that the best case scenario was getting the charges thrown out or if he was convicted he would seek to have Xavier's record expunged after a year, Xavier still had his fill of worries. First, it would take at least two more court dates before the final decision was made and Xavier was discouraged about this bit of news. He was not like his brother. He knew nothing about the criminal justice system and he hated the fact that he had been falsely accused. The cocaine found in the car must have belonged to his father or his brother but it certainly didn't belong to him. He hoped this lawyer Detria had hired on his behalf could deliver what he promised because a criminal record was nothing that Xavier thought he would be facing, not in a million years.

With Khalil making him Youth Director and Financial Administrator at Holy Rock, instead of it making him feel better, Xavier felt more inadequate and more than unworthy of his dual roles and new responsibilities. Sure, he would be making a ton of money, but his sites had never been on being involved in ministry like his father and now his brother. He wanted to go away to college and get as far away from his family as possible. He had a belief in God but not to the point that he wanted to commit his life to it. Christianity was too judgmental for him and he had no desire to be part of it, but here he was, thrown into the ministerial roles all because of his family. He loved his parents and he wanted to please them in any way that he could, but he didn't see how working at Holy Rock would do that.

After the hearing was over and done, Xavier said a quick goodbye and thank you to his attorney, Detria, and Khalil before he shot out of the courthouse and headed to see his father. He dreaded going but he knew again that this was something expected of him so he did it.

On the way to see Hezekiah, Xavier thanked God for the positive outcome he had in court. He thanked him for Detria footing the bill for his attorney fees, but if that woman thought that he had any real respect for her, then she was sadly mistaken. How could he when she was the cause of his mother and father's broken relationship. The woman was nothing more than a rich slut in Xavier's eyes. When she was around with Khalil, of course he acted respectful toward her, but inside, Xavier felt that Detria Graham didn't deserve his respect at all. He felt like a phony, a hypocrite whenever he was around her.

He had issues with Hezekiah, too. He had cheated on Fancy with the likes of Detria Graham. Xavier had lost respect for his father as well because here he was supposed to be a man of God, someone who professed that he loved his wife, yet he was going behind her back and the church's back and laying up with a Jezebel like Detria.

This visit was uneventful and Xavier had been there less than an hour when he told his father that he was going to leave. His mind was consumed with thoughts of the broken relationship between him and Raymone and the unhappiness he knew his mother felt over the actions of Hezekiah. Today, he just couldn't take anymore. He had to get out of that place.

"Take me...Holy Rock," Hezekiah said to his youngest son.

"Huh?"

"Holy Rock," his father said again. "Take...me." Hezekiah frowned as he spoke with force to Xavier.

"You want to go to church?" Xavier asked, hoping he didn't hear his father correctly. He did not want to be the one to take him to Holy Rock and if that's what Hezekiah wanted, then Xavier would just have to tell him that he would have to get somebody else to do that.

"Yes. Holy Rock. Want to go to Holy Rock," Hezekiah reiterated.

"I don't think I can do that. I won't do it." Xavier was just as forceful and adamant as he replied to his father's demand.

"Take me," Hezekiah yet repeated again.

This time Xavier snapped and all of his pinned up emotions spewed out like a geyser. "I'm not taking you anywhere. You think this is easy? Coming here to see you and sit with you, talk to you, when I know you're nothing but a lying, adulterous cheater? You've abused my mother; you've broken her heart, and you expect me to feel sympathy toward you? Well, I've had enough. I'm tired of pretending like everything is okay between you and me. Yeah, you listened to me when I told you some things I was going through, but you know what, Dad...I wonder what you'll have to say when I tell you that I'm gay!" Xavier shouted before he realized what he was saying. But he was fed up with so much. His family was not all of what he thought them to be. Khalil was power hungry and unrestrained just like their father. He felt that his mother was far too weak when it came to standing up against a man like Hezekiah, and Hezekiah was nothing more than a tyrant. Xavier hoped his words stung his father and from the look on Hezekiah's face, his words had done more than render a sting.

Hezekiah eyed his baby boy like he was his number one enemy. He began to grunt like a bear.

"Yeah, I thought that would get a rise out of you. To know that your son is gay." Xavier laughed. "Me and Raymone were in a relationship for two years until I made him a cripple. Now I have no one," Xavier cried. "He doesn't want anything to do with me and do you blame him?"

Hezekiah grunted and growled even louder before he screamed at his son… "Get out!"

"Nothing but a word," retorted Xavier as he turned around and left out of Hezekiah's room with the quickness.

Chapter 19

"I'm tired." Shelia Bell

Hezekiah had been in an uproar most of the morning. He demanded that he be released from the rehab facility and allowed to go home. If Fancy still had a stick up her...well if Fancy was still parading around like she was a victim when he was the one who had suffered a debilitating stroke, then he would just go to his downtown condo. He was fed up with being kept away like he was a common criminal. Being at the rehab slash nursing home reminded him of the six years that he spent behind bars. He felt just like prisoner number HM370972. He still remembered his prison number and he hated that feeling more than anything else in the world.

"Mr. McCoy, you still have a long way to go before you're able to even think of living on your own," the social worker who was called explained. "You are making some improvements, but let's not rush it. You have to be able to take care of yourself and you still require around the clock care."

Hezekiah had been taught over the past few weeks how to use an app called Verbally on an iPad to help him communicate since his speech still had not improved to any greater extent. Like text messaging, he was able to use his one good hand to choose the words he wanted to say. "I don't care, I want out."

"You must understand that if you are released from this facility that you will be leaving totally against doctor's orders."

"Don't want to spend another day here," he chose the words and letters with less difficulty than trying to actually pronounce them orally. "Do you understand me?" he said followed by several question marks and then guttural tones rising from his throat. Before using the app it had been difficult to know the exact words he tried to say, but now that he was adapting to the technology, it was far easier to decipher his words. They both took a step backward as if taking a precautionary step away from the angry man.

True, he had been at the facility going on a hundred days and he was more than mentally tired and drained. His wife and rarely anyone else came to see him. It was primarily his choice that no one visited him because he had made it clear and in no uncertain terms that he no longer wanted visitors and that he wanted to exercise his right to privacy.

After Hezekiah continued to act out, the nurse administered a mild sedative injection, which Hezekiah didn't like one bit. After several minutes, he drifted off to sleep.

"Mrs. McCoy," this is James Burlington from Primacy Parkway Nursing Home and Rehabilitation Center. I'm calling about your husband, Hezekiah McCoy. You and I have met on a couple of occasions when you came to our facility."

"Yes, I remember you, Mr. Burlington. How is my husband?" she asked. "He still refuses to see me. Have things changed?"

"I'm afraid not. And that's why I'm calling. Your husband has been very belligerent lately. Today he was determined to leave our facility. He says he wants to be on his own. He became so upset that it was necessary to administer a mild sedative. And as you know, he refused to see anyone. Several people from I believe his church have tried to visit him and call him but he's shut himself off."

"Tell me about it. You know he won't see me so I'm not surprised that he won't see anyone else. Mr. Burlington,"

"Please, call me James," the man offered.

"Well, James, as I was saying. My husband doesn't want to

see me either so I haven't been there in weeks. But like you said, he is totally incapable of doing anything on his own so coming back here or going God only knows where else, is impossible. He can't transport himself, can't get in and out of the bed to his chair on his own, has the limited use of only one arm and hand, has a catheter and he wears a grown up diaper, and he thinks he can go home! That stroke has affected him mentally."

"Uhhh," James Burlington cleared his throat, somewhat surprised at Fancy McCoy's explicit details of her husband's condition. "You are his wife, which is why I wanted to let you know that if he insists on leaving it will be totally against medical advice."

"He's not going anywhere. Thank you for letting me know what's going on, Mr. Burlington; I mean James. I'll handle things from here."

They ended the call and Fancy's phone rang again immediately after.

"Ma, have you read the contract Daddy had with the church?" asked Khalil.

"It's been a while. I mean, I haven't read it since Hezekiah became senior pastor. Why? What's going on?"

"A lot. Some good and some not so good. Xavier's here too. He's found out more information about Dad's financial obligations and funds. You might want to come to Holy Rock so we can sit down and talk."

"Khalil, I really don't feel up to it," Fancy replied grudgingly. "I'm tired mentally and emotionally. And on top of everything else I've been going through I just got a call from the nursing home. Your father is showing his behind up there, talking about he's leaving against the doctor's orders. I don't know how much more of this I can take." Fancy got up and started nervously pacing back and forth. She went downstairs to the kitchen, opened the refrigerator, and pulled out some leftover caramel cheesecake that Xavier had brought her yesterday from the Cheesecake Factory. She walked over to one of the cabinets, applying light pressure on it and it opened effortlessly and automatically. She reached inside for a fork, repeated her previous action and the cabinet drawer closed. "Can we do it some other time? Maybe later in the week, say Wednesday or Thursday?" She took a big forkful of the cheesecake and stuffed it inside her mouth as she waited on Khalil's response.

"Ma, are you going to be all right?"

"I told you…I'm sick and tired. This past year has been, well let's just say, I pray that something changes with the quickness. And as if your father acting a fool wasn't enough, I find out that he may not have to put pressure on them about leaving the nursing home because I just received a statement in the mail from them. There's an outstanding balance of seventy five hundred dollars that the insurance is not going to pay!"

"That's one of the things I wanted to talk to you about."

"You knew about it?" Fancy felt it hard to suppress her growing anger at Khalil knowing that he knew about the nursing home bill.

"I'm just learning a lot of things so don't get upset, Ma. I can hear it in your voice. Xavier's discovered a couple of things about Dad's finances and his medical insurance. I read over his contract with Holy Rock and things don't look so bright for the old guy," Khalil stated. "Look, why don't you chill out for now, Ma. I'll get with Zay and let him know the plan and I'll come over tonight. I'll even bring dinner with me and the three of us will sit down and work everything out. How 'bout it?"

Fancy exhaled, closed her eyes, and then answered her son. "You've always had a way of putting me at ease, even when you were a little boy. I love you, son."

"Love you, too, Ma. So, we're on for tonight, say around seven?"

"Seven is good. I think I'll go shopping and treat myself to a mani/pedi."

"Now that's what I'm talkin' about. See you tonight, Ma."

"See ya, Khalil." Fancy ended the call with a smile on her face. She was so thankful that she had two sons who looked out for her and who were more than capable enough of running a massive conglomerate like Holy Rock, no matter if it was a church.

She rushed upstairs, changed clothes, and then hurried back downstairs to go treat herself to some well-deserved *Fancy time.*

Detria walked into the building like she owned the place. She could tell that all eyes were on her as she strolled confidently through the double glass doors, up the hallway, and to the front counter where a white woman with long braided weave going down her back looked up at her and smirked.

"May I help you," the woman asked.

Detria eyed her up and down, rolled her eyes, and then said, "Yes, I'm here to see Hezekiah McCoy."

The girl rolled her eyes back at Detria, looked down at her computer sitting in front of her, and then back at Detria. He's on the third floor, room 336."

Detria mumbled a low "Thank you," and flippantly strolled off toward the elevator. This would be her first time seeing Hezekiah since he had his stroke almost a year ago. She was a little nervous because of that and she didn't know the reason that he had someone to call and tell her that he wanted to see her. She thought about the times they spent together in his private downtown getaway. She blushed as she stepped on the elevator. Memories flooded her mind and she smiled when she thought about their hot, steamy lovemaking. She didn't know who was better….him or his son. She surmised that Hezekiah's experience didn't have nothing on young Khalil McCoy's stamina mixed with his smooth conversation. She leaned against the elevator wall and the thoughts saturated her mind to the point she felt her body awakening. The elevator door opening brought her back to reality and two people stepped onto the elevator as she stepped off.

She looked at the signs for the room numbers and followed the arrow until she arrived in front of the closed door that said Room 336 – H. McCoy. She tapped lightly on the door with the back of her fisted hand.

When she didn't hear anyone respond, she tapped again, but a little harder, then lifted up on the handle of the door and pushed it open slightly. She stuck her head in and saw the open space that looked like a nice-sized efficiency apartment.

"Hezekiah?"

She ventured inside the space slowly and quietly. To the left was a small kitchenette, to the right an open door which she saw was a handicap accessible bathroom. Ahead of her was an open space and to the left and in the far end of the corner was a queen-sized bed. Across from the queen sized bed and on the right was a small sofa, a simple looking cloth covered chair and a table with a lamp on it. No sign of Hezekiah.

She turned around to leave. When she walked outside of the room and back out into the hall, she saw another nurses' station on the far end of the corridor on the right of her. She headed in that direction but just as she was about to go seek more information about Hezekiah's whereabouts, he drove up in his electric wheelchair.

"Are you here to see Mr. McCoy?" the woman walking beside him asked Detria.

"Yes." She looked at Hezekiah. "Hello, Pastor McCoy," she said, uncertain as to how familiar she should act considering she had no idea who the woman was that was with him.

Hezekiah's eyes appeared to bulge. He looked pleasantly surprised to see her. Not only did she look good, she smelled good. He imagined briefly that she was here to satisfy his sexual desire. She, after all, was a tigress in the bedroom and did things Fancy never dreamed of doing.

"Hi, D….D..Detreee," he managed to say.

"We were just returning from therapy," the woman explained

with a smile plastered across her high yellow acned face.

"Are you good, Hezekiah? Can you manage from here?"

"Yea...m...good," he said and slowly steered his wheelchair past Detria and up to the front of his door.

Detria stepped in front of the door as Hezekiah came to a stop. She leaned in and used her good arm to pull the latch up on the door and pushed it slightly open.

Hezekiah pushed the button on his wheelchair and it moved forward, pushing the door all the way open. He went inside and then turned the wheelchair around to face Detria.

"Come in," he said and then turned back around and went all the way into his studio space.

"Uhh, this is nice," Detria told him.

"Sit down," he said.

Dee went over to the couch that she'd seen when she entered his room earlier. She didn't bother to tell him that she had been inside. Instead she sat down and watched him try to remove something from one of the side pouches that hung from his wheelchair.

"Need some help?" she asked him as he seemed to struggle to get whatever it was out of the pouch. She eased up off the couch but stopped when she heard him speak.

"No," he practically yelled.

She immediately sat back down and hid her frustration as she watched him struggle to retrieve what she finally saw was a tablet. Once he was able to pull it from the pouch, he drove the wheelchair over toward his bed and laid the tablet on top of the bed. He then began to touch different words on the tablet which gave him a strange voice, and enabled him to talk to her with less of a struggle.

At first it was weird hearing the voice talk for him because the voice coming from the tablet sounded so robotic. She soon got used to it and at the end of their hour or so long visit, Detria understood the true reason Hezekiah wanted to see her.

"So, you want me to get in touch with George? The man has caused all of sorts of drama from what I've heard and yet you want to see him?"

Hezekiah shook his head up and down. "Get him."

Chapter 20

"Your bills be like…you ain't going out this weekend." Unknown

"This house is in Dad's name. Holy Rock added an additional amount to his annual cash salary to cover his mortgage payments, and a housing allowance is designated to cover his mortgage insurance, utilities, real estate taxes and maintenance, but records show that Holy Rock has been paying the utilities, insurance and maintenance in past years," explained Xavier like he was a professional businessman and CPA. Fancy felt proud once again listening and watching her son.

"Yes, but I'm not the one who handles our finances. Hezekiah has always handled the money aspect of things, and it's worked out so far so good. I mean I've never really ever wanted for anything that he hasn't provided."

"Yeah, but you just got that medical bill, and looking into the disability insurance provided by Holy Rock, for some reason it's lapsed. I'm still looking into that. But according to the disability papers, Dad should be receiving a percentage of his salary since he is disabled."

"I think that's it."

"What do you mean, Ma?" Khalil said as they sat around the dining room table eating Chinese food, drinking wine and chatting it up.

"Your father stopped accepting a salary and opted instead to receive love offerings. He said he fared much better than being paid a set salary. And as far as I know, I think he was right."

"Yeah, but the thing is, that means he probably was responsible for paying his own insurance and all the expenses of the house, mortgage, cars, etc." said Xavier.

"Oh, my God. Surely Hezekiah maintained the bills. He's always been so good with managing money—at least I've always thought so I guess because I've rarely ever seen a bill even before he took over as senior pastor."

"The one good thing I discovered is that he had written in his pastoral contract that if anything happened to him that you or one of us would take over as Senior Pastor of Holy Rock."

"Now that part I clearly remember because Hezekiah told me that on several occasions that if anything should ever happen to him that I had the power to step up as senior pastor or appoint one of you or anyone else of my choosing to replace him. Thank God, he's still alive even though he is physically incapacitated."

Khalil spoke up. "Mane, I don't know how daddy convinced the senior elders and trustees to agree to that, but hey, it is what it is and it looks ironclad too."

"So what about you and Dad's personal accounts? You straight, Ma?"

"I haven't had to max out my credit cards, if that's what you mean." Fancy giggled slightly, feeling the effects of her third glass of wine. "And as far as our bank accounts, I haven't checked to see what we have, but then again, it's not like I have many expenses either. My nails, my hair, clothes, groceries, going out to eat, stuff like that but I mostly use my credit card for that. When I do want to spend cash, I've never not been able to get it when I need it. Like I said, Hezekiah has always been a great provider even when he did wrong." She took a forkful of her Vegetable Chinese rice and then followed it up by taking a bite of a vegetable spring roll and washing the food down with another swallow of expensive white wine.

"I'll look into it some more but in the meantime, I need you to check you and Dad's bank accounts," Xavier told her. "Can you go by the bank tomorrow? I can go with you, if you'd like. Or you can call; whichever is easier."

"No, we can go to the bank in person. If I need to pay that bill, then I might as well go pay it tomorrow while I'm out. But what about Medicare? Can he get that since he's disabled?"

"We'll find out more about that when we go pay his bill. I think he might be able to get it though, now that you've mentioned it, and maybe even some type of Medicaid assistance," Xavier said, sounding much older than he was.

"I think some of that depends on your income, but no worries, Ma. We got you." Khalil added to help reassure her.

True to her word, Detria had made contact with George and told him about Hezekiah's need to see him. She and George signed Hezekiah out for a half-day visit.

He may not have been able to do much of anything, but it still felt amazing to be out of that nursing home and rehab facility and sitting in his downtown condo.

Sure, George had been a snake and a crook from what Fancy and his sons told him after he had the stroke, but then again, Hezekiah knew that at the end of the day, if the price was right, he could rely on George to do what he needed done. Today he needed to get away from Primacy Parkway Nursing Home and it was George that made it happen—well, George and Detria that is.

As far as he knew, Detria wasn't sleeping with Khalil anymore, and even if she was, at this point Hezekiah could care less. He needed her for what he needed her for and that was a little of her money and whatever honey he could get from her. As things were now, honey to him could mean only a kiss or letting him feel up on her since his manhood had suffered when he had the stroke. He tried not to think about his incapacities because if he did he would find himself in a deep well of depression like he had experienced quite a bit lately.

George had brought him a little something something to help him get in a better mood. They sat in the condo and Hezekiah and

Detria took a couple of hits from a blunt. Before long, Hezekiah was laughing and feeling better than he had in a long time.

He used his tablet to tell Detria that he needed her to pay George until he could get back on his feet. Detria was reluctant to do it at first, but stroke or no stroke, Detria knew better than to make trouble with Hezekiah, especially since George was back in his corner. Bad things could easily happen and she didn't want to be caught up in any unnecessary drama, nor did she want to find herself laid out in an alley or up in a hospital. George could be scandalous like that. She knew right off the bat that George had planted those drugs in Hezekiah's car. Initially, he had planned for Khalil to be driving the car with the tail light out, get pulled over, and then he was going to make sure that his juvenile record was revealed. He already had someone working with him on the inside who he knew could help him. George was not one to sit back and let somebody screw him over like dem McCoy boys were trying to do.

He had a good attorney to fight his case and he had also told Hezekiah about what his sons were trying to do. At least he told him his version while Detria took another draw from the coke-laced blunt and kept her mouth shut. She leaned in occasionally and kissed Hezekiah full on his lips to appease him, while George assured Hezekiah that as long as he was paid, that he would take care of things on the outside for him.

"I'll keep an eye on your boys for ya. I'm telling you, you won't be too pleased with the stuff they're trying to pull. And I hate to say it, but Fancy is in on screwing you too, and not in a good way. They don't want you to get better, man. Why do you think Fancy was in such a hurry to get you out of the house and put away at that nursing place? She's going to claim that you are mentally incapable and unable to handle your own affairs."

"She's already made that clear," Detria said as she laughed for no reason, and passed the laced blunt to Hezekiah.

George had a bottle of his favorite whiskey that he was indulging in, but he held back, not wanting to get too inebriated to the point he would be unable to drive Hezekiah back to the facility.

"What do you mean?" George asked, looking at Detria.

Detria directed her reply to Hezekiah as she eased closer to him. "Khalil told me that Fancy said that you were losing it and soon you would no longer be mentally able to handle your affairs. Honestly, I can't believe George was able to sign you out of the nursing home today. From what I understand, your little wifey has control over everything."

"Money talks," said George. "You should know that better than anyone, sweetheart," he said.

"So you paid somebody at the nursing home to turn a blind eye?"

"Whatever it takes," George nodded and smirked.

Hezekiah laughed himself this time. "She doesn't have the power she thinks she does." It felt good to laugh, to relax, and to be around people who understood his plight. Sure, George was a snake but the woman who he believed to be his biological mother all of these years used to tell him and her oldest son it's better to have an enemy who you know hates you instead of a friend who secretly stabs you in the back and puts you down. George was the enemy and his 'friends stabbing him in the back' were his wife and sons. What a terrible thing.

Hezekiah was going to make them pay and he would use Detria and George to bring them the kind of justice that they deserved for turning their backs on him. He didn't plan to be down forever. He was already improving and his speech was getting better, too. The day that Fancy and his sons would see him again, he planned to be back to his old self.

"So what's going on with Xavier's case?" George asked Detria while they sat at the table across from Hezekiah in his wheelchair.

"He's going to get him off, but this should be a sign to Xavier and Khalil just how easy it can be to get caught up."

"Yeah, that's what this was all about."

Hezekiah smiled wickedly. "Lessons hard."

"Yeah, you got that right, partner," George agreed and grinned. "It's good to know people in high places."

"Or people who have an extra set of keys to your ride," said Detria, chuckling and looking at George and then over at Hezekiah.

George had keys not only to the condo but he had a set of keys to Hezekiah's and Fancy's cars, too. It hadn't been much that he didn't have privy to as Hezekiah's former head of security. Knowing the power he had, he could have easily made things far worse for Xavier by planting a larger quantity of drugs in the car than what he did, but he basically wanted to test the waters first and hopefully let them young boys know that they were messing with the wrong guy. And to have Hezekiah on his side, and of course Hezekiah's little side-piece Detria, then he could only rise to the top like cream. Detria was paying for George's attorney too and just as Xavier was assured of getting off, George had just as much assurance that he wouldn't do a day behind bars himself. He expected to get probation if anything, with a suspended sentence and he could easily deal with that. He was glad he still had a few favors that he could call in from some of his law enforcement friends. It paid to not burn all your bridges. He took another drink of the brown liquor.

"One thing I'm glad about is that the house is in your name so if your first lady isn't careful, she could easily find herself on the streets. All you have to do is say the word, and it's good as done. And no one would suspect you had a thing to do with it."

Feeling the full effects of the laced blunt, Detria and Hezekiah laughed almost uncontrollably. "You're smarter than the average bear," she teased George.

"Go on and finish that blunt," he said to Hezekiah. "Y'all are high enough and I need to get you back. I don't want them sending out the dogs for ya," he said and laughed.

Hezekiah and Detria continued to laugh and make funny

remarks. They took a couple more hits of the blunt and relaxed until it was time to call it a day and head back.

Chapter 21

"I'm making changes in my life right now. If you don't hear from me, you're one of them." Iliketoquote.com

Xavier accompanied his mother to the bank. Less than half an hour later, they walked out of the bank with frozen looks plastered across their faces. Her name was not listed on anything belonging to Hezekiah McCoy. Sure, she had a debit card and a credit card, but the debit card was in Hezekiah's name, something she never thought two cents about. As long as she knew his pin number and could use the card whenever she pleased, there was no concern on her part. As far as the credit card, it was in her name. Hezekiah had made her an authorized user. That was the only thing she had access to. She walked out of the bank feeling betrayed. The bank officer would not divulge if someone else's name was on Hezekiah's account, but she did tell Xavier that he was not on any of the accounts either.

Any of his accounts? Just how many accounts does he have? Xavier wondered. Hezekiah was up to no good, and Xavier was going to do everything he could to find out what was going on. He decided to play things safe over the next few weeks until what he hoped would be his final court date. His attorney had assured him that it would be all over and done with when they returned to court soon. After that, he would be able to fully concentrate on his new role at Holy Rock and helping his mother get to the bottom of whatever it was that Hezekiah had done.

Xavier felt that he owed Detria Graham a lot, and though he didn't particularly like her, he still owed her for making sure he had the best attorney money could buy.

He dropped his mother off at home and then headed for Holy Rock to divulge the information of the day to his brother. He couldn't wait to see Khalil's reaction when he heard about his father's latest antics. This man was out of control. He and Khalil had to find a way to restore what rightfully belonged to their mother and to them as Hezekiah's sons.

"Eliana, how are you adjusting to working at Holy Rock?" Khalil asked his new administrative assistant.

"I like it and I'm learning quite a bit. And before she moved to the other area, Sista Mavis shared more than I expected her to. You know she wasn't too happy about me taking over her position."

"Yeah, but the good thing is she still has a job here; it's just that she's no longer working directly for me," he chuckled.

Eliana smiled. She found Khalil both handsome and charming and she wanted him. She loved his swagger, his casual style of dress of jeans and a button down shirt and loafers. He rarely wore suits like some pastors, but appealed to the younger crowd with his simplistic messages combined with his stylish up-to-date fashion sense. He kept his hair cut low and it didn't take much to see his natural waves. His chiseled jawline matched his strong voice. Oh and that smile. To Eliana, Khalil's smile was enough to set the soul of any woman on fire, herself included. She could see herself as the First Lady and if she played her cards just right, and not appear too eager, then she was sure she could eventually pull him.

"My brother is on his way. When he gets here, we're going to need some time alone. Will you move back any appointments I have scheduled?"

"Yes, you have a counseling session with Sista Wright and her daughter. I'll see if I can move it back until later this afternoon, unless you want me to cancel it altogether and make it for later this week."

"No, later this afternoon should be fine."

"I know she must be devastated to discover that her fourteen-year-old daughter is pregnant, and the poor girl doesn't even know who the father is." Eliana shook her head in sympathy for the girl's plight and for the teen's mother, too. This would be their third session with Khalil. One thing Eliana knew even when she heard such highly sensitive things was to keep her lips sealed. Unlike Sista Mavis, who told her about the little girl and her mother before she moved to work for the associate ministers' staff, Eliana was not one to gossip. Whatever she heard or saw going on at Holy Rock would stay inside the confines of Holy Rock if she had anything to do with it.

"Yeah, it's hard I'm sure to know that you've tried your best to do everything right and still your child goes astray. I'm a young pastor, but I can tell you that it was God that changed me. I was on a road of total destruction. If I can say something to this young lady to help her and to help give her mother something positive to hold on to, then that's what I'm going to do."

"I admire you, Pastor Khalil. And if you need me to talk to the girl, just let me know. I know it's not my place as your administrative assistant to sit in on counseling sessions or offer any advice, but being a young woman myself and growing up in a troubled home, well let's just say, I think I could share some things with the young girl."

Khalil was quite impressed. Not only was Eliana a beautiful, attractive, sexy woman, but she had compassion and feelings to go along with it, and that proved to be quite the combination for Khalil that might be beneficial for him later...and for her.

"Thank you, Eliana. That's good to know. Maybe we can arrange for you to talk to the youth sometimes. I think I made a positive impact when I shared my testimony with them. I was the youth director before I became senior pastor. I don't think it's a good idea for you to talk to this young lady, well not until I can sit down with her and her mother at least. But I'll definitely check with my brother and let him know to reach out to you about speaking to the youth."

"I would love that. And maybe my twin brother, Ian, can participate, too," she said and flashed a tempting smile his way as he turned to walk back to his office.

"Twin? You have a twin?" he said, stopping and turning around to face her again. He gave her his own hypnotic smile and if he could have seen inside her heart, he would have felt her swooning.

"Yep. And he's a great speaker and he has a remarkable testimony. I think Ian and I both have something to say that can help young people. My situation is a little different from my brother's but what we've gone through is a direct result of what happened or should I say didn't happen in our household."

Khalil could see the seriousness on her face as she spoke. Whatever she'd gone through certainly had a lasting impact on her, or so it seemed from the tone of her voice and the sadness that shown in her coffee brown eyes.

"Ian and I didn't exactly grow up in the best of environments. I mean, don't get me wrong, we were raised up in the church, we had successful parents, grew up as middle class kids, didn't have to want for much of anything…except love and acceptance, something my brother still wrestles with today. Being gay may be easier for some but in the black community it can still be quite a stigma placed on a person."

Khalil's heart dropped a notch. *Dang, she likes women? Man, what a waste.*

Eliana must have noticed the look of disappointment in his eyes because she immediately clarified her statement. "I love my brother; I don't care if he's gay or straight. But it just so happens that he's gay and he still gets bashed for it quite a lot. He's a schoolteacher and I think he's looked at strangely in his profession, you know, like he's a pervert or something. I feel like if he was famous then he'd be looked at totally different cause it seems like careers take off in Hollywood when you announce that you're gay. You know what I mean?"

"Yeah, unfortunately I agree with ya." Khalil thought about Xavier at that point. He loved his little brother but deep inside he hated the fact that dude was a homosexual. It tore at his insides every time he thought about it. Remembering those pictures of Xavier and Raymone made him even more disgusted, but he kept his feelings to himself. "God is the ultimate judge of us all. Who are we to point a finger of blame and ridicule at someone else?"

"Right. Anyway, I didn't mean to ramble, Pastor Khalil. But I do want you to know that I've got your back if you need me," she said as she smiled and then answered the ringing phone. She threw up her hand and concentrated on assisting the caller. "Holy Rock, this is Eliana. How may I help you?"

Khalil walked away feeling even more impressed by Eliana's openness. "Whew," he said as he stepped into his office and closed the door behind him. "Temptation, temptation, temptation," he whispered while he thought about her. "Got to have a taste of that."

Chapter 22

"As sure as God made black and white; what's done in the dark will be brought to the light." Johnny Cash

"Sista Mavis, where is Eliana?" Khalil asked as he approached Eliana's work area.

"She went downstairs to take some paperwork to some of the other ministers. She asked me to cover for her until she returned."

"Okay. Well, I'm going to run an errand. I shouldn't be gone too long. If Omar comes by, just tell him I'll get back with him," he said as he swiftly walked past her desk.

"Yes, Pastor Khalil," Mavis said, wondering what in the world was going on. *That young boy is on the move more than the wind changes direction.*

Khalil exited the church, got inside his car, and before turning the ignition, he reached into his pants pocket and pulled out the set of keys that had started this whole transition. His mother did not want him to have the keys, afraid that he would do something stupid. But what could he do that was worse than what his father, George, and Detria had done? Nothing, if you asked him.

Ever since his father's stroke almost a year ago Khalil had made good use of the keys his mother found that went to his father's secret condo, post office box, and safe deposit box.

Khalil checked the post office box regularly. On most

occasions Hezekiah received junk mail, but the main thing he received were bank statements from Bank of America. That's how Khalil found out the details of Hezekiah's Bank of America accounts that his mother was not listed anywhere on. His mother could not get access to any of that money. The accounts didn't have a lot of money in them, just a few thousand in each one. If his father was embezzling money from Holy Rock, then what was he doing with the money and where was he keeping his stash? Khalil was still determined to find that bit of information.

Khalil or Fancy could not check Hezekiah's safety deposit box either because that, too was a matter of privacy, so that key was useless. It appeared that Hezekiah knew exactly what he was doing before he succumbed to the stroke. He was definitely a low life and Khalil didn't like his father, not at all.

It hurt him to see his mother in a constant state of anguish over the way Hezekiah had hidden so much from her.

Today, Khalil decided it was time that he made another pop up visit to 3201 River Circle. He had only visited the condo a few times over the months since his father's stroke, but his spirit told him that he needed to stop what he was doing and go.

Khalil had thought long and hard about what he would do with this bit of information about the property being in Holy Rock's name. He convinced his mother to let him handle the situation and for her to stay as far removed from any of Hezekiah's shady sounding dealings. Each time he went to the condo, everything remained in place. It appeared that someone, however, was keeping the place clean and the refrigerator even had cold bottled water and a few sodas. The cabinets had some small nonperishable snacks which seemed like they were kept fresh, so Khalil knew someone was coming by there periodically. Yet, each time he popped up the only evidence that someone had entered the place was the fresh snacks and water. Perhaps, Hezekiah had someone on Holy Rock's staff or a private cleaning company that maintained the condo. Again, like everything else, he hadn't found out much of anything. His father was proving more and more that he lived a double life.

However, today, it dawned on Khalil, while he was working on his message for Sunday, that because the condo was in the church's name he may be able to use this bit of information to his advantage. He was going to change the locks and see what happened.

He arrived at the condo, unlocked the door, and was totally taken aback at the strong aroma that hit his nostrils when he walked inside. He'd lived the drug life long enough to know that smell – cocaine. He looked around cautiously, unsure if there was anyone inside.

"Hello," he called. No answer. "Hello," he called again as he moved further into the living room. He looked around but the place was empty. However, it had that stale smell to it and Khalil saw drug residue and a 750 ml bottle of Hennessy was sitting on the square, dark wood living room table. Next to the Hennessy was a glass that still held some of the liquor in it. The bottle was still pretty full so whoever had drunk some of it, hadn't indulged too much. There was also a clear glass bowl sitting on the table with residue in it. For the scent of drugs to still be in the atmosphere so strongly, Khalil surmised that whoever had been there had recently left. Maybe they would be returning to clean up since Khalil had never seen the condo in such disarray.

He looked around and saw that the bed was unmade in the one bedroom place. The bathroom shower looked like it had been recently used and a couple of bathroom towels were haphazardly draped over the towel rack.

Khalil pulled out drawers and opened cabinets throughout the twelve hundred square feet condo, not looking for anything in particular, but curious as to who was going in and out of his father's secret spot. Could it be George? Was he still walking around free after Khalil and Fancy had made the FEDS aware of what the pervert was doing? He hadn't seen George's wife at church lately. He figured that they had moved on and if she was still going to church, she had probably joined somewhere else to save herself the embarrassment of what was rumored to have happened with him.

He looked at the cabinets underneath the sink in the kitchen and then went back to the bedroom and searched for nothing in particular underneath the king bed. As he prepared to give up his useless search his eyes shifted and his mind went into overdrive as he looked at what at first sight looked like a regular HVAC vent in the bedroom. He looked closer, stooped down and studied the vent. He had read somewhere recently about vent safes. *Could this be one of those? Naw*, he thought. He got up and began to search around the room again, this time more thoroughly and more carefully. Even if it was one of those vent safes, he didn't see anything that looked like a remote or RFID or a Fob that would open a safe. He went back over to the vent and studied it. He tried to see how to open it, and after he couldn't, he became convinced more than ever that it was no ordinary vent. He searched and rummaged through Hezekiah's things for the next hour until he went into the walk-in bedroom closet for the fourth time. Without giving it thought, his eyes shifted to the breaker box inside the closet. He opened it for no good reason and bingo; hanging on a small latch inside the breaker box was a rectangular shaped RFID looking card. Khalil removed the card and walked back into the bedroom. He ran the card across the front of the so-called vent and just like that, the vent popped open.

"Yes! You sly dog!" he said aloud and pulled two bags out of the vent safe. He opened the smaller bag first. It contained a Rolex timepiece and a few other pieces of expensive jewelry. The face of the watch said it was a Rolex Oyster Perpetual Datejust. It was yellow gold with a diamond bezel and dial. Khalil already knew it had to cost a pretty penny, and it was a men's watch, no doubt belonging to his father. There was a Cartier white gold women's bracelet in the bag along with a men's white gold diamond link bracelet. He closed the bag back up and then opened the second bag and almost passed out when he saw the boatload of cash.

There were at least twenty stacks of money, if not more, bound by rubber bands and in various denominations from 20's to one hundred dollar bills. He had no idea how much money there was but he knew it was no small amount. It had to be in the tens of thousands because there were at least ten or eleven one-hundred dollar stacks and another eight to ten twenty-dollar stacks of money. Khalil suddenly felt himself getting a little nervous and paranoid; he looked around like he was expecting someone to look over his shoulder at any minute. He quickly got up, gathered the money, closed the vent safe back up, ran into the kitchen, and searched for a bag, anything to put his find inside. He found a box of small, kitchen-sized garbage bags. He hurriedly placed the bag of jewelry and the bag of money inside the trash bag, and got out of the condo as fast as he could, making sure he locked the door behind him. He looked around as he left to see if there was anyone suspicious lurking around, but the place was quiet and void of people like it usually was whenever he came.

He ran to his car which he had parked inside the parking garage. He got inside, started the car, and sped off as quickly as he could, stopping only long enough to pay his parking fee at the automated gate.

On the drive back to Holy Rock, he thought about himself and his father. The two of them were so much alike—smart, conniving, charming, and self-assured mixed with a little cockiness and conceit. He smiled at the thought but it didn't dispel his anger or suspicion. Something was going on at that condo and he added it to his list of things to uncover about his father. But as for now, the joke would definitely be on Hezekiah McCoy when he discovered that his stash of money and his jewelry keepsakes were gone.

"Thank you, God, for vengeance," he said as he made a turn onto the I-240 highway but instead of going in the direction of Holy Rock, without much thought, he took the opposite direction and headed to Primacy Parkway Rehabilitation and Nursing Facility. He was going to try to see his father again. Maybe, just maybe, if he could convince the receptionist to contact the nursing staff on his father's floor and tell them to tell his father that he really needed to see him; perhaps, Hezekiah would have a change of heart and agree to talk to him.

As he drove, he saw a yellow van pass by. He quickly memorized the number and immediately called it. It was a cleaning service truck that he'd seen countless times up and down the highways and streets of Memphis. He spoke to a pleasant young woman on the phone and told her his situation. By the end of the conversation, he'd arranged to meet a cleaning staff at the condo in a couple of hours. By the time they finished, it would have no sign of anyone having been there doing drugs. After that phone call, he made another call to the number stored in his phone.

"Holy Rock Ministries, Pastor McCoy's office. Eliana speaking. How may I help you?" she politely said into the phone.

"Eliana?"

"Oh, hello, Pastor Khalil."

"Hi, will you page Omar for me?"

"He happens to be right here. Hold on," she said.

Omar came to the phone

"Yes, Pastor K. How can I help you?"

"I need a personal favor and I need you to keep it under wraps."

"You got it," Omar replied.

Khalil explained that he needed him to meet him at 3201 River Circle. "I need you to check for any sign of surveillance equipment when you get there, and I need you to change the locks."

"Okay, got it," Omar said without asking any questions.

"I'll meet you there in a couple of hours."

"See you then," Omar said and they mutually ended the phone call.

Khalil arrived at the nursing and rehab facility. He found a parking space middle ways the parking area of the facility, and got out of his car. He was startled when just as he closed the car door and headed toward the entrance, he saw his father about to enter the building, being pushed in a manual wheelchair by none other than George. What shocked him even more was Detria walking next to George and his father.

He got out of his car and ran toward them. "Heyyyy, hold up," Khalil shouted.

George turned and looked back over his shoulder, and so did Detria.

"Get away from here. Your father doesn't want to see you," George ordered as he barely slowed his roll and continued pushing Hezekiah to the front entrance.

"So this is how it is, huh?" Khalil said as he caught up to them and eyed Detria with a nasty, evil look.

She looked away, cowering slightly, knowing she was caught in the middle of something she never wanted to be part of.

"What?" Hezekiah said. "You want?" he asked as he slightly held up a few fingers toward George, and George immediately stopped pushing him.

"You think these two got your back? You're a bigger fool than I thought. Here I am thinking you were the man, that you were the best at cunning people into believing whatever it is you want them to believe, but it's funny because you're the one being conned by these two. I just came back from the condo. I saw some interesting things when I was there."

Hezekiah looked uneasy. He had totally forgotten about the set of keys Fancy had found. He should have had the locks changed, switched his P. O. Box, and everything else those keys went to, but the stroke had stopped a lot of things. He wondered what Khalil did when he saw the place in disarray. George and Detria were going to go back to clean it up after they dropped him off. He could count the times on one hand when they left it the way they had, and of all times Khalil had shown up. *Dang.*

"You had no business there," George butted in.

"And you have no business saying anything to me," Khalil said, his chest puffed out. "And I have every right to be there. Technically it belongs to Holy Rock."

George cackled. "You're more stupid than you look."

"Be careful, I'm not one of your little boys. I can handle my own. Dad, I'm ordering you and your band of idiots here to stay off the property of Holy Rock. That condo is for the private, personal enjoyment and use of Holy Rock's Senior Pastor. That is what the lease and paperwork states. And unless you want the police called, I suggest you do what I say."

George released the handles of the wheelchair, folded his lips, balled his fist, and prepared to strike Khalil but Detria jumped in between them.

"No, George!" Detria bellowed immediately.

Khalil laughed this time, shook his head, turned around and walked off. "What a joke." As he walked away, he stopped and turned around. "Don't you ever in life let me see you again. You've served your purpose. It was a nice ride," he said to Detria. "In more ways than one." He laughed, turned back around and strolled confidently to his car.

The three of them remained outside the entrance. George slowly turned Hezekiah's wheelchair so he could see Khalil. They watched as he got in his car and drove off the parking lot.

"What…can…I…do?" Hezekiah forced the words out in bits and pieces.

"He's probably already had the locks changed," George said. "You shouldn't have to worry about anything in there, except for what we left on the table. You had a few clothes and a couple of pieces of jewelry, but you might as well accept that as a loss."

Hezekiah quickly became sick both physically and emotionally. George nor Detria, no one but him, realized that he had a whole lot more to lose than a watch and some clothes. He had over a hundred thousand reasons that his whole world had quickly taken a turn for the worse. This was worse than having a stroke. He felt his head become light and his stomach churned. "Inside," he said. "Take me…to room."

On his drive to Holy Rock, Khalil felt like he had been exonerated from a crime he never committed. He laughed heartily as he remembered the looks on the faces of his sorry daddy and his daddy's two goons. He could only imagine what Hezekiah was thinking. He was probably wondering if Khalil had actually found where he kept the money he embezzled. More than likely he probably thought that Khalil would never find it; but Khalil was his father's son and like Hezekiah, he was right to feel that the condo was more than a place where his father and George bedded their freaky women and George's young boys. And if there was any type of surveillance equipment or hidden cameras, which Khalil also believed there was, then Omar would be the one to find it. There had to be something there because how else did George have videos and tapes of Hezekiah's sordid rendezvous with that slut, Dee?

Once he arrived back at Holy Rock he parked in his own private space, and exhaled deeply. He laid his hand on his steering wheel, and thought about what had just happened. He smiled wickedly, as if he had won a playoff.

The tap on his window startled him. He looked up and saw Eliana.

"Eliana? What's up?" he smiled.

"I should be asking you that question. I saw you roll up in here like you were running from the boys in blue," she said, laughing and hugging herself from the mounting cold weather.

"Naw, I was trying to hurry up and get back here. I need to finish my message for Sunday and I have those counseling sessions later on. What are you doing?"

"I was about to go grab some lunch for me and Sista Mavis. Do you need me to bring you something back?"

"No. I'm straight. You go on and get out of this cold."

"Okay," she said and jogged off to her car with Khalil watching her every move with enjoyment.

Khalil remained inside the car. *Should I leave this in the car or take it into the church? Or do I need to take it to my apartment? Should I tell Ma?* Question after question raced through his mind. He had to find somewhere safe to put the money. He decided he wasn't going to tell anyone. He started up his car again and backed out of his parking spot. He drove off the lot and didn't stop this time until he made it to his apartment.

Once inside his apartment, he rushed to his master bathroom, and removed all of his toiletries from the bottom shelf. He ran back outside to his private storage area and gathered a couple of electrical tools.

Once back inside the bathroom, he cut out the bottom of the cabinet, lifted the piece of wood up carefully, and placed both bags in the bottom of the cabinet floor. Keeping out a stack of twenties and a stack of the hundred dollar bills, he stuffed the money into his pockets. That would be for his personal use. He carefully placed the wood piece that he originally sawed off back in its place. He used a couple of screws to screw it in place, and then put all of the toiletries back on top before he locked up his apartment and returned to Holy Rock.

Chapter 23

"Rejection teaches you how to reject." J. Winterson

Hezekiah laid back on the sofa in his room, still high and feeling the effects of smoking marijuana mixed with coke. It had felt good to get out of that nursing home slash prison. He was glad at this point that he had removed the list of people who had permission to come see him, Fancy included.

Hezekiah laughed at the thought of the look that would be on Fancy's face, and his sons faces too, when they realized that he was not one to be played, not by a long shot. Detria had agreed to connect him with a lawyer who could make sure his finances and bank accounts were ironclad against anyone who might try to claim any measure of his wealth.

He had money set aside in two separate money market accounts assuring him that money was the least of his worries. If Fancy and his sons had plans to undermine him and get him declared crazy, incompetent, or whatever, Hezekiah was already steps ahead of them. With Detria and George, crooked as they were, working with him, it would be hard if not impossible for him to lose.

"What you ….here?" Hezekiah looked to his right when he heard his door open and saw Fancy walk in.

"Who do you think you are, Hezekiah McCoy to betray me?" She said out of control as she walked all the way into his room, hands on hips, mouth poked out, and red in the face.

She was heated. Hezekiah knew that look and that sound in

her voice, but at this point, he didn't care how heated she was, he was not going to deal with her foolery.

"Go," he demanded.

"I'm not going anywhere. Why am I not on any of your bank accounts? Answer me, Hezekiah! We've been together twenty-five years and you do this to me? I have never had a reason to doubt you, but this past year and a half has been torture. I found out you were cheating on me with that slut, Detria Graham. Then you had this stroke and I realized that you are a mean and selfish person who cares nothing about me, or your sons, just yourself. You tried to run me down on more than one occasion with that... that—contraption." She pointed at his electric wheelchair parked next to the sofa.

Tears flowed continually down her face as her voice escalated. "But that's not all. How could you, Hezekiah?

"How...could...what?" he asked, looking cool as a fan.

She shoved the pieces of stapled paper into his one good hand."

While Hezekiah stared at the words on the paper, Fancy kept talking.

"Yea, I just got this in the mail. What do you have to say?" she screamed. "Someone sent it to me in the mail! A Will? I can't believe you would even be thinking of a Will at your age. And you have a Will that I knew nothing about! You left me nothing; you left your sons nothing? So who is she? Is she the one who sent it to me, Hezekiah?" Fancy continued screaming.

Hezekiah had no idea who would have sent Fancy a copy of a Will. He had made one out in jest one night months before he suffered his stroke. It was not meant to be taken seriously, at least not on his end. If anything, it was meant to temporarily appease the woman he was seeing on the side, not Detria. Detria had plenty of money of her own.

He never had any intentions of Fancy finding out about something he did so thoughtlessly at the time—and definitely not like this. As far as Fancy was concerned, he had a money market account that she was the beneficiary of so she wouldn't exactly be left broke if something happened to him.

Finances were something Hezekiah and Fancy didn't talk much about; he handled everything and made sure she got whatever her little heart desired.

Fancy had plenty of book sense, but very little common sense, which was why he easily convinced her after they got out of prison to let him handle the money affairs. They had been in trouble once, served time for embezzlement, so he used that as his reason for keeping the finances in his sole control. Just in case anything else jumped off, she would not be part of it; that's the lie he fed her. When it came to him, he knew how vulnerable and weak she was for him and Hezekiah used that weakness as his advantage. She trusted him to no end and he tried to make sure she always would trust him. What he did outside of his marriage, he tried to keep it that way. He treated Fancy well, doing whatever it took to make her feel safe and secure.

As for the Will, the woman he was messing around with had told him that she needed something in place to make her feel secure because anything could happen to him. She was good on the computer so one night after they had partied she made the Will up for him, but he never had it notarized, witnessed, nothing, so in his mind, it was merely a piece of paper. He'd long forgotten about it. As he thought back on it, he was high at the time, too.

The woman also had a kid and he was the father, no doubt—DNA had clearly proved that. After he found out she was pregnant, he told himself that he had to be more careful, especially when he was high. Getting high made him lose all sense of reasoning.

The only way he managed to keep the woman quiet about the kid was by taking care of her, paying the rent on her spot, and keeping her purse lined with money. The kid was a year old when he had the stroke, and since the stroke he hadn't seen the woman or his kid. George was still good for stuff like that. He checked on the woman and kid at least twice a month for Hezekiah, just as long as Hezekiah continued paying him.

George had raised a stink after Hezekiah initially had the stroke. He had threatened Fancy and his sons if they didn't keep paying him. They had no idea that George never missed a payment from Hezekiah. George was just playing his hand, trying to see if he could get more money from them. It didn't work, thanks to his boys. Dem McCoy boys were smart in their own right. The only thing is they were a little too smart because not only did they turn George in for being a pedophile but they had threatened their own father by telling Hezekiah that they were going to tell the church and the police that he was embezzling money.

So far, Hezekiah had heard nothing more about them going to the police on him. As for the woman and George, Hezekiah had a bank account set up for the woman and another one for George. The one for the woman was set up to transfer money into her account once a month. Now that money wasn't coming in like it did when he was the senior pastor of Holy Rock, he didn't know how much longer he could keep her quiet. As for George, he hoped that George would be going away real soon for a long spell to the federal penitentiary; before the money ran out that he was paying him. His trial was supposed to be coming up in the next month or two. George was definitely going to do some time; that much Hezekiah could bank on. Maybe a couple of years, but needless to say, a couple of years would give Hezekiah time to fully make a comeback from his stroke and get Holy Rock back from Khalil.

The stroke had opened a whole can of worms that he wasn't prepared to handle. Nevertheless, all of what Fancy said was basically true; he had made the Will and he had left most of his money and personal assets to the persons listed in it. He didn't expect to die anytime soon, he was only forty-two years old. He felt he had a nice long long life ahead of him. Sure, the stroke had set him back, but he believed that he would be back to himself sooner than anyone could imagine, but even if he was to die, then so be it because he wouldn't be around to see the fallout from his choices. But back to the Will...who would send his wife a copy of a Will he made when he was out on one of his drug fueled escapades? Something wasn't right.

Fancy walked up on him while all sorts of thoughts rushed through his mind. She was unable to control her rage and she slapped him with all her strength across his face.

Hezekiah yelped like a stricken puppy, taken off guard by her surge of violence. Fancy was a calm woman, and hardly ever displayed anger in such a vile manner.

"You did this? You did this to me? Everything? All of what you have goes to some other woman? You *are* crazy," she yelled. You are out of your mind. Who is she, Hezekiah? How long have you been screwing her? What is going on! How dare you!" She kept talking and yelling. "I don't have access to any finances if something happens to you. I'm out here trying to find ways to pay your medical bills and trying to make sure you're taken care of while you've left everything to some, to God knows who. And where did you get all of that money anyway? Wheereeee!" Her screams could be heard up and down the hallway.

Hezekiah didn't say a word. His demeanor had quickly changed from slight shock to almost comical as a weird smile appeared on his face. The drugs he'd ingested earlier had him still feeling cool as a fan and obviously unbothered. He did finally say, "Get...ouuutt." He tried to pull himself up to an upright position the way his therapist had taught him. He struggled longer than he probably would have but by him being high it thwarted his ability to maneuver. He struggled but he was able to sit upright. He tried to reach for his tablet on the side of his electric wheelchair but she hauled off and hit him again. This time not only did she slap him, she pounded him on top of his head with her purse. He cowered; she pounded. Tears poured from her eyes.

Suddenly someone bolted inside his room. It was a nurse followed by another nurse.

"Call Security," the first nurse ordered frantically. The second nurse ran back out of the room and screamed for someone else up the hall to call Security.

"Ma'am, stop it! What are you doing?" the nurse screamed, rushing up to Fancy and pulling her away from Hezekiah. "You're hurting him!"

Fancy was distraught and unhinged. She snatched the Will back from Hezekiah while she screamed and cussed like a mad woman, something totally out of her character. A security guard appeared within minutes, tore Fancy away from the nurse and Hezekiah. While dragging her away the second nurse reappeared, ran over to Hezekiah, and checked to make sure he was all right.

For the next several minutes Fancy ranted and raved as the guard forced her out of Hezekiah's room and up the hallway.

"You were supposed to have my back. I thought you loved me. You're a lying, cheating, dog. I hope you die up in here. I hope you rot in hell," she said, crying, screaming, and kicking. Several residents, who were physically able, gathered in the hallway and others stood inside the door of their rooms watching the scene. A few of the staff members were recording it with their phones.

The security officer pulled her on to the elevator and pushed the button to the first floor. While Fancy calmed down somewhat she was still howling like a wolf. The pain and rage she felt was too much to bear.

When the doors of the elevator opened, the officer led her outside.

"Where are you parked, ma'am?" he asked.

Still crying, she said, "Over there," and pointed to the parking area to the left of her.

The guard turned her loose but continued to walk beside her, following her to her car. "You need to get off this property and do not come back," he said in a serious, unrelenting tone. "If you do, you will be arrested. Do you understand?" he said forcefully. Fancy answered by nodding.

The security officer opened the door of her car when she walked up to it and hit the key fob to unlock the door. As he waited for her to get inside the car, she didn't see the man who had just parked and gotten out of his car.

"What's going on?" George mumbled and then proceeded to go inside the facility undetected by Fancy.

Fancy drove straight to Holy Rock almost blindly as her tears kept gushing. She arrived at the church, barely putting the car in PARK before opening the door and jumping out. She ran inside the church.

"First Lady McCoy, what's wrong? Are you okay?" Sista Mavis asked as Fancy almost knocked her down when Mavis pushed open the heavy door leading into the church offices. She had just left her desk and was headed for her car to take a late afternoon lunch when First Lady McCoy appeared. She saw that she was crying heavily and appeared totally distraught. Right away, Sista Mavis became nervous and uneasy. Despite being nosy and a gossip, Sista Mavis was genuinely concerned. She hoped and prayed that nothing bad had happened to Pastor Hezekiah.

First Lady McCoy didn't say a word to Sista Mavis after almost plowing the woman down. She fled past her and ran down the long hallway to her son's office while Sista Mavis dashed back inside and stood in front of the receptionist's counter.

The receptionist stood up from her counter and leaned over to watch as Fancy dashed up the hall. She and Sista Mavis watched until Fancy passed Eliana's area and then disappeared from sight as she rounded the curve obviously headed to see Khalil.

Fancy didn't stop until she arrived at Khalil's office. She turned the doorknob and walked inside. Xavier jumped up when he saw his mother and Khalil got up, ran from around his desk, and both of them rushed up to her.

"What in God's name is wrong?" Khalil asked.

"Ma, what happened?" Xavier asked and placed his arm around her.

A trembling, nervous, and shaken Fancy released a loud sob and almost fell to her knees, but her fall was halted by both of her sons planted on each side of her and holding her up.

They led her over to the sofa in Khalil's office and sat her down. Each of them sat down beside her.

"Ma, please, what is it?" Khalil pleaded.

Xavier got up and walked over to Khalil's desk and retrieved the box of tissue. He took the box and placed it in his mother's shaking hands.

Fancy accepted the box of tissue, pulled out a couple of them, and wiped her eyes and snotty nose.

"Ma, what happened?" Khalil pleaded.

Fancy slowly looked up and over at each one of her sons. She reached down inside the pocket of her tangerine peacoat jacket, removed the copy of Hezekiah's Will and put it in Khalil's hand.

Khalil scanned it, put his hand on his head, leaned back, and then passed it over to his brother. "That son of a…" he cursed as he pounced up off the seat and began walking across the office floor like a madman. "Just when you think he can't stoop any lower, he does something like this? Who is this woman? Do you know her, Ma?"

Fancy shook her head from side to side. "No," she murmured.

"Where did you get this?" asked Xavier, not sounding as upset as his brother. He was the calmer of the McCoy brothers. He had a tendency to weigh things out and seek answers before he acted out.

"It was in the mailbox."

"I guess there was no return address or anything, right?" Khalil followed.

"No, just a blank envelope," Fancy mumbled again, wiping the last of her tears away.

"And you have no idea who sent it or put it in the mailbox. You don't know the person listed in this Will?"

"No, of course I don't." Fancy's voice began to rise. She was getting sick of all the questions. She needed to go home, get away from everyone. She needed time to think, but she didn't move.

"Maybe it's a hoax," Khalil said. "It has to be. It's just some stupid person trying to get you upset, and it worked."

"I think it's authentic. Look over here on the last page," Fancy said, flipping to the last page of the copied document. "See these signatures of witnesses."

"I don't know. I'm with Khalil on this one. I think it's someone trying to stir up more drama in our family," Xavier said.

"I just left your father. He didn't deny it. He didn't deny keeping the bank accounts from me. He didn't deny anything. But he wouldn't admit who this woman is. He's crazy, I tell you. He has to be. And me, I…I lost it." She started sobbing again.

"Lost it how?" asked Xavier as Khalil continued pacing across the floor, clasping his hands and pursing his lips, signifying his growing anger toward his father.

"I hit him. The nurse called Security. It's a wonder they didn't have me carted off to jail. I was escorted off the property and told if I came back that the next time I *would* be arrested."

"Is Dad all right?" Xavier asked. "Did you hurt him?"

"You're asking if she hurt him? Who cares if she hurt him? He better be glad it wasn't me or I *would* be in jail and he'd be in the ground! Then we would see if that Will is real?" Khalil said, balling up and slamming his fist into the open palm of his other hand.

Xavier hugged his mother, pulling her against him. She laid her head on his shoulder and wiped more tears from her face. "It's going to be all right, Ma. I'm going to get to the bottom of this."

Khalil wasn't so understanding. "Ma, you're a grown woman. You mean to tell me that you had no idea that you weren't on any of Dad's bank accounts? Come on, now." Khalil threw up a hand in disgust and irritation.

Fancy looked up at her son. "I trusted Hezekiah. I had no reason not to. He said for my protection and benefit it was better if he handled things."

"And you fell for that bunch of crap?" Khalil shook his head.

"Back off, Khalil. Ma said she trusted him, and that was between Ma and Dad, so leave it alone."

"Yeah, but look who it's between now. Us! We have to sort through this mess. Might as well tell her what else you found out. Get it all out in the open."

Fancy raised her head and looked at Xavier and then at Khalil.

"What? I don't think I can take anything more."

"You need to know, Ma. And after this, you need to get a lawyer and take him for every penny he has," Khalil said.

"We'll talk about it some other time," Xavier said, looking at his brother and rolling his eyes.

"No, tell her now," Khalil demanded.

Xavier paused, exhaled, and then started talking. "You know those financial files I found showing that Dad was paying George and embezzling money from the church?"

"Yes. What?"

"Well, I kept digging and I found another hidden file. It was a PDF password protected file, but I managed to hack into it. I found close to a hundred thousand dollars unaccounted for, Ma." Xavier said.

"Oh, God, this can't be real. None of this can be real."

"I know for sure now that Dad's been embezzling money from Holy Rock." Xavier paused. "It's the only way he would have that kind of money."

"What? Where is this money?" Fancy asked.

"I don't know. Could be hidden at the house somewhere," answered Xavier.

"I'm confused. Where at home?" asked Fancy.

"I don't know if it's there or not. That's just my guess. It could be in that safety deposit box he has; at that condo; it could be anywhere. I doubt that he would put it in a bank. That would be too easy to trace."

"This is like a dream, no, it's more like a freaking nightmare.

Something off of Forty-eight Hours or Dateline," Fancy said. She placed her hand on the side of her like she was trying to keep herself from passing out.

"Xavier, take Ma home." Khalil ordered his brother like he was his father or something.

Xavier nodded, stood up, and reached down and took his mother's hand to help her stand.

"Ma, try to get some rest. Don't try to contact Dad. Don't say a word to anyone. Me and Xavier got this," Khalil tried to reassure her.

Fancy got up and slowly allowed Xavier to lead her to the door. "You know what? Now that I think about it, Hezekiah had some remodeling done when we first moved into that house. Maybe he put in a safe somewhere. I don't know," Fancy said, shaking her head.

"And let me guess," Khalil said sarcastically. "You had no idea what kind of remodeling because he kept you clueless, huh?"

"That's not fair," Fancy said.

"Give her a break, bruh," Xavier said forcefully, cutting his eyes at his brother.

"Okay, look, Ma," Khalil said and walked up to her. "I'm sorry. It's not your fault that you trusted him the way that you did. Anyway, I love you." He embraced his mother, and kissed her on her forehead. "Xavier, you drive Ma's car. If you want me to I'll get Omar to follow you and bring you back to the church so we can finish our talk."

"There's no need for Xavier to drive me home. I can make it by myself," Fancy tried to convince Khalil, but failed.

"No, Xavier will take you. You're too upset. Oh, and let Xavier keep that Will."

"Yeah, Ma. I'm going to see what I can find out," Xavier said.

"Tonight being Bible Study and mid-week praise, you won't hear from me until later or tomorrow morning," Khalil reminded her.

"That's fine. I'm going to go home, have a glass, or two, of wine, and lay it down."

"Are you going to be okay at home by yourself?" Khalil asked.

"Yeah, I'll be fine."

"I'll drop you off and then I'll come back home as soon as church is over, "Xavier also reassured her.

"You two are the best sons a mother could have. I love you so much," she said, still teary-eyed.

Chapter 24

"Muddy water is best cleared by leaving it alone." Alan Watts

Stiles sat, leaning back in his chair and thinking of this evening's message. He delivered his message around the passage of scripture in Matthew chapter five verse twenty-two.

"But I tell you that anyone who is angry with a brother or sister will be subject to judgment. Many of you have heard that I recently discovered that I have a brother. He's a couple of years younger than I am, and the manner in which we found out about one another was not a pleasant one. Nonetheless, I have a brother. I wish I could say that since this discovery that everything has been great and that we have bonded and are glad to be in each other's lives. But that has not been the case. My brother is angry. He is angry with me; he is angry with our father; he is angry I believe even at God. Now I don't want you to get it twisted. I'm not preaching this message this evening to war against my brother. I'm preaching this message to you or anyone out there who may be holding anger in your heart, harboring hate, or seeking revenge for a wrong that was done to you. I'm preaching to you who are stuck in the pit of despair because of the way you were unjustly treated, especially by a family member, maybe even your sibling, or your parents. I'm here to tell you, and to encourage you to release your anger. Release it to God. Do not allow your anger to fester and torment you. Do not be a fool. Release it. I'm trying as much as I possibly can to reach out to my brother; to let him know that I want a relationship with him. That I want to get to know him."

Stiles continued to share his powerful message with an attentive audience. The more he spoke, the more his own spirit was pricked.

He too was wrestling with feelings of anger. It wasn't just Hezekiah who was resentful; for Stiles it was the whole idea of how the realization came to be that they were brothers.

"This message is not just for you," he continued. "This message is for me as well. I'm still holding on to some unresolved issues that have turned into anger. I ask God daily to help me to let it go. I'm telling you that we need to pray for one another. We need to pray that we will let go of the anger we have, the malice, and the hate. Replace it with love, forgiveness, kindness, gentleness and compassion..."

After Stiles finished his weekly midweek message he returned to his church office to gather his things to go home for the evening, when Fancy and Hezekiah fell on his mind. He hadn't talked to either of them since his visit a few weeks prior. He had called his brother but like always, Hezekiah didn't want anything to do with him. Stiles understood how difficult it was for the guy to communicate verbally, but he still wanted to check in on him. For Hezekiah to treat him like he was the blame for what happened between Pastor and Margaret, Stiles couldn't understand that. He longed to have a relationship with Hezekiah. After everything and everyone he'd lost, it would be good to know that he still had family other than Pastor. He had lost Rena, his sister Francesca, Tim, the Jacksons, his baby girl, his mother, both of his mothers…he'd lost everything, even the love that could come from having a good woman in his life. He needed someone in his life who he could love again, trust again. That could be his brother, if only Hezekiah was willing, which he wasn't. It hurt Stiles all over again. The feelings of rejection seemed like too much to take at times, yet he knew that he had to persevere.

He picked up his cell phone from off of his desk and searched through his Contacts until he found Fancy's number. He had talked to her about a week ago and she told him that Hezekiah had refused to see her, their sons, and anyone associated with Holy Rock. Stiles couldn't understand Hezekiah's way of thinking. Perhaps, his mind was somewhat clouded because of the stroke. If that was the case, Stiles hoped that Fancy would check on getting the guy some counseling or a psych eval.

Pastor told Stiles that he too had gone to see Hezekiah, but like the others, he had been turned away and told that Hezekiah had visitor restrictions.

He pushed the Call button and listened as the phone started ringing.

A knock on his office door prompted him to end the call before Fancy answered.

"Yes, come in," he said to whoever was on the other side.

Stiles watched as the doorknob turned slightly and the door slowly opened.

Kareena stuck her head inside. "Hi, there. You busy?" she asked.

"No, come on in," he said slightly rising from his chair.

"Don't get up," she said before he completely stood and she walked inside his office. She closed the door behind her. "That was a great message. But then again, you are a powerful preacher, so all of your sermons are soul stirring," she complimented.

Stiles leaned back in his chair again. "Thank you, Kareena." Stiles smiled, and clasped his hands together.

"I was just checking to see if you'd like to go have dessert or coffee before you end your evening."

"Well, ummm I actually could use a little more than dessert. The food they served at the mid-week Fellowship this evening was good, but it didn't keep me full for very long; I'm still hungry."

"You're probably hungry because you preach so hard and you burn off those calories in no time. But if you want some company, then I'll be glad to go with you. What do you have a taste for?"

"And River?"

"Huh?" Kareena folded her arms and appeared confused.

"River? You two don't have plans this evening?"

"River and I are just friends. I've told you that before—many times before," she said, almost sounding a tad bit irritated. "But to answer your question, no, River and I do not have plans for tonight, tomorrow night or the next night."

Stiles raised both palms and made an awkward face at Kareena. "Sorry, I didn't mean to get the lady upset." He smiled and Kareena pouted her lips and unfolded her arms.

"What's it going to be?" she said.

Stiles picked up his phone, stood, walked from around the desk, and extended his hand out toward Kareena.

Kareena took hold of his hand and smiled.

"Shall we?" he said and escorted her to the door. "Do you want to follow me in your car, or ride with me? I can bring you back here to pick up your car after we're done. Better still, I'll follow you to your house to drop off your car. That way you don't have to worry about backtracking to the church. I can just take you home afterwards."

"Yeah, I like that idea better," she agreed.

"Tell you what. Why don't you go ahead. I'm going to put some things away and I'll be right behind you."

"Okay, I'm out of here. I'll see you in a few. Oh, did you decide where you want to go?" she asked.

"I was thinking we could go to Mikki's."

"Yum, sounds good. I'm working up an appetite myself now. See you in a little bit."

"Okay. I'm right behind you," Stiles said as Kareena walked out of the office and up the hallway.

He watched until she disappeared from his view and then stepped back into his office to make sure he shut down his laptop and put it away, among some other things. He closed his door and his phone rang.

He looked at it; it was Fancy.

"Fancy, how are you?"

"Hi, Stiles. I saw that you called. Things could be better, much better, but tell me how things are with you?"

"What is it, Fancy?" he asked, noting the tension in her voice.

Fancy explained everything to him. Hearing his voice on the other end of the phone was something that she needed. She had no one else who she felt that she could trust and really open up to about everything that was going on in her life with Hezekiah. Initially, when she saw that he had called, she told herself not to say a word about the latest drama going on, but as soon as she heard his voice on the other end of her phone, she suddenly found herself spilling her guts. She didn't spare any of the awful, hurting details.

He walked over to one of the chairs in his office, propped his feet on his desk and sat back, giving Fancy his full attention. For the next half hour or so she talked and Stiles listened. It was horrible what Hezekiah had done and this had nothing to do with him having a stroke. From the way Fancy explained things, the things Hezekiah had done were well in place before he got sick. Hearing about his affair with Detria to this new thing about a Will and stashed money was like a made for TV movie.

"Look, why don't I make a visit to Memphis. I'll try to talk to my brother....yet again. Plus, I can talk to the boys again, give them some advice if they want to accept it," Stiles offered.

"I don't think so, Stiles. You have a life and a church in Houston. I can't expect you to run to Memphis every time I have a situation. And your brother, well it would be different if he accepted you as his brother and you two had a relationship, but you and I both know that it's nothing like that."

"Yeah, you got that right. I just do not understand why he's so set against me when I'm in the same situation he's in. I had no idea about him. But the one thing that's different on my end is that I do want a relationship with him. I have nobody, absolutely nobody," Stiles lamented.

"What about your friend?"

"What friend? Leo? Leo is one of my closest friends. He's like a brother to me, but he's in Memphis, too and he has a wife, kid, a family of his own. And dudes don't run to other dudes with their problems like, well, like most women do."

"I was actually talking about the woman you're seeing there. What's her name? Karen?"

Stiles jumped up out of the chair.

"Oh, my gosh! Dang it," he yelled.

"Stiles, what is it?"

"It's Kareena. Her name is Kareena and I'm supposed to be picking her up for dinner. That was over half an hour ago. Look, I'll call you and let you know when I'm coming, okay, Fancy?"

"Okay, and I'm sorry I caused you to miss out on your date."

"It was no date, just dinner with a friend, but thanks. I gotta go. And I'll be praying for you. Talk to you later."

He ended the call, and rushed out of his office. He locked the door behind him and then ran up the hallway and outside to the private area where he parked his car. On the way, he called Kareena.

"Hello," she said, sounding like she was upset and rightfully so. "You could have just told me that you wanted to dine alone."

"Kareena, I'm sorry. I'm so sorry. A call came in from Memphis and I got caught up. I totally forgot that we were having dinner."

"Well, Mikki's is about to close anyway. I forgot they close at eight o'clock, so going to eat there is out of the question."

"We'll find somewhere to eat. This is Houston, remember?"

"Yeah, I guess. But that's only if you're sure you still want to go. Is everything all right in Memphis?" she asked. Her irritation turned to concern.

"Yeah, of course I still want to go. I'm even hungrier now," he said and chuckled lightly. "As for Memphis, well, things aren't too good," he replied as he got in his car and headed to Kareena's house as they continued talking. "There's a lot going on."

"I'm sorry to hear that."

"I'm sure I'll be taking a drive to the M-town in the next week or so."

"You sure are making a lot of trips to Memphis. Do you think that's healthy?"

"I don't know about healthy; but is it necessary? Yes. They're the only family I have left. I won't turn my back on them. Even if that means…"

"Means what, Stiles?" Kareena asked as she stood in the picture window of her living room glancing outside so she would see him when he drove up. "Moving back to Memphis?"

Stiles was quiet and silence filled the phone lines between them. "I'll be there in five minutes," he said, breaking the awkward silence and ending the call.

Kareena had brought up something that he hadn't thought about. Would he ever consider moving back to Memphis? Were things that crucial that he needed to at least contemplate moving and if he did what would he do if he returned? Start a church of his own? See if he could work at Holy Rock alongside Khalil, possibly groom his nephew? Be there for Fancy and help her in any way he could while trying to establish a real relationship with Hezekiah?

Stiles turned on the street leading to Kareena's neighborhood. He took several more turns before arriving at her apartment complex.

Chapter 25

"I wish I could go back to the day I first met you and just walk away." Unknown

"Are you sure about this?" Fancy asked.

"I'm more than sure. I'm not going to leave you to handle this on your own," Stiles explained. He planned a trip to Memphis after talking to Fancy and learning everything that had been going on. Whether Hezekiah liked it or not, he was going to talk to him. Hopefully, he could talk some sense into his brother. "I'll be driving up there Sunday afternoon after the end of worship service."

"Okay, I'll be looking forward to seeing you. Oh, and Stiles this time please accept my invitation to stay here at the house."

"Sure, Fancy, I'd be glad to." They ended their call and Stiles turned around and called his good friend, Leo to let him know that he would be in town. Leo and his wife Cynthia had remained members of Holy Rock. He was no longer a deacon, thanks to Hezekiah's choosing, but Leo still remained active in the ministry. He was a part of the Finance Ministry and the New Members Ministry.

Leo never particularly cared for Hezekiah because Hezekiah just didn't seem like a trustworthy man like Stiles, but Leo was not one to judge. He had his own skeletons to contend with so he did his best to work with Hezekiah. Serving on the Finance and New Members ministries was fulfilling for him and he felt less pressure than he did when he was a deacon under Stiles' leadership.

"I'll be looking for ya, bruh," Leo told Stiles. "Maybe we can catch a Grizzlies game while you're here."

"Yeah, you know it," was Stiles response.

The weather was still pleasant in Memphis even though it was mid-October. Stiles had his car packed and ready for the trip. He said his goodbyes to Kareena and once again headed up the highway to Memphis. He wondered would there ever be a time when he would move pass his past? Would Memphis forever hold him hostage and would it always be equated with pain and heartbreak? Hopefully, he would be able to find some peace and a little bit of happiness by building a relationship with his brother and nephews. He prayed for God to make it so.

Fancy had not returned to the nursing facility since her awful encounter with Hezekiah two and half weeks ago. Stroke or no stroke, he had really hurt her this time and it was going to be hard to forgive and forget.

Khalil had done some investigating of his own but he still hadn't found out who this mystery woman was that was listed on the fake Will Fancy received in her mailbox. He had spoken to Detria and he started to ask for her help again, but decided against it. She knew people and if she didn't know people she had a way of getting people to find out information. He understood that he couldn't tell her everything, just a select few things that he shared if he thought she could help him in anyway. He also thought that she could have been the one who sent it just to get under Fancy's skin. He could never tell about Dee; she had some strange ways which is why he would never trust her. Not to mention that if she slept with him and his daddy at the same time, then he didn't put anything pass her.

He had met her parents, the Mackey's, a few Sundays ago and found them to be nice and personable people. They were visiting Holy Rock. They explained that they had been members of Holy Rock for years but said they had moved their membership some time ago. Detria hadn't been to church since that one time a few months back but when her parents told her in passing conversation that they were going to go hear Holy Rock's new pastor, she told them to make sure they introduced themselves and let Khalil know who they were.

When the Mackey's greeted him after service one Sunday, and

introduced themselves, he realized that he had spoken to them once before since he became senior pastor; they only told him that they were Detria's parents this time.

For now, Khalil got dressed and prepared to head to the courthouse with Xavier. This was to be the end of the charge that had been levied against his baby brother.

Xavier was up early, dressed, and ready to hopefully go end an unwanted chapter written into his life. He spent the night with Khalil the night before to avoid answering questions from his mom about today's appearance. Fancy knew nothing about Detria hiring an attorney for him and he wanted to keep it that way. Khalil had told her that he'd found someone from Holy Rock to represent Xavier.

Xavier had lied to her, or rather avoided the truth about the actual day that he was to report back to court. When he came home today, he prayed that everything would be over and done with never to be heard of again. The main reason he didn't want her to know his court dates was because she would probably insist on coming and then she would run into Dee Graham, which was what he had avoided happening so far.

Khalil and Xavier exchanged little conversation on the drive to the courthouse. Xavier texted back and forth with Malik.

"OTW to a meeting," he texted Malik. "WYD?"

"OTW to work. Busy day," Malik texted back. "Want to meet me for lunch?"

"Don't know how long mtg going to last."

"Text me if you get done by one. Lunch my treat." Malik texted.

"Sure," Xavier texted and smiled.

"You all into that texting aren't you?" Khalil said. "Raymone?"

"Nope. Just a friend. I haven't heard from Raymone. We don't talk anymore. His mother did call me last week to tell me that they had settled with my insurance company."

"Cool."

"Yeah. I guess. Still won't make things the way they used to be. Nothing can do that."

"You got that right, which is why as bad as it hurts, you got to move on, bruh. Accept that and be thankful that your friend is alive. He has to come to terms with his new normal. You've tried to reach out to him time and time again, but he can't cope with things the way they are right now. You just got to respect that man's privacy and if he doesn't want to see you, he doesn't want to see you. Send up a prayer for him. That's about the best you can do. You feel me?"

"Yeah."

They arrived downtown, turned on Court Street, and drove to the parking lot adjacent to the courthouse. Khalil drove around and around until they were on the top floor of the packed garage. He found a space and the brothers got out and walked to the courthouse in silence.

Just as they walked inside, Xavier spotted Dee and the attorney. "There old girl is," he told Khalil.

"Who?"

"Your girl, Dee. See her over there standing next to my attorney."

"First off, she's not my girl. You know what's up. Don't act like you don't."

"Yeah, whatever, man."

Khalil looked in the direction Xavier was headed and that's when he saw her. Dee was an attractive woman. Her clothes fit her body to a fault. Her hair was always in place and she always, always smelled like a slice of heaven.

Khalil walked up to her, leaned in, and said devilishly. "Hey, what's up, you? I don't see your two bodyguards 'round here." He pretended to scan the courthouse.

"Khalil, don't do this. Not here. I've tried to explain that what you saw is not how things looked. I was basically forced to go to see Hezekiah that day."

"You're right. This is not the time or place to talk about it. Anyway, it is what it is. I'm here to support my li'l brother."

Dee looked at him, grabbed hold of his hand, and Khalil jerked away and walked toward the court room.

Dee stood alone, looking heartbroken and then proceeded to

walk in behind Khalil and Xavier.

Court lasted until close to noon. Just as Xavier's attorney said, everything was settled and Xavier walked out with the case having been dropped.

He thanked Dee and his attorney again as he couldn't shield the huge smile on his face. "Thank you, Miss Dee. Thank you so much." He turned to the attorney standing next to Dee, shook his hand again, and gave him dap.

As he walked off, he texted Malik. "Meeting just ended. Still wanna meet for lunch?"

"Look, thanks for helping my brother," Khalil told Dee. "I'm outta here."

"Khalil, wait. I thought we could spend some time together," she said. "You know, celebrate and all."

"I'm headed to the church after I drop him off. You might wanna celebrate with my dad and George. Might be a better fit for you, baby girl," he said smugly. For whatever reason, Khalil kissed her on her cheek and proceeded to walk off, leaving Dee standing next to the lawyer who quickly excused himself.

"If you'll excuse me, I see my other client," he said to Dee. "Have a good day, Miss Graham. Call me if you need my services again."

Detria stood outside of the courtroom sulking. Her text notifier chimed. "Why you looking like you lost your best friend?"

Dee turned around to see who was watching her. She looked and looked through the maze of people and then she saw him—George.

They walked toward each other until they met up. "What are you doing here?" he asked.

"I could ask you the same thing, but I already know why you're here. I thought your case had been moved upstairs to criminal court."

"It has. I'm on my way up there now. I just walked in here and I knew you were probably somewhere lurking when I saw the McCoy punks leaving out of here. Is that why you're here? For Xavier?"

"Yeah."

"How did that go?"

"He got off," she answered, looking over her shoulder as if hoping Khalil suddenly reappeared and whisked her off her feet.

"That was just a little something to shake em up," George said and laughed.

"I'm sure yours won't be as easy. You looking at how much time?" Dee asked, secretly bathing in the fact that soon he would be locked up somewhere and out of her life and business.

"A couple of years at the most, but it should still be a while before it goes to trial so don't write me off just yet," he said boastfully.

"Leave them young boys alone and you wouldn't be in all of this mess," she said nonchalantly.

"Hey, we all have our hang-ups'."

"George, you're a scumbag, but I'm sure you already know that," Dee said and prepared to walk off.

"So I've been told. I'll see you later. I've got to get upstairs. Remember I'm supposed to pick up your boy tomorrow for an offsite visit. I'll see you at the condo."

'I don't know about that. I have plans tomorrow."

"It's not like I asked you. Be there around ten. I'm picking him up at nine."

Dee rolled her eyes and walked off, and headed outside to her car.

George laughed wickedly as he walked in the opposite direction toward the escalators.

Khalil queried Xavier as he drove him back to his apartment.

"I'm running things. You understand? Right now Ma don't know her head from her tail. We have to look out for her."

"And how is trying to find Dad's money looking out for her?"

"First of all, it ain't Dad's money. It belongs to Holy Rock if you want to get all technical about it. He needs to be held accountable and before you say something, I don't feel sorry for him. No wonder he had a stroke. Either way, I'm gonna find it and when I do I'll invest it in something. Make it grow. Maybe even give it back to the church. But regardless of what I do, how I do it, or when I do it, I don't want you to say a word to Ma about none of this. You hear me?"

"You can't be serious. Keeping stuff from Ma ain't right," Xavier said, looking at his brother like he didn't know who he was sitting next to.

"Yeah, I'm way serious. You'll be sorry if you breathe a word to Ma or anybody, you hear me?"

"Heyyy, don't put me in it. When Dad finds out that you're just as big of a traitor as he is, he'll flip. And Ma is gonna find out. You're asking for trouble, Khalil."

"Dad is going to pay. He's going down for embezzling church funds. Stroke or no stroke. The way he's done Ma and us, he deserves to go back to prison, and I'm going to see that he does. You can be with me or you can go act like a little girl somewhere. I don't care."

Xavier balled up his fist and tried to strike Khalil but Khalil blocked his blow, swerving on the highway but he maintained control of his ride.

"Don't you ever in life raise your hand up at me. I swear, I'll take your head off if you ever…"

Khalil pushed the pedal to the metal and flew down the highway. He didn't let up on his speed until he got off the interstate and into the residential area where his apartment was located. He drove up to the apartment, jumped out, and ran around to the door where Xavier was getting out of the car. Before Xavier could fully step out, Khalil jerked him by his jacket and practically pulled him out of the car. He hit him so hard in the chest that it practically knocked the wind out of Xavier.

"You got me messed up. You don't run jack. You hear me?" he warned Xavier. "I got this. I run this! Now get your li'l punk behind away from me. Get yourself some business and stay out of mine."

Xavier didn't say a word. He gathered himself, held his chest, and stumbled off toward his car.

Inside his car, he wiped the tears from his eyes while Khalil got back in his car and sped away. Xavier sat in the car for a few minutes or so until he got himself together. A text drew him out of his feelings.

"Mexican place on Hacks half an hour?"

"Cool," Xavier texted back.

"See you soon." Malik texted back.

Xavier cleared his throat, looked around the parking lot area like he was expecting someone to be looking at him, then started his car and drove off. His brother had always played the tough guy, but he'd better be careful because payback could never be good after doing wrong toward someone else. He pulled himself together and headed to meet Malik.

This would be the first time he and Malik met up outside of Holy Rock. The day that he was in the meeting at Holy Rock being appointed as one of the new part-time associate ministers, Malik also took Xavier up on his offer to help with the Youth Department. Since that day, two months prior, Malik had asked him out a few times, but Xavier turned him down every time, until today.

Malik had reached out to him after midweek praise service the other night and asked him again about going out. Trying to make sure he was as discreet as possible around Holy Rock, Xavier told him to text him the next day, which Malik did, and this time Xavier accepted the invitation. It was time that he totally wiped Raymone out of his mind and move on in his life. It wasn't that Malik had come on to him; but Xavier could read between the lines. Just from the short conversation the two men had and from the flirtatious looks Malik had given him, he knew that Malik was gay the same as him, but was he really attracted to him? He was a fairly good looking man, a few years older than Xavier, dressed nicely, and had a pleasant persona about himself, but Xavier was not physically attracted to him.

They had a half way decent lunch, but the more they talked, the less they talked. Malik was too flamboyant for Xavier's liking and he looked at every man that walked past them and into the restaurant. He also cussed like a sailor and that was a total turn off for Xavier. Being outside the doors of Holy Rock showed who and what this guy was all about.

Xavier excused himself almost as soon as he finished eating his meal. He had already had an eventful and stressful morning and listening to Malik's foul mouth and watching his wandering eyes was just not what he had planned.

When Malik asked him about them hooking up again, Xavier politely dismissed him by telling him that he had very little time to engage in a relationship and that his roles at Holy Rock plus his family affairs took up most of his free time.

Malik responded as if he already understood, and he did, that Xavier was turning him down and being polite about it. Malik didn't care one way or the other because his only mission anyway was to get Xavier between the sheets, if only for one night.

The two of them exchanged casual goodbyes after they finished lunch and agreed that they would continue to work to improve the youth ministry at Holy Rock in every way that they could.

Back at Holy Rock, Xavier went straight to his office. He had nothing to say to his brother. He was still quite upset for the way Khalil had treated him; like he was some nobody off the streets. He sat behind his desk and went over some of the notes and contact information for those who had offered suggestions about how to improve the youth ministry. Quite a number of people had been signing up each Sunday to show their interest in working with the youth and young adults. That was a good thing and Xavier was exceptionally glad about it.

After he made some suggestions and comments, himself, he switched roles and sat in front of his computer to go through the latest financial files that he had the finance secretary send him. While he went through the files with a fine-toothed comb, there was a knock on the door.

"Yes, come in," he said.

"Brother Xavier," Leo said as he stuck his head inside the door.

"Oh, hello, Brother Leo. Come in. What can I do for you?"

"I wanted to know if you needed any more volunteers for Wednesday night Youth Jam. I think it's going to go off with a bang."

Leo enjoyed working with the youth and also served on the finance committee and several other ministries around Holy Rock. He was one of those members that spoke up and volunteered for just about everything that went on at Holy Rock. His wife, Cynthia, and their little girl who was a little older than Detria Graham's kid, were faithful members.

Youth Jam was a new youth and young adult program that Xavier was going to start up in the next couple weeks. It was just another form of ministry to attract and retain young people and keep them off the streets, give them a place to have fun, come together, chat it up, play games, watch movies, eat, study the Word and just have good clean fun.

"We can always use help," Xavier told him, standing up and walking from behind his desk. "You and your wife already do so much around here. I wouldn't want y'all to get burned out."

"Cynthia loves this church just as much as I do," Leo said, walking further into the office as he closed the door behind him.

"I don't know you or your wife that well on a personal level, Brother Leo, but I see you around here all of the time. You do seem committed to Holy Rock and from what I've heard you used to be a deacon under uhhh….my uncle.

"Yes, Stiles and I are like brothers. I got major love for him. Things changed at Holy Rock but it doesn't change my love for this church."

"That's good."

"So, aren't you supposed to be leaving for college? I heard you got a full ride to Xavier University."

"Yeah, I did, but God had other things in mind. I'm needed here." Xavier turned slightly away from Leo as the tone of his voice lightened.

Leo walked up to him and placed a hand on his shoulder.

Xavier looked back at Leo.

"Look, man. Don't give up on your dreams for anybody. If you're hanging around here because of what happened to your father, then I'm just saying you need to think about what you're doing long and hard."

Xavier sat at the edge of his desk. "This is where I'm supposed to be."

"I hope you're sure about that," Leo said. "But hey, it's your life, your decision. Just know that if you need someone to talk to, someone to listen, then I'm here." Leo placed his hand close to Xavier's inner thigh, allowing it to linger momentarily before he lightly squeezed it while he looked him directly in the eyes.

Xavier stood abruptly. "Uhhh, thank you, Brother Leo. I'll keep that in mind," he said and walked to his office door and opened it. "Now, if you'll excuse me, I have a lot of work to finish up."

"Sure, God bless you, brother," Leo replied as he stepped outside of the door and into the hall just as Sista Mavis walked up the hallway.

"Hello, Brother Leo, Brother Xavier," she said and kept walking without waiting on either of them to respond.

Xavier was beside himself. He felt like he wanted to do something really bad to Leo for assuming that he could touch him inappropriately. Xavier didn't understand what was up with that. Did he put off some type of vibe that gave men like Leo the impression that he was gay, and even being gay, did he give the impression to others that they could touch him or say cruel and vile things to him or about him?

He didn't display feminine traits like some gay guys or lesbian girls portrayed. He loved dressing like a man and acting like a man; he just happened to be a man who liked other men. He had wrestled with his sexuality since he was a young teen. He hated that he was like this and he had prayed and asked God to deliver him time and time again. He couldn't understand why he still had feelings toward men and not women.

He didn't know if he should confront Brother Leo about what had happened or just leave it alone. *I guess, if I was going to do something about it, I would have said something when he did it. Maybe, Khalil is right. I am weak as water. I can't even defend myself.*

He went back into his office and locked the door. He put his hands on his head and wept and prayed to God to forgive him for being the way that he was.

Chapter 26

"Because I am free...because I am whole...and I will tell everyone I know." Gospel singer/songwriter Anthony Brown, *Song is "Worth"*

"Lying lips are an abomination to the Lord, but those who act faithfully are his delight. That's what the word of God says in Proverbs twelve and twenty-two. Holy Rock, when I first accepted the role as senior pastor of this great church, I was fearful. I felt inadequate, unprepared, and less than. I wanted so badly to do a good job, wanted everyone to like and accept me. I mean, look at me...I'm nothing like my father or like the pastor before him, Stiles Graham, or even the pastor before him, Chauncey Graham. I'm just a young buck as some of the older dudes have called me, but I've also been called names like dope fiend, hustler, thug, never-gone-mount-to-nothing, and a few names I won't repeat in this sanctuary." Khalil laughed lightly and continued his message with the congregation glued to his every word like they were watching an Oscar winning performance.

"I'm still a young man; I have a long way to go in this life, but I'm relying on God to change me, to make me a better person. You all know what happened here a little over a year and half ago? A massacre, that's what it was. People call it the Jubilee Tragedy, and it was definitely tragic. You see, my father's biological mother murdered seven people and many more were injured. And do you know the main reason that happened?"

The congregation remained glued to Khalil.

Khalil scanned the large congregation. The sanctuary was filled to over capacity. He tried to hide his frown when he saw his father rolling in on his electric wheelchair with none other than George and George's wife next to him. They remained by the door in the very back of the large, sanctuary.

He continued his message after pausing for a few seconds while reverting his eyes away from his father. He zeroed in on his mother sitting comfortably and with pride on the second row in front of where Khalil stood.

"That woman was disturbed mentally, true enough, but it was more to it than that. She had been mistreated, pushed aside, lied to, lied on, and deceived for years until she had had enough. What I'm saying to you, Holy Rock, is my desire is that each of you and Holy Rock as a whole, have a discerning spirit. I know you all had mad love for my father, and I don't want to tarnish that for you, but I also don't want you to go for years without knowing some of what went on behind closed doors. My mother told me and my brother when we were growing up that God don't like ugly. I didn't know what she meant by that until…well until some years ago when I spent time behind bars for doing some bad things to other people. Well, some of you have heard about my father's past as well. He isn't exactly squeaky clean either. But the difference in the two of us is that I learned from my mistakes while my father has continued to fool and deceive people and that includes deceiving you."

The congregation gasped and a few people got up, shook their heads as if in disgust, and walked out the doors.

"If you don't want to hear the truth then you are certainly free to leave, but God says in one of my favorite books of the Bible, as I'm sure you can tell," Khalil smiled and looked in the direction of where he had originally seen his father and George. He no longer saw them, but as he continued to look across the sanctuary he saw the Mackey family and next to Brother and Sister Mackey sat Detria and a little boy who appeared to be about four or five years old. Khalil immediately assumed that it must have been Detria's son or then again maybe it was her sister's child. He didn't know and at this point, he couldn't give the little boy and certainly not Detria much thought. He had to expose his father once and for all and make sure that he would never be welcomed at Holy Rock again, at least not in the position of pastor.

"Whoever conceals his transgressions will not prosper, but he who confesses and forsakes them will obtain mercy. I've not only asked God for mercy, I confess my sins and my faults to you and I ask you for mercy as your pastor. My father, however, has done just the opposite. You would think that out of everything that has happened in this church that he would be the man of God he says he was called to be. You would think that after God brought him to his sick bed with a debilitating stroke that he would want forgiveness, and that he would want to do what is right. But he's done just the opposite, Holy Rock."

Fancy listened to her son. As much as she hated that he was about to expose his father, she had little sympathy for Hezekiah. He had brought this on himself by being a lying, cheating, violent and selfish man and it was time he paid for it.

"Unfortunately, and with sadness I have to tell you that it has been discovered that my father, your pastor or former pastor I should say, has been embezzling money from Holy Rock ever since he was first appointed as senior pastor."

You could hear the oohs and aahs going through the church. My brother, Xavier McCoy," Khalil pointed over to where Xavier sat in the row of pews across from their mother among a large group of young men and women. "who you know is the new financial administrator, uncovered this sad truth. We went to him and asked him to confess, to tell the trustees and deacons at Holy Rock but he refused. I just looked out in the sanctuary, and I saw him being brought into the church by the former head of security, George Reeves. George unfortunately is no better than my father. He may be even worse, but then again, sin is sin. I don't see either of them now; it appears that they must have left. You know the truth can hurt. I don't know at this time what charges, if any, will be brought against him in a court of law, but I do know that whereas we can forgive Hezekiah McCoy, it is going to be hard. We are human; my mother is hurt and ashamed by my father's actions and enough is enough. I ask that you keep her in prayer. Keep our family in prayer and keep me in prayer. I want to be a man after God's own heart," Khalil said, as he forced tears to form in his eyes and wiped them with a handkerchief he pulled out of his jeans pocket.

Xavier eyed his brother angrily. He had not forgotten their physical encounter and he knew his brother like the back of his hand. Khalil was putting on the performance of a lifetime and as Xavier looked around, he could tell that the people were buying every word Khalil spoke.

Detria shook her head, and then leaned in and said something to her son. She had called Skip the night before and asked if she could pick up her son and take him to church with her. His grandparents had practically begged Detria to call and ask Skip to let him come. They planned on spending the afternoon with him, take him out to eat, and then he would come over to their house for a while. Like Detria, they did not have a good relationship with Skip or his wife, Meaghan, and it was rare that they reached out to Skip to inquire about little Elijah.

Detria looked around the vast sanctuary, too, surprised to hear Khalil say that Hezekiah and George had been in worship service. George had said nothing about bringing Hezekiah to Holy Rock when she talked to him yesterday. George had called her to tell her that he went to Hezekiah's condo the day before only to discover that the locks had been changed.

Khalil broke down and began weeping while the organist started playing a touching song by Anthony Brown called "Worth." Khalil, in addition to his charm and good looks, had a beautiful, melodic voice that could drive a woman to her knees. He began singing the song and the sanctuary seemed to catch on fire with praising, shouting, singing, and worshipping.

"You thought I was worth saving, so you came and changed my life....You thought I was worth keeping...So I could be free, so..." Khalil song with the voice of an angel. He song with conviction. His voice was powerful, and the lyrics to the song set a spiritual blaze throughout the church. He held the mic in his hand and walked down the three steps and out of the pulpit, and along the sanctuary

singing and crying as if he was truly crying out to God.

The church was on fire and the ushers earned their positions on this day. Hezekiah looked and listened from the vestibule of the church as he directed George to take him out of the church.

When Khalil's deacons and associate ministers stood and opened the doors of the church, a drove of people poured to the front of the sanctuary.

At the close of the dynamic service, Khalil stood at the exit of the sanctuary to shake hands and be given hugs by women young, old, and in between. Many placed their numbers inside his hand or jean pocket as they leaned in to hug him. Some whispered X-rated words into his ears, all of which Khalil was used to by now. He'd received countless propositions that it was sometimes humorous to him.

He saw her approaching and as she hugged him, he felt the tears against his cheek. "Pastor, that message was so powerful. You have no idea how much it touched my spirit," she cried. "And I've never heard you sing. You have the most powerful voice. God used you today."

"I give all glory to God," Khalil told her and embraced her tightly and kissed her on her tear-filled cheek. "God bless you, Sister Eliana," he said and then quickly glanced at the handsome young man standing next to her. He felt his heart drop a notch as he thought *Dang, she brought her man up in here. Oh well, guess that means I just have to step up my game.*

"Pastor Khalil, I want to introduce you. This is my twin brother, Ian" she said and introduced him to Ian. "Ian, this is Pastor Khalil."

"Welcome to Holy Rock, Ian. We love having your sister as part of our staff," he complimented Eliana and looked at her and smiled. He reached out and used the ball of his thumb to wipe away a tear from her face.

"Thank you," Ian said. "I really enjoyed the service and your message, and that song is one of my favorites."

"I'm glad you enjoyed it," Khalil said. "Please consider joining us."

The armor bearer whispered to Khalil that they needed to keep things moving because there was still a long line of people anxious to greet him.

"I'll see you tomorrow," Khalil said to Eliana, as he reached out and held her hand a little longer than necessary.

"Okay," she said demurely, batting her long lashes at Khalil in a subtle but flirtatious gesture.

The line continued on and Khalil received word after word of praise. One or two people whispered in his ear that he should be ashamed of what he'd said about Hezekiah, but Khalil wasn't bothered. He expected there to always be somebody who would not be a fan of his. The line continued and then Khalil saw Detria and her parents approaching. He said something to the armor bearer standing to his left. As the Mackey's approached, Sister Mackey praised him and Detria's father gave him a firm handshake and a nod of the head. When Detria came up, she tried unsuccessfully to lean in and whisper in his ear, but Khalil wasn't having it.

"Good to see you, Sister Graham," he said with fake enthusiasm and slightly pushed her in the center of her back forcing her to move forward. The armor bearer gently took hold of her and led her forward and away from Khalil.

Detria was furious. She had still been texting and calling Khalil and still he ignored her, but she wasn't going to give up. She had to convince him that the only reason she was with Hezekiah and George was out of fear. George wasn't exactly the nicest guy and neither was Hezekiah and she didn't want to cross either of them. Plus, George kept her supplied with what she loved and craved the most – cocaine.

Ever since her accident and her daughter's death, she'd been on drugs. It started innocently with her becoming addicted to painkillers, which she was on for almost two years. When the doctor refused to write her any more prescriptions and she'd become unable to buy them as much as she once did from off the street, she tried cocaine and she had been using it ever since. She soon put the pain pills aside and became a faithful user. When she met George through Hezekiah, who she discovered enjoyed lacing his weed with the white powder, she traded her pill addiction for cocaine. The only persons outside of George and Hezekiah who knew about her habit was Priscilla, but she could count on Priscilla to keep her mouth shut. She paid the woman enough and because of that Priscilla was loyal.

As the armor bearer practically forced her past Khalil, Detria looked back at him and rolled her eyes. The armor bearer stayed by her side and escorted her and her son out of the sanctuary and into the vestibule. He stood at the door until he was sure she was not going to try to back track into the sanctuary. Detria followed her parents out of the church, and onto the crowded parking lot. She spotted George; he was loading Hezekiah's wheelchair in the back of his SUV. She couldn't see Hezekiah but assumed that he was already inside the vehicle.

She walked with her parents unnoticed by George but Hezekiah watched them. He smiled wickedly and then began watching the other people come outside the church.

There were several people who saw him before he got into the SUV but surprisingly their welcome wasn't as warm and inviting as he had expected. Khalil and Fancy seemed to have done a good job turning his flock against him and for that he wanted them to pay, and he would do it by striking out at them where he knew it would hurt the most. For Fancy that meant money and he would start with that house. As for Khalil and Xavier, he would get George to help him devise something against his sons and he hoped to do it soon because George would be leaving for his stint behind bars relatively soon.

And him going back to prison was out of the question for Hezekiah. No way would he let Khalil set him up to go back there and if he did, Hezekiah thought to himself, *I'll take Fancy with me and you too, boy if I have to.*

.

Chapter 27

"The only people I owe my loyalty to are those who never made me question theirs." Loveoflifequotes.com

As planned, Stiles arrived Sunday afternoon, and Fancy couldn't be happier to see him. After today's earlier events at Holy Rock, she needed a reprieve of some sort and who better than Stiles to help her regain a clear head. Khalil had said that he'd seen Hezekiah and that slime ball, George, at church, but he seemed to have vanished before she saw him.

Though Fancy didn't see Hezekiah, she did see Detria Graham with her parents. The poor Mackey's. To have someone like Detria Graham as a daughter was something Fancy wouldn't wish on her worst enemy. She noticed the little boy standing next to Detria when she was in line to greet Khalil. He favored Detria to the point that Fancy assumed it must have been Detria's son. Fancy heard that the boy lived with his father because Detria didn't have time to be a mother. She didn't want to say that she hated anyone, but what Fancy would say is that Detria was on a very short list of people she disliked immensely.

"It's good to see you. I'm glad you had a good trip," Fancy told Stiles as she gladly welcomed him into her home.

"Thanks, I'm glad I'm here, too. How are you?" he asked.

"We'll talk about that later. For now, are you hungry?"

"Yep, I sure am." He patted his stomach. "Have you already had dinner?" he asked.

"No, not dinner, just a light lunch after church. Would you like to go out to eat or would you like me to order something to pick up to eat here?"

"Let's go pick something up. Better yet, I can go and I'll bring it back."

"No, I'll go with you, and I'll drive; you've been on the road for the past nine hours at least."

Stiles raised up a hand to show his palms. "Nooo, I thought I told you. I've decided to stop trying to make that drive. I booked a flight and of course got here in a couple of hours. I had a rental car reserved, swooped it up, and here I am. I can't do that driving thing anymore, especially since it seems that I'm coming to Memphis so often "

"Good for you. I'm glad you didn't drive. You're right; it can be exhausting. It's not like it's a two hour drive. Come on and sit down for a minute and we can decide what to eat. You can leave your bag right there. We'll move it later. I'm not expecting anyone to come barging over here. You know what I mean?"

Stiles laughed, sat down his bag, and followed Fancy into the family room.

"You want to take off your coat?" she asked.

"Yeah, sure. It's getting cold out there, isn't it?" he said, making small talk as he took off his overcoat.

"Yeah, it is. Who knows; we might have an early winter," she remarked, and took his coat as he removed it. She hung it up on a brush bronzed coat rack standing inside the entrance into the family room.

"So, how are things going?" he asked again.

"So much has happened. I told you quite a bit already over the phone and through text, but you know there's nothing like that one on one, face to face kinda talk." She giggled nervously. "But let's talk first about what you want to eat."

"Umm, something light will work for me. I can eat Subway. I noticed one on the way over here."

"You can do better than that. What about calling a take out from Chili's? They have a special—two appetizers, two entrees and a dessert for twenty bucks."

"Sounds like a winner," he said and laughed lightly. He enjoyed Fancy's company as much as she enjoyed his. It felt good to have someone to talk to and to have someone who easily confided in him. He cared deeply for Kareena but he didn't think he would talk to her as openly as he did around Fancy. It was probably because he and Fancy had Holy Rock in common and he'd gotten to know her when he was the senior pastor. Added to that, she was an attractive woman, she was smart, funny and she had a way of making him feel at ease when they talked.

"Okay, I'll pull up the menu on my phone and we can decide what we're going to order."

She sat down next to him on the loveseat and they perused the menu until they decided what they would order. Fancy ordered their food online and then they chatted for a few more minutes afterward before they got ready to go pick up their dinner.

"I'll be right back. I'm going to run upstairs and get my jacket. Oh, you can come with me. Get your luggage and I'll show you your room."

"Good deal," he said and went into the foyer and retrieved his luggage.

Fancy felt comfortable around Stiles, but he also had a way of making her a little giddy too, and she didn't know why. Perhaps it was because it was the only time she seemed to laugh. Everything was so serious and she hardly ever had the chance to just relax and laugh. Stiles could bring that part out of her. He was someone she felt that she could easily talk to and she needed that person; someone to openly confide in without having the feeling that her trust would be betrayed.

On the way to Chili's they made small talk. He told her that all of the evacuees were gone from Full of Grace and the church was finally returning to normal. He shared with her about the membership growth and even though it was slow, he was grateful to God for any growth.

"And what about Kareena? How are the two of you getting along?" Fancy asked as they turned on to Chili's parking lot and drove up to Takeout Parking to wait for the server to bring their order to the car.

"She won't admit it, but I think she really likes this River guy.

And that's cool. Kareena is a good girl and she deserves someone that's ready for a relationship. I think this could be the guy."

"What makes you say that?"

"I don't know. I mean, who wouldn't be interested in Kareena? She's a beautiful woman inside and out." Stiles said.

"If she's so beautiful why don't you tell her how you feel about her? How can you just up and let some other guy move in on her when you know you have feelings for the woman?"

"I…I just can't do it."

"Maybe what you really mean is you just can't do it with Kareena."

The carhop appeared at the window with their order, which had already been paid for online. Fancy checked it to make sure they'd gotten everything right before they left and returned home.

"Let's sit in the dining room," Fancy suggested.

"Okay."

They took a seat across from each other at the rectangular table. Fancy got two glasses of ice and brought them to the table along with a pitcher of sweet tea with lemons and some silverware. The carhop had put plastic utensils inside the bag but Fancy preferred using regular silverware if she had the choice. She went back into the kitchen and retrieved two dinner plates and began opening the bags of food and placing them onto the plates.

Stiles immediately poured himself a glass of tea while Fancy transferred the food onto the plates.

"Ummm, this is good," he complimented.

"Thanks. Hezekiah loves sweet tea with lemons, and so do the boys."

"Well, now you can add this guy to that list," Stiles said and took another deep swallow. "You made this?"

"Of course, I made it. I used fresh tea bags too, no instant tea."

"You should consider marketing this. It's just that good." He took another swallow and the glass of tea was gone.

"Help yourself," she said as she began to uncover her food and he poured himself another glass of tea.

She finally sat down. Stiles blessed their food and they

immediately started eating. After several bites of food they started talking, Fancy first. She told him everything about the fake Will, the bank accounts that she had discovered that she didn't have access to, all the way up to the dynamic sermon Khalil had shared today.

Stiles had a way of helping her find that peaceful place. Their phone conversations had increased over time and each time they spoke, she ended the phone conversation feeling calmer and less stressed. He didn't preach to her but he somehow had the uncanny ability to talk to her in such a manner that it soothed her spirit. She needed soothing and she needed peace more than ever. Knowing that her husband of the past twenty-four years was a cheater, a scam artist, and a liar had hurt her to the core.

"I bet Holy Rock went wild after hearing that message, and for him to say that about his own father, my brother, well that part I don't know about."

"What is it you don't know about?" Khalil said, as he suddenly appeared in the doorway of the dining room, startling both Fancy and Stiles.

"Oh, well good evening Pastor McCoy. How are you?" Stiles said with a mouthful of food, he'd just placed in his mouth after he spoke his last sentence.

Stiles chewed his food while Khalil leaned down and gingerly kissed his mother on her cheek. "Hi, Ma. I was on my way home and thought I'd swoop by right quick. I saw this strange car and wondered who was here. But I have my answer. So, what is it you don't know about?"

"Your mother was telling me about the message you delivered today. I'm proud of you. If you let God direct your steps, you can't fail. If you put yourself into the equation and you tell your sheep what you want them to hear, then you can find yourself on a road of despair."

"So you're saying that what I said about my father was not God talking, but it was me?" Khalil looked at Stiles, folded his arms, and stood beside his mother, while looking Stiles face on.

"You said that, not me. Who am I to second guess what you preach about? That's between you and God. I'm just saying, study to show thyself approved. Always listen and expect to hear from God and then follow his directions. Second Timothy four and two says preach the word; be ready in season and out of season; reprove, rebuke, exhort, with great patience and instruction. You got that," Stiles said, covering his mouth with the paper napkin he pulled out of the Chili's bag and swallowing the last bit of remaining food in his mouth.

"Okay, let's not get into preaching tonight. Stiles came for a few days; he's going to see if he can see Hezekiah….again," Fancy said, sounding discouraged.

"Good luck on that," Khalil said. "To be honest, I don't even know why you're wasting your time trying to have a relationship with him. He's gone mad or something. I don't think it's worth it; especially with you coming all the way from Houston every few weeks—unless you have another agenda." Khalil eyed Stiles suspiciously.

"Khalil, stop it," Fancy said, interrupting her son's words that echoed his obvious distrust of Stiles.

"I'm outta here. Oh, where you staying?" Khalil asked Stiles as he stopped and turned around before leaving from out of the living room.

"Not that it's any of your business, but I invited him to stay here," Fancy answered again.

Khalil smirked. "Gnite, Ma."

"Gnite, son." She wiped her mouth and stood up from the table. "Excuse me, Stiles."

"Don't worry about me. I'm good. Take your time," Stiles replied and started eating again.

"Have you seen your brother?"

"No, not since I left church. He said he was going to hang out with some of the guys from the youth ministry. Did you call or text him?"

"No, I didn't. I don't want to treat him like he's a baby. He always has complained that I do, so I'm trying to give him breathing space."

"Good for you, Ma. Let him grow up. Maybe it'll make a man outta him. I mean a real man," Khalil said and smiled.

"Stop that, Khalil. Don't make fun of your brother. That's not nice."

"Who's making fun of him? I'm just sayin'."

His text message notifier started chiming and then his phone started vibrating. He looked at it quickly but he really didn't need to because he already knew who it was—Dee. She was acting like a maniac, like a stalker. She had been blowing up his phone ever since he caught her with his father and George. Did she think he was sitting on stupid or something? Did she think the sex was that good that he would fool with her after what he saw? He'd already backtracked once to help his brother get out of the mess he'd gotten himself into, but now that all of that was over, he had no use or concern for the likes of Detria Graham ever again.

Gnite again, Ma. You don't have to walk me to the door. I'll lock up," Khalil said and walked through the foyer and out of the front door.

As soon as he opened the door and walked outside and up to his car, the headlights of another car sparkled brightly, almost blinding him. He raised a hand to his head to see if he could make out who was pulling up on him in front of his mother's house. Xavier, he thought. The lights went out and Khalil proceeded to look around before he fully opened the door to his ride. It wasn't his brother; it was Detria.

"What the...what are you doing here?" Khalil said. "Are you crazy?"

Detria got out of the car. It was very seldom that she drove because of her one arm and because she said she didn't like driving that much since the accident, which proved that much more to Khalil that this broad was nuts.

"What you doing driving?"

"I can drive you know. I just don't like to drive. But since a certain someone has been avoiding me I thought I should pay that certain someone a visit, a personal visit. You know?'

"Which means you had to be following me, or how else would you know I was here?"

"I wouldn't say that. Let's just say, your car does stand out, so when I saw it, I thought I'd trail you to see if I could steal a minute of your precious time."

Khalil walked up on Detria, put his hand around her neck, and squeezed it to the point that her feet almost left the ground. She gagged and turned a deep purplish red in the face. "You must not know who you messing with, Dee. I'm warning you, leave me alone. I don't want to see you, I don't want you at Holy Rock, I don't want you anywhere you might even think I might be. Do you hear me?" He released her and she fell to her knees and onto the ground next to her car. Tears gushed from her eyes.

"Khalil, I'm sorry. I promise you there's nothing going on between your father and me. It's not like you think."

"That's it…I don't think anything, Dee. I don't care about you, my father, George, none of y'all. You're nothing to me. Oh, and one more thing." He left her struggling to get up while he walked over to his car, opened the door, and reached into the center console for his wallet. He got the wallet, opened it, and pulled out a card. He walked back over to Detria and just as she stood up, still trembling and crying, he threw the card at her. "It's maxed out. I don't need it anymore. I got everything I wanted. Now get off my mother's property before I call the police and have you arrested for littering 'cause you're nothing but trash."

He walked back to his car, leaving Dee standing there crying. She bent down and picked up the card and got inside her car. He watched as she used her one arm to try to put on her seatbelt, but she failed at the attempt, probably because she was physically and emotionally upset. He chuckled, shook his head, and drove off.

"Stupid broad," he mumbled and shot off down the street, leaving her far far behind.

Detria cried all the way home. She almost had several close call accidents, clouded by her teary vision and her broken heart. She'd yet again gotten herself involved with another man who didn't care about her the way she cared about him, but she blamed herself for this one. She was stupid and dumb to get involved with both Hezekiah and Khalil anyway. She hated herself right now.

When she stopped at the traffic light, she hurriedly reached into her purse and pulled out the tiny round and pink single pill compact. She opened it with expertise using her one hand and leaned down, and put a big scoop of white powder underneath her longest fingernail and brought it up to her nose, and like magic the white substance disappeared. She shook her head from side to side as she felt the rush. Quickly she closed the compact and set it on her lap just as the light changed from red to green.

Her tears continued to pour, but she began to feel some calm as she sped down the cold, dark highway.

Her car phone rang. It was Skip. "What is it?" she said as soon as she pushed the answer button on her steering wheel.

"Where is my son?" he bellowed.

Detria had forgotten all about Elijah. He was still at her parents' house where she left him after church.

"Uhhh, he's at my parents," she answered with much attitude.

"You were supposed to have him home hours ago. Bring him home. Now," Skip ordered into the phone.

"I'm not bringing him anywhere. You want him. You go get him," she screamed back and abruptly ended the call.

Skip called back several more times and each time, Detria hit the IGNORE button as her tears turned to laughter and she sped home.

Hours later, Xavier pulled into the driveway and hit the remote control to the three-car garage. He saw the black Toyota Prius parked to the side and wondered who could be at the house at this time of night.

"Ma, you got company or nah?" Xavier texted.

He pulled into the garage but his mother hadn't responded. He called her on the phone. He didn't want to walk in on any surprises. It wasn't like he expected his mother to have some man up in the house, but he wanted to know for his own sake whose car that was before he just up and walked inside.

"Xavier, I was just about to answer your text. Where are you?"

"I'm about to come in the house. Whose ride is that?"

"It's your uncle's."

"My who?"

"Stiles," she giggled into the phone.

"Why is she all giggles? he asked himself. "What's he doing here at this time of night? It's one thirty in the morning.

"He came to Memphis for a few days to try and see Hezekiah again, so I invited him to stay here. Anyway, come on in the house. Why are we talking on the phone if you're downstairs?"

"Yeah, okay." Xavier ended the call, hit the remote to let down the garage, and walked inside the door leading into the kitchen from the garage.

He stopped to get himself a cold bottle of water out of the fridge but opted for pouring himself a tall glass of sweet tea when he saw his mother had made a pitcher. He took off up the stairs, two at a time, and headed toward his room.

"Xavier," his mother said, peeping her head out of her bedroom door. "Everything okay?"

"Yeah. Why you ask that?" He turned around to face her.

"I haven't seen you since this morning at church. Out with friends?" she asked curiously, stepping into the hall with folded arms dressed in a pink sleeveless gown that rested right above her knees.

"Yeah, I was with some friends," he quickly answered like he didn't want to get into a conversation about it. "Anyway, good night, Ma."

"Goodnight, Zay," she said and went back into her bedroom, closing the door behind her.

Xavier took a shower and prepared himself for bed. He had a long, fulfilling day and he was ready to lay it down. For the first time in a while, he had been able to let loose and put aside some of the things that had been troubling in his life. He was especially glad that the drug case was over and done with because he felt he could move on with his life. It was a new norm for him because he wasn't going to be at Xavier University like he had dreamed and he wasn't going to be with Raymone like he once thought, but hanging with Eliana, her twin brother, Ian and some other people from Holy Rock, had made him feel that maybe he could have a rewarding, successful life right where he was, at least for the time being.

He wasn't expecting to meet Ian, but when another girl in the group asked Eliana if she wanted to join them for a later lunch after church, Eliana accepted and asked if she could bring her brother along. Of course, no one had objections about that; the more the merrier. About ten of them went out to eat and from there they spent the rest of the evening together. Eliana invited everybody to come over to her house to play some board games. Out of the ten of them five accepted her invitation and the others said they already had other plans. Xavier was one of those who accepted her invitation.

Eliana had a one-bedroom apartment that was cute and quaint. Everyone gathered in her cramped living room on the floor and laughed, talked, and played Monikers, a fun board game followed by a couple rounds of Uno Deluxe.

By ten o'clock everyone was saying goodnight because most had to work the following Monday morning.

Ian and Xavier hit it off almost immediately when Eliana introduced them to each other. They laughed, talked, and had fun playing the board games and cards. They left out with the rest of the party.

"It was nice meeting you," Xavier told Ian. Both of them were shy, which was apparent in the soft tone of their voices. Standing outside in the cold air, they continued to make small talk.

"It was nice meeting you too. My sister is usually a good judge of character, so when she told me she had someone she wanted me to meet I felt like she would be cool."

"She?" Xavier frowned.

Ian laughed. "Yeah. She's always trying to set me up with some girl or other, but this time, well this time, it wasn't a girl...it was you." He looked at Xavier and then quickly looked away.

Xavier remained quiet. "Your sister seems cool. I haven't talked to her that much. I see her at Holy Rock but she's my brother's admin so she doesn't have to do much for me. But today I saw her in a whole new light. She's funny and actually very likeable."

"Yep, that's Eliana for you. I'm not as open as she is. I know we're twins, but people aren't drawn to me the same way they seem drawn to her. She meets no strangers." Ian chuckled.

"Yeah, my brother is like that too. He's the senior pastor of Holy Rock, Pastor Khalil McCoy. I'm amazed at how he gets up there Sunday after Sunday and preaches, and then he's so charismatic and people love him."

"I guess we have our own good qualities," Ian said. "For instance, you're funny yourself. I had a good time tonight watching you laugh and have fun. And when we were partners on one of the games, that was fun."

"Yeah, it was," Xavier said. "You live close by?" he asked Ian.

"I live in this same complex, on the other end and closer to the leasing office. What about you? Where do you live?"

"I'm still at home with my mother. My father had a stroke and he's in a nursing home, so she's in that big house all alone, well, except I live there with her, you know. It's about thirty minutes from here, closer to Holy Rock but on the other side."

"Cool."

"You wanna have a nightcap before you strike out for home?" offered Ian. "And by nightcap I mean coffee, soda or hot chocolate." He smiled and showed off a perfect set of pearly white teeth. "I don't drink, except on very special occasions," he clarified.

"Neither do I," said Xavier. "Umm, that's something we have in common." He smiled.

"Okay, hop in your car and follow me."

They arrived at Ian's apartment in less than three minutes. He lived in an upstairs unit just like Eliana. Ian unlocked the door to his apartment and ushered his new friend inside allowing him to freely look around the six hundred and fifty square foot space.

Ian's apartment was about the same size and layout of his sister's. It was perfectly designed and the layout was welcoming and masculine with pops of color and quaint pieces of art lining the walls.

"Nice place," Xavier complimented. "I can't wait to move into my own space."

"You prefer hot chocolate, soda, water, or coffee?"

"A bottle of water and some hot chocolate would be right on time."

"Okay, hot chocolate coming up, with whip cream on top and a bottled water," Ian said and laughed then offered him a seat on the sofa in the living room, which flowed into the open kitchen area.

Xavier sat down and continued to look around.

"What's holding you up?"

"Huh?"

"What's keeping you from moving into your own spot? Ian asked.

"I don't know. I think I'm using my mother being alone as an excuse, and then I thought I would be away from Memphis by this time."

"Away where?"

"New Orleans."

"The Big Easy, huh? Doing what?" replied Ian.

"I was going to attend Xavier University this fall."

"Oh, yea. What happened?" Ian asked with genuine curiosity.

Xavier gave him a shortened version of his reasons for not attending the college.

"Well, like I'm sure you've heard a ton of times, all things happen for a reason."

"Yeah, I've heard it more than I care to hear it."

"Here you go," Ian said, bringing the cup of hot chocolate with whipped cream and bottled water to Xavier on a small serving tray.

"Thanks," Xavier said, reaching for the tray and setting it on the table in front of him.

They talked while both of them sipped on hot chocolate and cold water. It was after one a.m. before Xavier and Ian parted ways with promises to see each other again real soon.

Chapter 28

"Those who don't know the value of loyalty can never appreciate the cost of betrayal." Unknown

Stiles got up, took a hot shower, and got dressed in a pair of casual slacks and a polo shirt. He tidied up the guest room by picking up behind himself and making up the queen bed. He had a peaceful sleep and was ready to tackle the day. He sat in the bedroom chair after he was done dressing and cleaning, retrieved his Bible from off the nightstand where he'd put it the night before, and opened it up to read his morning scriptures and devotional. That took about an hour and when he was done; he opened his bedroom door, peaked out in the hallway, and was met by silence. He stepped into the hall and went downstairs quietly into the kitchen.

The aroma of fresh brewing coffee hit his nostrils as he got midway down the steps. He walked toward the kitchen and stopped when he saw Fancy in the kitchen preparing breakfast. She was humming a song and her voice was angelic. Must have been where Khalil got his pipes from. He watched and listened as she swished around in a long sleeved, loose fitting, one piece, over-the-head dress that fell just below her upper thighs. Her pedicured feet were encased in a pair of open-toed slippers.

She continued humming and then broke out into actual song. *"There's a sweet sweet spirit in this place, and I know that it's the spirit of the Lord."*

Stiles watched and listened until he heard someone approaching from behind. He turned and met Xavier's stare as the young man came toward him and walked past him.

"Good morning, Ma," he said, looking back at Stiles. "Hello, Past...uh, Uncle Stiles."

"Good morning, Xavier."

Xavier hugged his mother while she looked at him and kissed him on his forehead as he leaned in.

"Good morning, Stiles," she said after she acknowledged her son. "I hope you had a good night's rest."

"I did. That bed is super comfortable. Thank you for allowing me to stay here."

"I'm making spinach, tomato and cheese omelets. Would you like one?"

"Yes, sounds good."

"Help yourself to coffee. Everything you need should be over there at the coffee station," she said, pointing to the area on her far left.

Stiles walked over and made himself coffee with lots of cream and sugar and then walked over to the huge peninsula island and took a seat.

"Xavier, here you go," she said, passing him a giant omelet with toast on the side.

"Thanks, Ma." He sat at the other end of the island, blessed his food and then before he started eating, he got back up and walked over to the refrigerator and brought out a giant pitcher of iced tea with lemon slices floating on the top.

"That's some addictive stuff right there," Stiles pointed at the tea and chuckled.

Xavier laughed too. "You know it."

"Y'all are something else. Anyway, here you go, Stiles." Fancy put his omelet and a couple slices of toast in front of him. "Would you like anything else?" she said.

"A fork maybe," he said.

"Oh my goodness. I forgot about silverware. She walked to the nearby cabinet, pulled out a drawer and removed a couple of forks and butter knives and sat them on the island.

She slid one of them down toward Xavier before turning around and going back to the stove to prepare an omelet for herself.

The three of them enjoyed breakfast together. Fancy felt happier than she had in a long, long time.

"Fancy, you have a beautiful voice. I don't remember you singing when you were first lady."

"That's because I'm one of those *in the shower* singers or *sing while I cook* persons. I don't have the kind of voice people want to hear in public," she laughed at herself.

"From what I heard, that's not true. People would be moved by your singing."

"Thank you, Stiles." She smiled coyly while Xavier looked at his mother and then at Stiles.

"So, are you planning to go see my father today?" Xavier asked, changing the subject.

"Yeah. I'm praying that he will accept my visit. Oh, and I called Pastor last night before I went to bed."

Fancy stopped eating and looked up at Stiles.

"You know he wants to see Hezekiah, too."

"And you should know by now that Hezekiah is stubborn and selfish. You're going to have a hard enough time getting him to accept a visit from you, and you think he would see his father? That's asking a lot," Fancy said, shaking her head in doubt.

"Yeah, he's turned all of us away, and at this point, I don't care. Let him do what he do," said Xavier. "That's on him."

"I can't give up. Not until the Holy Spirit tells me otherwise," Stiles said, and took a bite of his omelet.

Fancy and Xavier remained quiet.

Xavier finished eating, got up from the island, and proceeded to leave the kitchen.

"Aren't you forgetting something?" Fancy called out.

"What?" Xavier stopped, turned around, looking confused.

Fancy's eyes said it all as she used them to point to his plate and glass.

Xavier got his plate, his glass, and wiped the particles off of it before he put it inside the dishwasher. He then returned the pitcher of iced tea to the refrigerator. "Satisfied?"

"Satisfied," she said and smiled. "Have a good day"

"Thanks, Ma. It's going to be a full one. I'm going to meet some friends at the church gym and work out first, and then I have a meeting later this morning to talk about the upcoming Youth and Young Adult Summit."

"I'm sure it's going to be good."

"Thanks, Ma. Anyway, I'm going to go finish getting ready and then I'm outta here. Good luck, Pastor Stiles, I mean Stiles on seeing my father."

"Thanks, nephew. Have a good day. I'll try to stop by the church later on and see how things are going. That summit sounds like it might be something I'd like to incorporate at Full of Grace. We're trying to grow our youth and young adult ministry."

"Sure thing," Xavier said. "Anything I can do to help," and he dashed out of the kitchen and could be heard bolting up the stairs.

Stiles arrived at Primacy Parkway Nursing and Rehabilitation Facility. He approached the front desk like he'd done several times before and once again he was told that his name was not on Hezekiah's visitors' list. He tried unsuccessfully to persuade the receptionist to call Hezekiah and let him know that he had an out of town visitor, but she refused.

He turned to leave, feeling defeated and fed up. If this was the way Hezekiah wanted things to be, then he was ready to give up and let him have it his way.

He sat in his car on the parking lot outside of the nursing home facility and dialed the number he had saved under Contacts for Hezekiah. It hadn't worked the past several times he'd tried calling Hezekiah, but maybe, just maybe, it would work now. The phone rang until the usual voice came on. "*The number you've dialed is not a working number*," the automated robotic- like voice announced. With a heavy sigh and slouched over shoulders, Stiles ended the call, and then called Pastor to let him know that he was headed to his house.

Pastor and Stiles enjoyed each other's company for most of the afternoon.

"Son, I'm sorry that Hezekiah is behaving this way. I've tried seeing him and calling him but after he kept refusing to see me or talk to me, I gave him over to the Lord. Only the good Lord can change his heart."

"I just can't figure him out though. Did you know that it's not just you and me that he won't see; this dude won't even see his wife and sons? He's shut himself off from everybody, everybody except that fellow named George who Fancy said used to be head of Security at Holy Rock until Khalil got rid of him. Fancy said he's a crook who hides behind his sweet wife's skirt tails and the fact that he's a retired police detective."

"George *was* quite the character. He was one of a few white members we had at Holy Rock, and the only one on staff. Although he was more of an employee than a member, but he and Hezekiah were awfully close. Just as close as you and Leo."

"Yeah, from what Fancy told me, that closeness wasn't the result of a kindred spirit of friendship like me and Leo. We're like brothers and Hezekiah and George are more like they're united by the spirit of evil," Stiles said.

"If that's the case then they both have to pay for any wrong doing. I don't go that often to Holy Rock, but Josie tells me that someone called her yesterday after church and told her that one of dem McCoy boys, the one that took over his daddy's pastorship...."

"That would be the oldest son, Khalil."

"Well, anyway, she said someone told her that he said some harsh things about his father yesterday during church service. Said Hezekiah has been embezzling money from Holy Rock. Now I don't know if that's true, but I guess the boy has done his homework. At least I hope he did before he got up and accused his father of something like that. I tell you, that family is troubled. It wasn't bad enough that woman did what she did, killed all those innocent people, my daughter and son-in-law in particular but now Hezekiah seems to be on a path of destruction too. Lord, have mercy" Pastor said, resting his head in his hands.

"That was Margaret."

"Huh?" Pastor said.

"That woman you're talking about, her name is Margaret. My

biological mother." Stiles prompted Pastor. Another red flag raised when Stiles realized that Pastor had forgotten Margaret's name.

"Yeah, Margaret. That's what I said," Pastor replied.

"Well, like you said, we have to give him over to God. He's the only one who can handle this, Pastor," Stiles said just as sadly. "I feel bad for Fancy. God knows what's going to happen to her. She says she's definitely thinking seriously about divorcing Hezekiah. I can't say I blame her, but I wish they could work it out."

"I know but she has to do what she feels is best for her. Anyway, changing the subject and speaking of Leo, have you seen or talked to him lately? He would call me and Josie every now and then but it's been a while since we've heard from him."

"He's good. Matter of fact, I'm going to go hang out with him when I leave here. He's at Holy Rock just as much as he was when I was pastor. He and Cynthia love that church. When he isn't there, he's either at work or spending time with the family. Leo is an all around good guy. I'm glad he's my best friend."

"He's always been a nice young man," Pastor said. "Never a bad word about him."

"You're right. Never a bad word." Stiles agreed.

Stiles and Leo watched a Grizzlies game in Leo's man cave at his house. They kicked it, talked smack about the two teams and caught up on what had been going on lately. Not much had changed with Leo. He always had lots to say about his family. He adored his kid and he loved Cynthia to no end.

"Do you think you'll ever come back to Memphis and to Holy Rock?"

"Me? Naw, man. I don't see that happening. Now, if God says something different then I'll have to be obedient, but I don't feel that anything is about to change. I'm trying to grow the ministry in Houston."

"I think they need you man. Pastor Khalil is a good kid, and he has a powerful message, but he still needs a mentor, someone to guide him and teach him. You'll be good at that."

"I don't know about coming back to Memphis to mentor some young kid, even though he is my nephew. I'll do whatever I can to help him, but I don't have to move back here to do that."

"I hear you. What do you think about your other nephew?"

"Who? Xavier?"

"Yeah."

"I think he's a good kid, too. Smart, driven, but a little on the timid side. He needs to develop a little more backbone. I mean, he had his sights set on attending Xavier University, but he felt pressured into staying here. I mean, if that's what he really feels that God has directed him to do, then who am I to say otherwise. I just get the feeling that he'd rather not be here."

"I think it's because he's dealing with the fact that he's gay," Leo said.

"Gay? Do you really think that he is? I mean, I've heard it said but I haven't paid much attention, if any, to whether he is or he isn't."

"I don't know how you can miss seeing that. But, hey, he is who he is. Long as he stay in his place," Leo said.

Stiles looked at Leo strangely, and took a swig of his bottled beer. "What do you mean? He hasn't made a play at you, has he?" Stiles laughed.

"Man, don't make me go there. Are you serious? No way. He'd be laid out somewhere. All I'm saying is that tongues wag up in Holy Rock and he better watch his back."

"Yeah, I hear ya. Look at that man. Did you see him miss that free throw? He's sorry!" Stiles yelled, pointing to the big screen TV.

They continued watching the game, not mentioning anything else about Xavier or Holy Rock.

After the game ended, Stiles texted Fancy. "I'm about to head that way. Need anything?"

"No. I'm good. Front door key under big flower pot on porch. Put key on key ring in foyer when you come inside. Going to bed early. Food in fridge. Help yourself to whatever."

Fancy had prepared a light supper since Xavier had called and said he wouldn't be home. She didn't pry her son with questions, but she did wonder who and where he was spending the night. He was grown, and she tried to remind herself of that, but she still worried about both of her sons.

After reading her text, Stiles was a bit concerned. She had been through so much and he hoped nothing else had happened to make things worse. "Look, man. It was nice seeing you. I'll try to see you again before I leave." He gave Leo dap and Leo opened the door for Stiles to leave.

"When are you heading back to Houston?"

"Wednesday afternoon. If I had known Hezekiah was going to pull this same crap again and not see me or anyone else, I could have saved this trip. But then again, I guess I can look at the brighter side. I *am* getting to know my nephews and Fancy, too. And I did get to see Pastor, Josie and you of course. Man, your little dude is growing like a weed." Stiles and Leo stood at the front door as Stiles prepared to leave.

"Yeah, tell me about it. Might as well tell you now."

"Tell me what?"

"Cynthia is pregnant. We're having another kid."

"Congratulations, man. That's great news."

"Yeah, it is," Leo said, smiling proudly and thinking of his encounter with Xavier at the same time.

Stiles woke up in the middle of the night hungry as a bear. He opened the door to his bedroom. Clad in his pajama bottoms he went up the empty hallway and down the stairs to the kitchen.

He decided to warm up a bowl of spaghetti Fancy had made. He got a couple pieces of bread, poured himself a glass of tea and sat at the island and ate until his belly was satisfied. He washed out the bowl and utensils and his glass before he went back upstairs.

At the top of the stairs, he thought he heard something. He paused and looked around after not hearing anything. As he approached Fancy's bedroom door, he paused again because he heard something again. He wasn't trying to eavesdrop, but he heard the sound coming from her room.

She must have company, was his first thought. He smiled at the thought because he wouldn't blame her if she was seeing someone.

It wouldn't exactly be right because she was still a married woman, but she was young, vibrant, and probably lonely. Hezekiah didn't make the situation any better by turning his back on her either. He took another step toward his bedroom, but this time he realized that the sound he heard was that of someone crying. He intently listened just to make sure. He was right. Fancy was crying. He didn't know if he should keep to his room or knock on her door to see if he could console her. Her sobs grew a little louder and then he heard a loud thud, like she had thrown something. He heard her saying something, but couldn't decipher what it was she was saying. Stiles decided to leave her alone and allow her to release some of her pinned up emotions. He couldn't blame her for how she was probably feeling. He'd been through heartache himself and he didn't wish his pain on anyone.

Stiles went to his room, closed the door, got on his knees and began to pray for Fancy and for Hezekiah. He prayed for Kareena and for clarity about what God wanted him to do for his own life. He remained on his knees for quite some time making his petitions known to God. A knock on his door halted his prayers.

He listened to be sure that a knock was what he heard. The tap came again. "Stiles," he heard her say.

He ended his prayer, told the Lord, "thank you," got up off his knees, and went to the door. He opened it slowly.

Fancy stood on the other side. She looked shrunken and frail. Her eyes were fire red, her hair was disheveled, and tears had left streaks down her face.

"Fancy? What is it?" Stiles asked opening the door all the way up.

"I can't take anymore," she broke out and sobbed.

Stiles grabbed her and held her close to him when he saw her almost collapse into the floor. He held her against his bare chest, rubbing her hair gently back and forth.

"Shhh, everything will be all right. Don't cry. God's gotcha."

"I don't know where I'm going to go," she said as she continued to lay her head against his smooth chest and her tears poured down his taut belly.

"What do you mean?"

"The mortgage hasn't been paid in months. Hezekiah got a letter in the mail today. It had a forwarding address on it, but the letter still came to the house. Thank God, He never leaves His children in the dark."

"What did it say?" Stiles asked, pulling her slightly away from him but holding her by her shoulders like she was a delicate flower.

"The mortgage company is going to start the foreclosure process if the arrearages on the mortgage aren't paid by the end of the month. I was wondering why none of his mail was coming here, and now I see why. He must have had the mail forwarded. How could he do this? I didn't even know that he wasn't paying the mortgage. He always said it came directly from the bank account."

"That…self-centered…" Stiles mumbled to himself, trying to hold back his disgust toward his brother. "That stroke had to affect his mind. I can't see him allowing this to happen if he was mentally stable."

"There's a lot I don't understand lately when it comes to Hezekiah and his actions." Fancy continued crying.

Stiles grabbed her again, pulled her against his chest again, and planted butterfly kisses on the top of her head as he caressed her back in a circular motion. "I'm here," he said. "I'll help you, Fancy. I promise I will. Try to get some rest. I know it's hard, but we're going to figure this out." He took her hand and led her to her bedroom. He stood in the doorway and watched her until she got in the bed, and then slowly closed her bedroom door.

Back in his room, he pounded his fist into the palm of his hand over and over again to release some of his anger at Hezekiah. This fool was the one who had disrupted Fancy's life by cheating on her and now this. It was men like Hezekiah who made it hard for men like Stiles. He paced the floor of the room, thinking about how he could help Fancy. First, she needed to find out whose name was on that mortgage which that would be easy because the letter showed that. He didn't want to pry too much, but he was curious as to how much in arrears the mortgage actually was. He didn't have a lot of money, but he still got paid a portion of his salary from Holy Rock and a meager salary from Full of Grace. That wouldn't begin to cover any portion of what the mortgage probably was on this house.

He had to leave Wednesday, but he already knew that he would be returning as soon as possible. Fancy needed him and as her brother-in-law and the only family he had, he was not about to turn his back on her.

He finally settled down and climbed into the bed, tossing and turning until sleep overtook him.

Fancy cried herself to sleep. She loved Hezekiah but the things he had done and what he was doing now was slowly destroying that love little by little. Maybe Stiles was right; maybe Hezekiah was mentally unstable. Maybe the stroke had affected him mentally because the Hezekiah she knew would never jeopardize her well-being. But then again, the Hezekiah she thought she knew, the one she'd loved since she was a young teen, would never cheat on her and physically abuse her either, but this Hezekiah did all of those things and more.

Chapter 29

"The right one will know all your weaknesses and never use them on you." Unknown

After a restless night, Stiles woke up early, got dressed, and went downstairs. Fancy's bedroom door was still closed, and there was no aroma of brewing coffee like he woke up to every morning since his arrival.

He went downstairs into the kitchen, and over to the coffee station where he began making coffee for himself. He then looked in the refrigerator and pulled out some breakfast items and began to prepare a breakfast of bacon, eggs, and toast. He could burn a little, enough to keep from starving, and breakfast was one of the easier meals to cook in his opinion.

After he was done cooking and Fancy still hadn't come downstairs, he looked inside the pantry and found a breakfast tray, put the food on the tray, along with a cup of coffee and some apple juice and moments afterward, he was upstairs at Fancy's bedroom door.

He balanced the tray on one hand and knocked with the other a couple of times before he heard her soft, reticent voice.

"Yes?"'

"It's me," he said. "May I come in?"

"Uhhh, yes," she said.

He opened the door to find her still lying in the bed. Though her eyes were still red and slightly swollen from crying, she looked radiant. The room was dark but she seemed to brighten it up. He walked over to the bedside with the tray of food.

"What is this?" she said, and cracked a slight smile.

"Breakfast, of course. Breakfast in bed for a special lady," Stiles told her.

"This was nice of you. Thank you, Stiles, but I'm not really hungry."

"You have to eat," he said. He walked over to the window and opened the curtains. A light snow was falling. "It's snowing."

"What? Snowing?" Fancy looked over toward the window.

"It's just a mist and it doesn't look like it's sticking, but it's snowing, none the less," he said, smiling. He turned around and looked at her. "Go on, eat. I promise it won't make you sick."

"Can I at least get up and brush my teeth first?"

He chuckled and replied. "I guess that would be appropriate."

He turned to face the window so he wouldn't see her when she got out of the bed.

Fancy got up and went into the bathroom and groomed herself and then returned to sit on the side of the bed.

"This looks yummy."

Stiles turned and looked at her. She was still dressed in her gown.

"I hope it's as good as it looks."

"What about you? Aren't you eating?"

"Oh, I already ate."

Suddenly, the doorbell ringing startled Fancy and Stiles looked around.

"Who could that be?" she said.

"Maybe it's Khalil or Xavier."

"No, both of them have their keys." She placed the tray of food back on the nightstand and prepared to get up but Stiles halted her.

"I'll get the door while you get dressed," he offered.

"Thank you," she said.

He took off out of her room and down the stairs to the front door.

"How may I help you?" he asked when he opened the door and saw a man standing at the door. He looked over the man's shoulder and saw a utility truck.

"The electricity is scheduled for cut off at this residence. I'm just letting you know that I was outside," he said.

Fancy appeared behind Stiles. "You have the wrong house," she told the utility worker.

The utility worker showed her the order. "But you can't do this," she said. "You can't just come up here and turn off my electricity like this."

"I'm sorry, ma'am. You'll have to contact the utility company and discuss that. Have a good day," he said and walked off, disappearing on the side of the house. Within minutes, the lights were out. He reappeared, tilted his utility hat, and got in his truck and drove off.

Fancy broke down again, and again Stiles tried to console her.

"My phone. I need to call Khalil," she said.

Stiles pulled his phone out of his pants pocket and called Khalil himself. "Your mother needs you over here," he said when Khalil answered.

"Is everything all right?"

"Just get over here," Stiles said and ended the call.

Xavier walked inside the house and found his mother and Stiles in the family room. He saw that she was upset and was crying.

"Ma, what's wrong? What happened?" he asked, rushing over to his mother and looking at Stiles at the same time.

Fancy explained about the mortgage letter and the utilities, and Xavier showed his obvious anger by slamming his fist into his hand, the same way Stiles had done the night before. He bit down on his bottom lip.

"Don't worry; I'll find out what's up with the lights. I'm sure it's just an oversight. I'll get the bill paid."

Khalil appeared about forty-five minutes later and was told what had happened. Like Xavier, he was furious, only he added a few expletives to his explosive outburst. Stiles tried to calm him down and it worked somewhat. He got on the phone and contacted the utility company. There was an outstanding utility bill in the amount of eight hundred and something dollars but that was not why the utilities had been disconnected. Hezekiah had the electricity cut off on purpose. The person on the phone said if they wanted the electricity back on then someone would have to come down and put the utilities in their name, but they would have to present a lease or mortgage statement showing that the house was in their name.

The snow had stopped falling and the sun aggressively pushed its way from behind the clouds, but it felt like the cold was quickly settling inside the house.

While Fancy went upstairs to compose herself and finish getting dressed, Khalil, Xavier, and Stiles gathered in the home office and discussed the plan of action. He had Xavier compose a lease in the three of their names.

Xavier was good at things like this and it took less than an hour to make the new lease. Stiles was impressed with how the young men stepped up and handled their business.

"After we get the utilities back on, I'll contact the mortgage company and see what we can do about the arrearages and getting the house out of a foreclosure status," Khalil told his mother when she returned from upstairs fully dressed and groomed.

"Let's go do this," he said to his mother.

"Stiles, it's getting cold in this house. Do you want to go with us?"

"No, I'm good. I'll be fine. If it gets too chilly, I'll strike out and head over to Pastor's house. Y'all go ahead and handle your business."

"I'm going to Holy Rock after I change clothes," Xavier said.

"Okay, hold everything down. Oh, and let Eliana know that I'll be there later and to push back any appointments I have."

"Sure," said Xavier to his brother.

On the way downtown to the utility company, Khalil talked to his mother. "Ma, you might have to move out of that house. If it's in Dad's name, the only way you'll have any say so is if he adds you to the mortgage or quit claims the house over to you, and you already know that if he's making moves like this then that's the last thing he's going to do. Dude is crazy."

"I think something *is* wrong with him, Khalil. Hezekiah would never do anything like this. Never. He's always looked out for me and for you and Xavier."

"Well, he's not looking out for you now. And thing is, we can't get to this dude. He's changed his phone number; he's barred us from seeing him at the nursing facility and that crook, George guards him like a hound dog."

"George? How do you know that? I can't believe he would fool with that guy after everything he's done to this family."

"Without going into detail, I'm just telling you that George, and I hate to tell you this, but Detria Graham, too, are the ones Dad has in his life. It's time you accept that, and start thinking about what you wanna do. I say you need to be looking for another place to lay your head. Holy Rock isn't going to keep shelling out a salary to Dad either. That's over and done with. And I'm telling you now that Dad might be getting a visit from the Feds any time now."

"From the Feds? Why? Is it because of what you accused him of – embezzling from Holy Rock?"

"It's not what I accused him of, Ma. It's fact. He's going down. I told you I was going to make sure of that."

"But he's your father," Fancy said, getting visibly upset again.

"After everything he's done and that he's still doing to you, to this family, and you still want to protect him?"

"He's my husband; he's your father. "Khalil!"

"You can feel sorry for him all you want, and you can be angry at me all you want, but he's going to pay. The fact that he's still dealing with George and screwing Detria, well, if that isn't enough for you to flip the script on him, then nothing will. But it's not going to stop me or Xavier from doing what we have to do to make him pay for this."

Fancy shook her head and cried. "He's still messing with that woman?" She suddenly sniffled, wiped her tears away, and looked at her son.

"I know God doesn't want us to seek vengeance, but revenge is overdue for Pastor Hezekiah McCoy," Khalil said.

"I don't like to call it revenge—returning the favor sounds nicer," Fancy said with a look of vengeance sealed in her eyes.

It took a couple of hours but at the end, Fancy and Khalil talked to one of the customer service representatives and the utilities were placed in Khalil's name. The representative told them the utilities would be on by eleven o'clock p.m.

They left the utility office and Khalil dropped his mother back off at the house.

"Ma, I want you to start looking at where you want to move."

"I don't have any income, Khalil."

"Don't worry about that. If I have to put you on Holy Rock's staff and payroll, that's what I'll do. And even so, me and Xavier got you, Ma. Just find a place to move. Apartment, house, condo, whatever. Just do it as soon as possible."

"Okay," she said as they arrived at the house. She got out of the car and headed up to the front door.

"Call me later," Khalil hollered out the window before he drove off.

"Did everything go all right?" Stiles asked when he saw her enter into the house.

"Yes, the utilities should be back on by eleven o'clock tonight."

"That's a long time. Do you want to go out somewhere? We can do lunch, I can take you to the mall, anywhere you want to go to pass some time."

"Has Xavier left?"

"Yes,' he's been gone about thirty minutes."

"Khalil says that I need to start looking for somewhere to move."

"I think that's a good idea. If this house is in Hezekiah's name alone then you have no real say so about anything. Even if you divorced him, and asked for the house, that's a long process. I'm sorry all of this is happening to you, Fancy. I really am."

"Thank you, but you can't be any sorrier than me. I'm going to sit here I guess and look on my phone for places where I can move."

"Okay, you do that and when you find a few, then we'll get in the car and go check 'em out. How's that?"

"You are such a great person. I don't know what I would do without you here."

"Speaking of that, you know my flight leaves tomorrow."

"I understand. You have a life in Houston, a church, a girl."

Stiles showed both palms. "Hold up. I do not have a girl."

"Okay, whatever you say, but either way, you have your own life to live. I just appreciate you being here now."

"I'll be back as soon as I can. I don't want you to worry. And it's a blessing that you have Khalil and Xavier looking out for you. Those two are not going to let Hezekiah or anyone else mess over their momma."

"You have that right." Fancy laughed in agreement.

Chapter 30

"The axe forgets but the tree remembers." African Proverb

"Your message this past Sunday was awesome, Pastor Khalil," Eliana told him when he arrived at the church. "And I had no idea you had an amazing singing voice like that."

"There's a lot you don't know about me," he said and gave her a charming smile.

"Is that right?" she responded as innocently as she could without sounding like she was coming on to him.

"Yes, that's exactly right. I bet there's a lot I don't know about you either," he said.

"Well, sounds like we have a lot of learning to do about each other. Guess I'll have to carve out some time on your busy calendar for some one on one sessions."

"You know it," he replied. "But before you do that, we have some serious business to discuss."

She stood up from her desk to stand next to him as he started walking toward his office. "What's going on?"

"As soon as Xavier comes, or he might already be here; the three of us need to get together. I have some things I want to share with you. I don't have to remind you that whatever we discuss is strictly confidential, Eliana."

"You're correct; you don't need to remind me. I take my job seriously, and I respect the procedures. I'll go check to see if Xavier is here. I'll be right back," she said and turned around.

Khalil watched her as she walked away. She had the right curves, the right moves, the right everything and he couldn't wait until their one-on-one, but for now, he had to address the issue at hand—filing charges against his father for embezzlement.

While he sat in his office waiting on Xavier and Eliana to come, he thought about the stockpile of money he had uncovered. Then it dawned on him; his mother could move in the condo. That thought was quickly dispelled as he thought about how uncomfortable that would probably make Fancy, knowing that was where his father bedded Detria and God knows who else. Khalil was also concerned about who else knew about the condo. Since he found drugs there, he could only speculate that perhaps the dope man knew about the place. He decided that after this thing was settled with his father that he would talk to Xavier and the trustees about getting rid of the condo. He could always get something else, since his pastoral contract included the purchase or leasing of a house for him. He had yet to take advantage of that, but he planned to jump on it in the next few months. His contract, somewhat different than the one his father had drawn up, included payment on or the outright purchase of a vehicle for the senior pastor every two years, a full gym membership, health, medical, and disability insurance, and if he was terminated or retired, Holy Rock would continue to pay him forty-five percent of his base salary of $125,000. Not bad for a young buck of twenty-two. Not bad at all.

The knock on the door interrupted his pleasant thoughts of success. "Come in."

Xavier and Eliana walked inside.

"Please have a seat." Khalil looked at his brother and immediately thought about the incident a couple of weeks ago where he'd punched him. He felt sorry for doing that, but he couldn't stand it when Xavier came off like a weakling. He dismissed the thought as they both took a seat in the comfortable high back chairs in front of his desk.

"Xavier, you've been combing through the financial records ever since you took on the role of Financial Administrator, and I want to commend you for the outstanding job you're doing."

"Thanks," Xavier said and nodded.

Eliana smiled.

"Though most of the church records and finances are in order, unfortunately you've uncovered some less than pleasing findings, and those findings pertain to our father."

"Sooo, what exactly are you saying? Are you talking about what you said during Sunday's sermon? The part about your father embezzling money from Holy Rock?" Eliana spoke up.

"Yes, that's what I'm talking about. It hurts me and it hurts my family as a whole, but it hurts God and Holy Rock even more. This is going to be difficult to do, but we have to do what's right."

"What do you want to do about it?" Xavier asked, looking questioningly at his brother.

"I think you already know."

"We have to turn him in to the proper authorities and bring charges," Xavier added.

"What choice do we have? If we keep quiet, then we're just as guilty as he is."

"And you can't keep quiet anyway, not after you shared it with the congregation. People have already been calling trying to get on your calendar to talk to you. Some of them have outright said they want to know what's going to be done. I've been referring the calls to the associate ministers, fielding them out as much as I can."

"Good for you, Eliana. You are truly valuable and you always seem to think ahead. I like that. I like that a lot, which is why I'm offering you a permanent position as my administrative assistant. We'll talk more about that later."

"Thank you, Pastor," she said with excitement. "I'm just doing my job."

Xavier spoke up. "Well, if we're going to do this, then let me get some printouts. The police will want to see evidence. We don't have access to his bank accounts, but the authorities can seize that information. But I don't think that he was stupid enough to put all of that money he stole into a bank account. Not our father. He has it hidden somewhere."

Khalil remained quiet, clasping his hands together, and listening. Maybe he didn't have all of the money his father had stolen, but he was glad that he had found what he had and he wasn't sharing it with anybody; not his mother or his brother. He deserved that money and that jewelry and he didn't feel the least bit bad about not telling them anything.

"My speculation is that he's spent a lot of it," said Khalil and he probably has cash hidden away in some safe or some other kind of investments he's made. That's not our worry or concern. I just want him to pay for what he's done."

"I know it's my father, but I have to agree with you on this. Wrong is wrong and it's not us he did wrong, it's this church, the people who have paid their money and tithes, who've been committed to supporting this ministry," said Xavier.

"Exactly, so Eliana, I want you to work with Xavier. He's going to need someone he can trust to work with him to get those reports done. Let's get on this right away. I want to call in the authorities as soon as you're done," Khalil said.

"You got it," Xavier said. "Anything else?"

"No, that's it for now. Let me know when you two are done."

"Sure thing."

Xavier and Eliana got up and left out of the office, closing the door behind them.

Khalil smiled, and said in a wicked tone out loud. "It's payback time."

Chapter 31

"Sometimes I wish I'd never become so close to you, that way it wouldn't be so hard saying goodbye." Unknown

The following day was Wednesday, and Stiles finished packing his things and prepared to leave for the airport.

Fancy hated to see him go. He had been like a rock to her and without him by her side, she felt that she would have crumbled after learning all of what Hezekiah had done behind her back.

They went to several spots the day before and she found a couple of places that she liked. One was a three-bedroom house in a small private subdivision off the river in downtown Memphis. It had a beautiful lanai with views of the river and the Memphis-Arkansas bridge. There was another place that was also downtown but it was a townhouse. She liked it too, but she preferred single-family living. The third place Stiles had taken her to see was far out in Covington, Tennessee. The home was gorgeous; four bedrooms, four baths, an outdoor kitchen, and it had pocket doors that opened up to the huge backyard that overlooked a lake. The thing about that house was its distance from Holy Rock. She didn't know if she wanted to drive that far to church. She planned on looking at some other properties after Stiles left and hoped to make a decision in the next few days. It was going to be hard to move out of the dream house that Hezekiah had made possible. But what else could she do when he had chosen to dismiss her the way that he had.

She had an appointment with an attorney in a few days to discuss what she needed to do. Fancy really wanted to have Hezekiah declared as incompetent and mentally incapable of making decisions for himself. She didn't know how difficult it would be, but she knew that an attorney could help her either way.

"I'll call you when I make it home," Stiles told her as they stood inside the front door of her house. The weather had warmed up again and there was no hint or trace that it had snowed a couple of days prior.

"Please do that," she said.

"Well, I better get out of here. I have to turn in the rental car so I want to get to the airport in plenty of time."

"It's not like the airport is crowded like it used to be, so I don't think you have anything to worry about. Now when you get to Houston, that's a whole other story. I've never been there but I have been to that Dallas Fort Worth Airport and that place is like a city within a city. It's nothing but hustle and bustle nonstop."

"Same thing in Houston. Look, Fancy," Stiles said, turning the conversation to a more serious tone. He placed one hand on her shoulder. "Remember what I told you. I'm here for you. I'll come back as often as I can."

"I know, but I don't expect you to run back here and babysit me. I'm a big girl. I'll get through this."

His phone rang. He looked at it. "This is Khalil," he said to Fancy. "Hello, Khalil. How can I help you?"

"I know you're about to leave soon, right?"

"Yes, I was just saying goodbye to your mother. What's up?"

"I need to holla at you. It won't take long. Do you think you'll have time to stop by here on your way to the airport?" Khalil asked.

"I'll make the time. I'll see you in about fifteen minutes."

"Cool," Khalil responded and they ended their call.

"What is it? Is everything all right?" Fancy inquired.

"Yeah, I'm sure that it is. Khalil wants me to run by Holy Rock before I leave. That means I need to get out of here now. Anyway, like I was saying, I'll be back as soon as I can, probably in a couple of weeks. In the meantime, call me or text me. I don't care what time of day or night. If you need me, call me."

"Okay, okay, I will," she said. She stood on tiptoes and kissed him lightly on his lips.

Stiles frowned slightly, surprised by the gesture.

She looked him in his eyes, rubbed his check with her soft hands, and said, "Thank you. God bless you, Stiles Graham."

Stiles averted his eyes, dismissed the awkward kiss, and darted off to his car.

Fancy stood in the doorway and waved as he drove off. *Why would you do that? You don't want him thinking that you were coming on to him because you weren't. You're lonely and you're heartbroken. That's it.* She inhaled and then slowly exhaled, then turned and walked into the house and broke down in tears.

Eliana showed Stiles to Khalil's office.

Khalil shook Stiles' hand as he entered the office.

"Thanks for stopping by. I know you're headed to the airport, but I didn't want you to leave without me having the chance to tell you thanks for everything."

"You're welcome although I don't know what I did to warrant thanks," Stiles replied, standing and not sitting.

"You've been there for my mother. You know better than anyone how busy this position is. It takes a lot of time. Thank God I don't have a wife or children because I understand how being the senior pastor of a church this size requires around-the-clock commitment and dedication."

"Yeah, working for the Lord isn't always easy." Stiles smiled in agreement. "But I believe in the end it'll all be worth it."

Khalil nodded.

"My mother trusts you. She trusts you a lot. She doesn't have friends, not any real friends. It's hard being in her position and after everything my father has put her through, it makes it even harder for her to confide in others you know?"

"Yeah, I do. That's unfortunate, too. She's a good lady. She deserves to be happy and to have friends and just enjoy her life. I hate what Hezekiah is doing to her."

"So do I. Look, you've reached out to me on several occasions to offer me guidance and give me some insight into being a successful senior pastor. The more I do this, the more I realize just how valuable you are. You're a dynamic speaker, and I believe that you are a man after God's heart. From the outside looking in, you're someone whose footsteps I'd like to follow."

Stiles appeared stunned to hear such glowing words from of all people Khalil McCoy. It was true; he had tried to reach out to the young man from time to time, but to him, Stiles didn't think Khalil could care less about what he had to say. Seems like that wasn't the case after all. It just proved to Stiles even more that a person never knows who's watching them from afar. He felt good inside knowing that Khalil had gained something positive from him."

"Thank you, Khalil. Your words mean more than you can ever know. I want to be here for you. I want to be someone who you feel comfortable coming to for advice, guidance, and direction. I can't say that I'll always have the answers, but I can promise you that I will always take my advice and counsel before the Lord. And you're talking about me and my messages to the congregation, well from what I've recently been told you have one of those preacher singing voices." Stiles and Khalil both burst out in laughter.

"You know folks love to have a preacher that can sing, especially one that really sings well. They say you sound like a cross between Marvin Sapp and Bishop Paul Morton mixed in with a little Tyrese and Drake!"

Khalil and Stiles burst out laughing even louder and harder.

"See, that's what I'm talking about. You understand where I'm coming from. That's why I have something important I want you to consider." Khalil stopped laughing and his facial expression grew serious once again.

"Okay, ask. I've really got to get outta here and head to the airport."

"Since you say you're a praying man, and I believe that you are, I want you to pray about coming back to Memphis."

Stiles' eyes grew large. "What?"

"Yes. I want you to pray about coming back to Memphis. I want you to come back to Holy Rock and serve on the board of trustees and be the associate pastor. Now, I know you might think it's a step down being the associate pastor, but I could use a good Godly man like you by my side. The pay will be good; that I can promise you."

"I…I don't know what to say."

"Just say that you'll pray about it. Don't look at it as a step down or a demotion. I believe this can really work. My father will not be returning to Holy Rock. That I know for sure."

"It's not that. It's like you said I guess. From senior pastor to associate pastor. I…well, I don't know what to say. And to move back to Memphis. That would mean giving up Full of Grace, the church I've been working hard to build."

"Not necessarily. You can still fly between here and Houston. Preachers do it all the time. It's not like I'll need you to preach every Sunday. We can hold meetings through video chat and you can be here physically a couple of times a month. What I'm saying is that we can work all that out. Look, you better leave if you don't want to miss your flight. Pray on it and call me when you've had time to think about it."

Khalil walked up on Stiles and stretched out his hand. Stiles shook Khalil's' hand and they gave each other a deep brotherly hug.

"God bless you," Stiles said.

"Have a safe flight," Khalil responded.

Stiles walked out of the office and out of Holy Rock with a whole different mindset. He couldn't believe what Khalil had just offered him. Come back to Memphis? Come back to Holy Rock? This was definitely something that would have to be a God thing.

He got inside the rental car, exhaled a minute, then started the ignition. He put the car in DRIVE and drove off the parking lot. Still not believing what had just occurred, he prayed, "Show me the right path, point out the road for me to follow."

Words from the Author

Dem McCoy Boys! Wow! Each time I complete a story and I read back through it, I am so in awe and so amazed at what God has given me to write. I don't understand sometimes why he directs me to right 'on the edge' stories like this, especially when I consider them to be under the realm or on the border of Christian fiction. Yes, I have come to understand more and more that God is the one who directs my steps and he has his purpose in everything I write.

As I've said so many times before, no one is perfect. We all fall short and that includes the pastor. We all are human, and we all have God that we need to vindicate us and give us another chance. Yes, I know there are some things that some readers might consider controversial or may not agree with, but I believe God uses what I write not only to entertain people, but to prick the spirits and hearts of people; to show people that no one is beyond sin and no one is beyond saving.

The characters in Dem McCoy Boys have a bevy of issues in life that they are contending with, and as I continue to write this series, I pray that they each find their God-given paths in their fictional lives.

I also pray that you will be able to glean whatever it is God wants you to glean from this story.

Thank you for coming back again and again to support the *My Son's Wife* series as well as my other literary works!

No me without You!

Shelia E. Bell
God's Amazing Girl

This is My Confession

My name is Shelia Bell. I confess that
I am a writer.
I am an author.
I am God's amazing girl.
I confess that I write perfect stores about imperfect people like
The McCoys and The Grahams, and guess what? Like Me....and
YOU!

Thanks for reading another Shelia E. Bell novel!

Contact information
www.sheliaebell.net
www.sheliawritesbooks.com
sheliawritesbooks@yahoo.com
www.facebook.com/sheliawritesbooks
@sheliaebell (Twitter & Instagram)
@literacyrocks (Instagram)

Please join my mailing list for literary updates and new book release
information
www.sheliawritesbooks.com

If you enjoyed this book (or even if you did not) please go to your
favorite review site
and leave a review!

More Titles by Shelia Bell
*Some titles are written under former name of Shelia Lipsey

<u>YA Titles</u>
House of Cars
The Life of Payne
The Lollipop Girls

<u>Novels</u>
Show A Little Love (*out of print*)
Always Now and Forever Love Hurts
Into Each Life
Sinsatiable
What's Blood Got To Do With It?
Only In My Dreams
The House Husband
Cross Road (Coming Winter 2018)

<u>Series Books</u>

Beautiful Ugly
True Beauty (*sequel to Beautiful Ugly*)

<u>My Son's Wife Series</u>
My Son's Wife
My Son's Ex-Wife: The Aftermath
My Son's Next Wife
My Sister My Momma My Wife
My Wife My Baby…And Him
The McCoys of Holy Rock
Dem McCoy Boys

Adverse City Series
The Real Housewives of Adverse City
The Real Housewives of Adverse City 2
The Real Housewives of Adverse City 3 (Coming Winter 2017)

Anthologies
Bended Knees
Weary to Will
Learning to Love Me

Nonfiction
A Christian's Perspective: Journey Through Grief
How to Life Your Life Like It's Golden

COMING 2018

SERIES
Book VIII of My Son's Wife series

The Real Housewives of Adverse City 3
Adverse City Series

STANDALONE NOVELS

Cross Road

NONFICTION

How to Live Your Life Like It's Golden
"Even if there is no pot of gold at the end of the rainbow"

CPSIA information can be obtained
at www.ICGtesting.com
Printed in the USA
LVOW12s1631291217
561233LV00001B/109/P

9 781944 643041